Copyright 2017

Laurence E Dahners

Kindle Edition

ISBN: 978-1978111479
ASIN: B0761S5Y46

Bioterror

An Ell Donsaii story #14

Laurence E Dahners

Author's Note

This book is the fourteenth in the series, the "Ell Donsaii stories."

Though this book *can* "stand alone" it'll be *much* easier to understand if read as part of the series including

"Quicker (an Ell Donsaii story)"
"Smarter (an Ell Donsaii story #2)"
"Lieutenant (an Ell Donsaii story #3)"
"Rocket (an Ell Donsaii story #4)"
"Comet! (an Ell Donsaii story #5)"
"Tau Ceti (an Ell Donsaii story #6)"
"Habitats (an Ell Donsaii story #7)"
"Allotropes (an Ell Donsaii story #8)"
"Defiant (an Ell Donsaii story #9)"
"Wanted (an Ell Donsaii story #10)"
"Rescue (an Ell Donsaii story #11)"
"Impact (an Ell Donsaii story #12)" and
"DNA (an Ell Donsaii story #13)"

I've minimized the repetition of explanations that would be redundant to the earlier books in order to provide a better reading experience for those of you who are reading the series.

Other Books and Series
by Laurence E Dahners

Series
The Hyllis Family series
The Vaz series
The Bonesetter series
The Blindspot series
The Proton Field series

Single books (not in series)
The Transmuter's Daughter
Six Bits
Shy Kids Can Make Friends Too

For the most up to date information go to
Laury.Dahners.com/stories.html

Table of Contents

Preprologue

Ell's father, Allan Donsaii, was an unusually gifted quarterback. Startlingly strong, and a phenomenally accurate passer, during his college career he finished two full seasons without any interceptions and two games with 100 percent completions. Unfortunately, he wasn't big enough to be drafted by the pros.

Extraordinarily quick, Ell's mother, Kristen Taylor captained her college soccer team and rarely played a game without a steal.

Allan and Kristen dated

more and more seriously through college, marrying at the end of their senior year. Their friends teased them that they'd only married in order to start their own sports dynasty.

Their daughter Ell got Kristen's quickness, magnified by Allan's surprising strength and highly accurate coordination.

She also has a new mutation that affects the myelin sheaths of her nerves. This mutation produces nerve transmission speeds nearly double those of normal neurons. With faster nerve impulse transmission, she has far quicker reflexes. Yet her new type of myelin sheath is also thinner, allowing more axons, and therefore more neurons, to be packed into the same sized skull. These two factors result in a brain with more neurons, though it isn't larger, and a faster processing speed, akin to a computer with a smaller, faster CPU architecture.

Most importantly, under the influence of adrenalin in a fight or flight situation, her nerves transmit even more rapidly than their normally remarkable speed.

Much more rapidly...

Prologue

"Hey Stupid. What happened to your neck?"

Carley realized her hair must have fallen aside to expose the bruise on her neck. A year ahead of her in school, Johnny lived to bully kids younger and smaller than himself. When he'd gotten into the seat behind her she'd felt dismay. Trying to ignore him, Carley lifted a hand and combed fingers through her lank brown hair in an attempt to straighten it over the dark purple spot.

With dismay, she felt her hair being pulled aside as Johnny moved it so he could see her neck. Carley couldn't keep from cringing aside a little. The kid said, "Gross. Don't you ever wash your hair?"

Carley felt like she was dying inside. She couldn't think how to respond, but her shoulders turtled up of their own accord to protect her neck.

Johnny said, "Ooh, gross. That's a hickey, isn't it?"

Carley didn't know what a hickey was, but from the sound of Johnny's voice it seemed like something even worse than a bruise. She slid lower in her seat, willing herself to disappear.

Refusing to let it drop, Johnny loudly asked, "Is it a hickey? You letting guys suck on your neck Carley?"

Suck on my neck? Carley thought in horror. *Why would anyone do that?!* She slid even lower in the seat, willing Johnny to climb back into whatever hole he crawled out of every morning.

Sounding like a klaxon to her ears, Johnny said, "I'm talkin' to you Carley!" She realized he'd never let it drop.

Suddenly Carley's younger brother Eli stood up in the seat beside her.

Eli turned.

Carley suddenly realized that things actually could get worse than being humiliated by Johnny Folsom. "No Eli!" she hissed, reaching toward her brother.

Too late. Eli'd already punched out with all the force he had.

Carley surged up out of her seat, ready to do what she could to protect her little brother from Johnny.

To Carley's astonishment Johnny had his hand up covering his nose. His eyes looked startled for a moment, then they welled with tears. A moment later he bent forward and buried his sobbing face between his knees.

***

As the years passed, Carley never quite knew what to make of the events of that day. Johnny never again said anything directly to her, which seemed like a plus. But she could tell he said things about her to others, spreading ugly rumors which may've been more devastating than any face to face taunts.

Nonetheless, her younger brother had defended her and she loved him for it...

***

Bioterror

Carley woke to the sound of her mother screaming.

Trembling, she rolled out of bed. This wasn't the first time her mother had screamed in the night, but somehow... somehow this time her mother's cries seemed even more terrified than usual.

Carley found herself at the top of the stairs, heart thumping, knees shaking. She could barely understand her mother's screams but thought they were begging the house AI (Artificial Intelligence) to call 911.

Carley leaned down to peer out into the kitchen from the stairs. Carley's dad sat astride her mother's torso, holding her mother's AI headband out of reach. Her Mom's face was bloody. Her hair was a mess suggesting that Dad had been manhandling her by a grip on her hair like he'd done before.

Like he did to Carley sometimes.

Carley's dad laughed. In a slurred tone he said, "Ya stupid bitch. Think *I'm* dumb enough that I'd leave the house AI powered up when I came in to have this little talk with you?"

He pulled his fist back.

Carley started running down the stairs—to do she knew not what.

Her dad's hand flashed forward and her mother's head flopped to one side. It lay unnaturally still. He pulled back his other hand.

Carley turned to the closet where her dad kept his baseball bat.

***

Carley huddled on the stairs, arms around a trembling Eli. She heard the woman say she was from

Child Protective Services. The woman was talking quietly to a policeman and to someone who seemed to be the policeman's boss. She thought they were talking quietly so Carley wouldn't be able to hear them, but she still understood them. The woman asked, "Is she dangerous?"

The man who wasn't in uniform shrugged, "Pretty sure she's the one that bashed the guy's head in with the baseball bat. I guess that makes her dangerous, but it seems like she had just cause to do it."

"The man was beating the woman?"

Another nod, "Bruises and tooth marks on his knuckles. Crushed facial bones and broken jaw on the woman. Probably a broken neck's what killed her." His eyes turned to Carley's mother whose head still lay twisted unnaturally beneath the sheet. Carley still felt her mom's unseeing stare. In a sad tone, the man continued, "He beat her mother to death *before* the girl bashed in his skull."

"Is the man related?"

"She says he's her dad."

"Any other relatives?"

"The girl says the only relatives she's ever known are her brother, mom, and dad. Just the brother now I guess. Hopefully you can find someone else. Gotta hope there's someone decent in the family somewhere."

The woman sighed and glanced at Carley. She said thanks to the policemen and started Carley's direction. "Hi Carley," she said in a friendly tone, "I'm Ariel..."

***

Carley sat at a table in the kitchen while Ariel talked

to the couple in the living room. They were speaking quietly. Like on that terrible night, they apparently didn't think Carley'd be able to hear what they said. This seemed to happen to Carley a lot and she'd started wondering whether people commonly misjudged each other's hearing, or whether perhaps she actually heard better than other people. In any case, she was able to hear and understand almost everything they said. The woman had her eyes on Carley, but turned them to Ariel. "She seems very sweet. Has she been a problem?"

Ariel shook her head, "No. She's been very polite to adults and caring toward other children."

"How's she doing in school?"

"Her teachers say she does well. They think she's smart enough to do far better. Unfortunately, it seems that kids at her previous school picked on her. She's been clothed shabbily and wasn't allowed to bathe very often… that probably had something to do with it."

"Oh!" the woman said with a distressed glance at Carley, covering her mouth with her hand. "That's so sad." After a moment her eyes turned back to Ariel. "What's going to happen to her brother? Will he come here later?"

Ariel looked at Carley as she said, "I hope so. Carley hasn't seen her brother for weeks and she's been despondent about it. The judge though… He's worried about keeping them together. Sibling rivalry and fights occur in even the most loving of circumstances and after what happened to Carley's dad, he… he thinks she might be a danger to him."

The man, who hadn't been saying anything so far, glanced over at Carley then turned his eyes back to Ariel. "She killed her own father?!"

Ariel got a pinched look on her face, "While he was killing her mother, yes."

"How?! For God's sake, the girl's a toothpick!"

Ariel looked at him for a long moment as if considering whether to tell him or not. Finally, she said, "She hit him on the back of the head with a baseball bat while he was kneeling over her mother, beating the poor woman to death."

There was a long silence. Eventually the man said, "She doesn't have to go to prison for that?"

Ariel slowly shook her head, "It's called justifiable homicide..."

***

Mrs. Heune and the lady from the principal's office walked Carley to her new class. Carley glanced over at her, thinking she liked Mrs. Heune. Carley wasn't sure about Mr. Heune yet. She thought he still worried about the fact that Carley'd killed her own father and wondered if he might be next. But Mrs. Heune, a little overweight and almost always pleasantly smiling, she seemed to like Carley. After spending her life being despised by her drunken father and distressed by her mother's moods, Carley found Mrs. Heune pretty easy to tolerate.

In fact, Carley'd characterize her life as the best it'd ever been... if the judge would just let Eli join her at the Heune's. She wished she knew where her brother was and how he was doing.

She wanted to see him again.

Very badly.

But, from what she'd heard the adults say when they

thought she couldn't hear, the biggest reason she and Eli weren't together was the persistent fear that Carley might hurt him like she'd hurt her father. They didn't understand how much Carley loved her brother, or how much she'd hated her dad. Carley worked every day to *be* a perfect girl. The kind of girl that they'd believe would never hurt her brother.

Maybe they'd allow a *model* child to form a family with her brother.

Mrs. Heune had gone to some lengths to get Carley some clothes that might help her fit in. They'd sat outside Carley's new school last week and watched the other kids to see what they were wearing. Mrs. Heune had listened to Carley's requests and had even taken her to a thrift shop so they could get her some clothes that didn't look brand-new. New clothes were nice, but Carley thought that *nothing but* new clothes would seem… snobby. Instead of being embarrassed about her clothes like Carley'd always been before, today Carley felt comfortable in new jeans and an old but clean knit shirt.

And she was clean! At the Heunes' Carley got to take a shower every day. Her hair glistened and bounced with a reddish tint Ms. Heune called auburn.

The lady from the office knocked on the classroom door and Carley felt her heart beat a little faster. A woman opened the door and gave her a bright smile. She said, "Hello, you must be Carley Bolin?"

Carley nodded and the teacher held the door wide. She said, "Come on in, we've saved a seat just for you."

Once Carley sat down, the teacher told the other kids Carley's name and asked her classmates to help her catch up with her schoolwork. The girl seated next to Carley whispered, "I can help. I'm Mazie Carter, maybe we can be friends?"

As a warm feeling flowed over her, Carley nodded again.

***

Shadan Farsq walked down the street carrying a reusable grocery bag, one apparently full of groceries. On top was a head of romaine lettuce and a bunch of bananas. If someone had lifted those out, they'd have seen a carton of milk. The fact that the milk had been dumped out and several pounds of smokeless rifle cartridge powder put in its place wouldn't have been evident. Surrounding the milk carton was a bag of marbles and dark glass beer bottles, each of which had had their beer poured out and replaced with kerosene. Someone would've had to lift out the wine bottle to realize it trailed wires into the milk carton and had a switch on its side to start its five-minute timer.

Shadan walked up to the back of the crowd that was protesting a recent terrorist attack. He set his grocery bag down on top of a concrete planter just inside the edge of the crowd, surreptitiously flipping the switch on the timer.

He raised his hands into the air and took up the crowd's chant, working his way through the press of bodies toward the other side. By the time the five minutes was up he had hundreds of bodies between himself and the bomb.

He stopped and turned his head toward the bomb so the cameras on his AI headband would capture the explosion.

Of course, the microphones would also pick up the

sweet sound of the screams.

Islam Akbar! he chanted to himself.

***

Carley Heune's knee jittered up and down as she sat on the stage and looked out over all the faces in the auditorium. Her mom, Martha Heune, the woman who'd served as her foster mother for two years and then adopted Carley, smiled happily up at her. Sitting next to her mom, Larry Heune—who she still tended to think of as Mr. Heune even though he'd adopted her as well—gave her a smile and a little wave. Over the years she'd learned to like him and even call him "Dad," but she mostly did so because her mom asked her to.

Carley's eyes drifted over the mass of other students. Mazie Carter's curly bright-red hair made her easy to pick out. Mazie'd been her friend from that day so many years ago when Carley'd first arrived at the school. Over the years Mazie'd become much more than a friend. At college next year they were going to be roommates.

Mr. Bradshaw leaned closer to the mic. "And now a few words from our valedictorian." Bradshaw turned to give Carley an admiring look, then turned back to his audience. "Many of you know that Carley's life was not always a bed of roses. Valedictorian by a substantial margin, she's certainly blossomed here at Carpenter High. She's also been a member of the student council and a star on the softball team. She's won a full ride Morehead scholarship and we expect her to do Carpenter proud at the University next year." He turned and opened his hand toward her, "Carley?"

***

Adin Farsq stared sightlessly out over the cold gray sea, trying to remember the details of his son Shadan's life. Though he did this often, to his horror those details kept fading.

Though his name, Shadan, meant happy, the boy'd seldom been so. Small and slender, he'd been bullied in school. Devout in his Islamic faith, he'd been taunted for practicing it. A period of time during which he'd tried to practice his daily prayers in the school room had cemented his status as an object of the Christian boys' scorn and physical assaults. The girls weren't any better. Apparently they'd ignored him as if he weren't there, or worse, moved to avoid being near him. Though Shadan had started out as a friendly child, he'd slowly withdrawn into his shell as repeated adolescent emotional traumas gradually destroyed his spirit.

When Adin's introverted child reached manhood and abruptly declared himself to be one of God's warriors, Adin had been as surprised as anyone else. The quiet son, now suddenly and frighteningly intense. The son who'd once asked Adin why *he* believed, now become the son so fierce in his own faith that Adin was ashamed to express his doubts.

Adin had thought his son was merely strong in his faith. One so devoted that he refused to stray from the dictates in any way. Someone who might occasionally embarrass Adin for his own weaknesses. Someone who'd chastise others when they strayed from the path.

Adin'd had no idea that his son intended to take up arms against the nonbelievers.

Bioterror

Then Homeland Security came to Adin's door.

At first Adin thought they'd made a mistake. That his son couldn't have been involved in the ways that they claimed he'd been.

He couldn't have been planting bombs. Bombs Adin had read about with horror, not knowing his own son had been the one building and setting them.

But the agents forced the Farsq family's computers to give up their secrets. An agent showed Adin that his son had visited Islam Akbar's websites. A hyper violent Islamic splinter group, Islam Akbar advocated terrorism as the solution to almost every problem. Almost every other group in Islam had repudiated and distanced itself from the crazies that populated Islam Akbar.

They were hated everywhere, by everyone. They were despicable human beings.

Shadan had spent a great deal of time on websites that advocated horrifically violent holy war. Men from Homeland Security showed Adin the files his son had downloaded. Files describing methods for bomb building amongst what seemed like a thousand other heinous means of attack.

Homeland Security showed Adin communications between his son and others. Men who'd exhorted his son to consider more and more violent attacks on those who believed in false gods. They wanted him to join the holy war against the idolaters who'd been at war with the true believers for centuries. At first Adin had hated those who'd led his son onward, but as he read through some of the communications he came to realize that his son had been goading the others as much, if not more, than they had pressed him.

The men from the government had taken Adin's son away, leaving a black despair in Adin's soul. Adin had hired good lawyers who'd told Adin the evidence was overwhelming. They'd work toward a short sentence but couldn't put forth any hope that there might be a dismissal of the charges. If Adin's son could be an exemplary prisoner, perhaps he could be out in several decades.

Grasping at that straw, Adin visited his son frequently, encouraging good behavior and talking of what they'd do after Shadan was released.

But then Adin's son was dead...

He'd attacked a guard, they said. Shouting Allah's name and suicidally attacking one of two armed guards. He'd tried to take the man's pistol.

The other guard had killed Shadan, Adin's only son, leaving Adin's soul impoverished and bleak.

***

It'd taken months for Adin to realize that his son had been a warrior till the end.

Even prison hadn't been able to blunt Shadan's will. Even in the penitentiary Adin's son had kept attacking his enemy as represented in the nonbeliever guards.

After much soul searching Adin decided to take up arms in his son's war himself. Surprisingly Homeland Security hadn't removed the material his son had downloaded onto their house AI. Adin disconnected that AI from the Internet and bought another one to replace it. Then, keeping the old AI isolated from the Internet, Adin used it to learn about Islam Akbar and God's fiery will without going onto the net himself.

Adin would take the place of his son as one of God's warriors. He'd do it in such a way that Homeland

Bioterror

Security wouldn't ever realize what was coming.

The sword Adin could wield was mightier than any that'd ever been forged from steel.

Adin was a virologist...

Paris, France—Another cheating scandal erupted at the Tour de France today when officials discovered that yellow jersey rider Emile Vargas had oxygen transmitting ports glued to the back surface of his molars. Initially angry at Vargas, when the doctors for the Tour insisted on inspecting everyone's teeth, many riders began objecting that it was an invasion of their privacy.

In total, seventeen other riders were also found to have oxygenating ports...

Adin walked down the hall with Jerry Scott, one of the techs who worked in the BSL-4 (Biosafety Level 4 lab). They'd been talking about soccer, a favorite pastime for both of them though Adin preferred to call it fútbol. Adin rattled on about one of the players while Jerry coded in his password. The keypad had a shield to keep people from watching password entries, but Adin had practiced watching videos of people's hands while they entered passwords. He'd gotten pretty good at telling what password was keyed from the way a hand moved.

As Jerry said goodbye and went on into the BSL-4 Adin repeatedly recited the password in his mind to be sure he'd remember it.

***

A couple of weeks later Adin stopped back by the lab late one night—not at all unusual behavior for him. An hour later he palmed the door plate so his implanted RFID would key him out of the building. Pushing the door open he jammed it with a shoe and stepped back inside. He attached a thin steel plate to the magnetic door sensor so the building's AI would think the door had closed again. The plate had a thin, Kevlar string hanging from it. He put a piece of duct tape over the latch on the door so it wouldn't lock when it closed. Knowing his AI'd have had a handshake with the building's AI as he left, he walked all the way to his car. There he was far enough from the door that the building's AI'd lose direct contact and think he was completely gone from the campus. Shutting off his own AI, he changed his clothes, put on a hood and pulled on some blue lab gloves which would both prevent fingerprints and disguise his skin color. Sending his car home, he returned and reentered the building. The duct tape on the latch meant he didn't have to use his RFID key to get back in.

He had a copy of Jerry's fingerprint he'd lifted off a glass. Adin'd glued copies of the fingerprint to several of the digits on the lab gloves before he left home. He made a quick detour to the line of hooks in the hall where everyone kept their white coats. Jerry, squeamish about needles, had never been RFID implanted so his RFID was in his photo ID badge. Jerry was supposed to keep the badge with him at all times, but he often forgot it. Adin knew Jerry'd left the badge on his coat today because he'd been looking for it every day when they left work for weeks. Adin always hung his own coat on the hook adjacent to Jerry's. Now he plucked up Jerry's coat instead of his own and put it on. The presence of the badge was the reason Adin was here on this particular night. Arriving at the BSL-4, he tapped the palm pad with Jerry's card, carefully holding the card in his left hand so the pad wouldn't sense his own RFID. Then Adin applied the glove finger with Jerry's fingerprint to the sensor next to the pad. Finally, with a little shudder of nerves, he keyed in what he believed to be Jerry's password.

Adin exhaled in relief as the door unlocked. Inside the BSL he stepped over to the -80° freezer. He'd been in the room last month with one of the other investigators, so he knew what to expect. Pulling open one of the freezer drawers he looked in the back of it where a door was locked over the bin containing reference cultures for highly pathogenic organisms. Adin used a screwdriver he'd brought to scrape the frost away from the front edge of the bin.

Adin didn't have a key, but the screwdriver also served to pop the door open. As he'd known from studying the freezer in his own lab, the latches on the locked bins were total crap. He lifted out a rack of vials and studied their labels, wondering whether there'd be something dangerous enough in the bin to justify the risks he'd taken to break into it. To his astonishment he saw one of the vials was labeled *Variola major*!

Samples of *Variola major*, or smallpox, thought to have been eradicated in the wild, were only supposed to be kept in the CDC in Atlanta, and the Center of Virology and Biotechnology in Russia. As a disease, smallpox spread rapidly from person to person and had a mortality of over thirty percent. With trembling hands he lifted out the smallpox culture. After a moment spent staring at the innocent looking vial of death, he dropped it in his pocket and put an empty vial into the bin in its place.

Back in his own lab, Adin quickly scraped the smallpox label off the vial and covered it with a label for adenovirus B-28. Such a virus didn't exist, so he could be relatively sure no one would come looking for it and take his vial by mistake. On the other hand, if someone *found* the vial and wondered about it, they'd probably just assume that someone had been *told* to write out a label for D-28. It'd be easy to understand how they might've heard B instead of D and written B-28 on the label instead.

After taking off Jerry's coat, he hustled down the stairs and picked up the Kevlar string dangling from the steel plate that was spoofing the magnetic door sensor.

Pushing the door open, Adin trailed the Kevlar string from the magnet out through the gap in the door. He pulled the duct tape off the door latch and gently closed the door. Once the door was shut and attracting the sensor itself, he used his Kevlar string to pull the plate off the sensor and out the door gap.

Taking a deep breath, he started the long walk home. His car had, as instructed, driven itself home shortly after he left the building the first time. This'd give him an alibi if, or rather when, someone detected his second spate of activity in the building. At various locations on the long walk home he disposed of the mask, the fingerprints, and the gloves, each in separate trash cans.

***

Carley looked around Dr. Barnes' lab, wondering if she could ever learn how to use all the equipment. She'd done very well as an undergraduate at UNC, getting bachelor's degrees in both biochemistry and microbiology during the four years covered by her Morehead scholarship. She'd decided that her real interest lay in the study of DNA, so she'd applied to Duke University's PhD program in genetics.

When she started her first semester of grad school she'd been hoping to get into Dr. Hodges' lab. She'd been disappointed when he hadn't accepted her. Instead she'd wound up with Dr. Barnes who'd been her second choice. As she'd learned more about the two researchers however, she'd decided that fate had smiled upon her. Hodges was supposed to be quite the jerk. Apparently, he seldom accepted women grad students and most people thought he was pretty misogynistic.

And, just plain mean.

Barnes had a great reputation for being very nice. Nice or not, everyone said she was a genius.

Carley hoped she could measure up to Barnes' standards.

***

Adin opened the -80° freezer in his lab. It'd been a couple of months since he'd stolen the smallpox sample and so far no alarm had been raised. At first he'd feared someone would notice the broken latch on the bin containing the pathogen reference cultures. However, it hadn't happened. He suspected that, since no one in the lab had worked with high end pathogens for years, no one'd had an occasion to try to open the bin and thus notice its latch was broken. Even if they did, the frost in a minus eighty freezer could sometimes jam up a bin so that it needed to be pried open anyway. They might attribute the broken latch to their own efforts in opening it. Now that months had passed, if someone did notice it'd take extensive detective work to even determine when the freezer had been broken into, much less track it to Adin.

As well, when he'd pondered why a sample of smallpox still existed in their freezers, he realized that there was a good chance no one'd been in the highly pathogenic organism drawer for years, possibly decades. If anyone knowledgeable had seen the *Variola major* label they'd have known that the lab wasn't allowed to store it. Though, he supposed it was possible someone had simply been flouting the law.

Adin felt a little bit nervous to be working with such a dangerous organism when the biosafety set-up in his own lab would only qualify as level 2. However, he'd spent some time upgrading the filters and seals in the safety cabinet and had purchased high quality disposable protective clothing. In his own mind he thought of his lab as a level 3. It met most of the standards anyway. Besides, *Adin* was immune.

Like most people born since the early 1970s, Adin had never been vaccinated for smallpox, so working with the sample was really dangerous. However, he'd also found a sample of cowpox. Cowpox was a milder virus which had been what was used to vaccinate people for smallpox since immunity to cowpox provided immunity to smallpox. Thus, after growing up some of the cowpox, he'd been able to vaccinate himself with it.

Now it was time to sequence the *Variola major* virus. As unbelievable as it might seem, a few decades ago, he could've avoided all the cloak and dagger required to steal the actual virus and just downloaded its DNA sequence off the Internet. However, in the past decade a significant effort had been made to remove such sequences from publicly available databases. Adin suspected that if he'd searched the web hard enough he might've found a sequence hidden away on some server somewhere, however, he also suspected that the NSA kept a careful watch for people who were making such searches.

He'd just have to get the sequence the old-fashioned way...

***

Carley'd stolen some time to do yet another web search for her brother Eli. Eli's name might be unusual, but there were plenty of Elis to sort through, especially considering that she had no idea what his last name would be now. Searches for Eli Bolin hadn't turned up anything so she assumed he'd been adopted and changed his last name like she had. Requests to the court system for information about her brother's current name or location had all been rejected.

She looked up as Alice dropped into the lab chair near her. Alice was a more senior grad student who Carley frequently looked to for advice. She looked excited so Carley said, "What's up?"

Alice lifted an eyebrow, "Know where Dr. Barnes is this afternoon?"

Carley shook her head.

"D5R!" Alice said in an awed tone. "She said she had an appointment with Ell Donsaii herself."

Carley stared for a moment, "Are we going to be working with extraterrestrial DNA?"

"Maybe?" Alice said. "I can't imagine why else Donsaii'd want to talk to Reggie!" Alice leaned closer and lowered her voice a little, "Better yet, Dr. Hodges came by in one of his moods. He buttonholed me, wanting to know where Barnes was. I got to tell him that she was out at D5R talking to Donsaii. You'd have thought I'd shit on his shoes!"

Not wanting to encourage it, Carley suppressed a giggle over Alice's crudity. She'd already learned to dislike Hodges though, so she couldn't help but smile at the image. "ET DNA," she said, pretending that was the reason for the smile. "Wow, that could be very cool."

***

Adin Farsq leaned back in his chair and admired the results of his labors. In the months since he'd discovered the smallpox sample he'd managed to get himself established as an Orthopoxvirus researcher—Orthopoxvirus being the genus which included the smallpox, cowpox, monkeypox, buffalopox and camelpox species. Ostensibly, he was working on them because of the health and economic problems caused by cowpox and camelpox. Cowpox, or *Variolae vaccinae* was actually what the practice of vaccination was named after. In 1796 Jenner'd begun advocating the inoculation of people with material from cowpox lesions in order to prevent smallpox. Cowpox could attack an unusually wide range of animal hosts—in fact the cows it was named after were one of the animals it least frequently attacked—and vaccine derived versions of cowpox had spread all around the world during the efforts to eradicate smallpox. Camelpox was quite virulent for camels and caused trouble in various nomadic communities which depended on the animals.

With this as his justification for studying the

Orthopoxviruses, Adin had been growing up cultures of the various species, decoding their DNA and manipulating them in ways that he posited might make them less pathogenic to their hosts. This was in keeping with his desire to develop a milder form of cowpox that he could use to vaccinate the faithful before he began to spread his weaponized version of smallpox. The original use of cowpox as a vaccination had been much more dangerous than subsequent modern vaccinations for other diseases. It invoked substantial risks because it was a live virus which caused a substantial illness in a small percentage of people vaccinated with it. A small percentage of those vaccinated actually died from cowpox. The risks of being vaccinated had contributed substantially to the argument for stopping vaccinations once smallpox had been eliminated—other than in laboratory storage. If there'd been a safer vaccination, the presence of smallpox in various biowarfare stockpiles might have caused countries to continue vaccinating their citizens.

There were, however, some downsides to stopping smallpox vaccination because the vaccination provided some level of protection from HIV. In fact, though it wasn't clear why, asthma, malignant melanoma and various other infectious disease hospitalizations were lower in people who'd been vaccinated—both asthma and HIV having notably become much more of a problem in the decades subsequent to when the smallpox vaccinations were stopped. In fact, even after smallpox had been eliminated; in low income countries, adults who had smallpox vaccination scars had a substantially lower overall mortality than adults who hadn't been vaccinated—for reasons that weren't fully understood.

Thus Adin had been able to couch his proposals to study Orthopoxvirus species in terms of the economic benefits that might be achieved from a camel vaccination program and the human health benefits that might be achieved through development of a less dangerous cowpox vaccination for humans.

Hidden amongst his viral specimen and viral genomes were the specimens and genomes of smallpox. He'd mislabeled them *Variolae vaccinae GER-1999*, a version of cowpox that didn't exist. Because the cowpox and smallpox viruses were related, it'd take a high level of suspicion and a concerted effort for someone to prove that his GER-1999 was in fact smallpox or *Variola major* and not *Variolae vaccinae*.

Now he felt safe beginning his work to develop a safer version of cowpox and a more lethal version of smallpox...

Chapter One

Vanessa knocked on the frame of Dr. Turner's open door. When he looked up inquisitively she said, "It's about Zage."

"What's he done now?"

"As he'd anticipated, his peptide made the obese rats lose weight."

Turner barked a frustrated laugh. "When's that kid going to hypothesize something that *doesn't* prove to be true?!"

Vanessa shook her head, "Damned if I know. Wish it'd rub off on me."

Letting out a sigh, Turner said, "You going to help him write up a paper?"

"Already done."

"Whoa, you got right on that."

"I didn't do it. Zage just sent it to me this morning."

Turner shrugged, "You up to whipping it into shape then?"

She shook her head, "Nothing to whip that I can find. I wish I could write that well."

Turner laughed again, "The kid's going to drive me to drink! Send it on to me. Hopefully I can find something to change. We don't want him getting a swelled head."

~~~

After Vanessa left, Turner thought, *I suppose we'd*

better file that peptide with the University's patent office...

***

Adin's AI chimed a reminder and he got up to put the book back on its shelf. As he made his way out of the medical library he took care to do nothing that might bring attention to himself. Leaving before it got so late that he'd be one of very few patrons left was the first step of this. Adin did have library access, but when he entered the library he waited for the approach of another patron and followed closely enough behind them that he could slip in without extending his hand and letting the library's AI read his RFID. So far, only one person had frowned back over their shoulder at him as if they thought it odd that he'd followed them so closely. He exited the building in the same fashion.

Adin took great care not to use the library's electronic resources. He never asked the librarian for advice. He avoided the employee's eyes. He spent his time in a corner on the third floor, reading about smallpox and cowpox in printed versions of textbooks and journal articles. Though sadly the library stocked fewer and fewer journals in print form as the years went by, every one he found in print meant one less electronic access that might be tracked by Homeland Security if they were watching for someone who was *too* interested in smallpox. Fortunately, the library still seemed to be stocking new versions of major textbooks.

Adin used an elderly tablet on which he'd disabled the internet connection to take photographs of pages he thought he might need to refer to in the future. The tablet was encrypted, an encryption for which he used a very long and highly secure password.

All these efforts—reading only print versions, staying off the Internet, keeping documents on a single encrypted and unconnected device—were directed toward keeping any government surveillance systems from recognizing how intently he was studying the two viruses. When he did have to search for information he couldn't find in print form, he used AIs at the public libraries around town, signing in as any one of a number of other people. He'd invested significant effort in watching for and committing to memory the sign in information of a number of complete strangers.

Though his soul felt impatient, he regularly reminded himself that he was playing the long game.

He should never be rushed.

Instead of walking directly to his car, he detoured and stopped at a corner. There he looked three different directions as if puzzled, then hesitantly turned to the north. After walking about thirty feet, he stopped, looked about, then started back to the south. Fifty feet to the south, he turned between two buildings and stopped.

Ten minutes later, another man entered the other end of the gap between the two buildings. As agreed, they met in a dark alcove. "Harvey?" the man said.

To complete the query and response, Adin said, "No, Marley." He stepped forward and felt the man's head to make sure he wore no AI. Then he handed the man the end of a length of surgical tubing and mimed putting it in his ear. Once the man was holding it in place, Adin spoke quietly into the rubber cup at the other end of the tube. "You're from Islam-Akbar?" The man nodded, a puzzled expression on his face. Adin continued, "Speak to me through this so we can be completely certain that no microphones can pick up our conversation." He handed the cup to the man and took the end of the tube to insert hold to his own ear.

The man said, "You are ready for jihad?" He held the cup out to Adin.

Without taking the cup Adin merely nodded, slipping his left hand into his coat pocket and around his pistol.

The man lifted the cup again, "Are you willing to wear a suicide vest?"

Adin shook his head and took the cup. "I'm building a weapon much, much more powerful than a suicide vest," Adin said. "Can *you* deliver *it*?" In the dim light he couldn't assess the man's reaction and wondered once again how he could be absolutely certain the man didn't belong to Homeland Security. True, Adin had found him through one of his dead son's contacts, but of course he couldn't be sure that the contact hadn't been the one responsible for his son's exposure, capture, and death. Adin slid off the pistol's safety.

After a long pause, the man took the cup again. He said, "A larger bomb?"

Adin shook his head.

"Chemical or nuclear weapon?"

Adin shook his head again.

"A disease?" the man breathed.

Adin nodded and took the cup, "It'll kill *billions* of the unbelievers."

"It will kill believers too, no?"

Adin shrugged as he took the cup again, "Yes, some noble sacrifices. We'll vaccinate our people before releasing it."

The man stood motionlessly for minutes as Adin's

finger tightened slowly and inexorably on the trigger. Finally the man took the cup. He said, "I'll have to talk to others. Contact me again in a week."

***

Adin felt proud as he walked down the street, thinking that the research phase of his task might well be done. After extensive review of every relevant piece of printed literature that he could access, as well as careful perusal of a few papers he could only find online and therefore'd had to read in various public libraries, he believed that he'd identified a pivotal enzyme produced by both *Variola major* and *Variolae vaccinae*. Different isoforms of this enzyme seemed to be associated with the virulence of the species in which they were found. A highly virulent smallpox virus isolated in Bangladesh in 1975 had an isoform at one end of the spectrum while the most benign form of the vaccination version of cowpox had an isoform of the enzyme that fell at the other end of the spectrum.

A second fruit of his investigations had been the recognition that one of the proteins coded for by the viral DNA in both viruses was associated with respiratory expression and therefore communicability.

A little genome editing should produce a more benign cowpox and a more malignant smallpox, both of which were more easily spread by respiratory transmission.

Finally, he knew which proteins the two viruses shared and believed that he'd identified the ones on the external surface of the virus which were recognized by the human immune system. He could cut out and insert modifications of the genes for those proteins in his more lethal variola strain and simply insert modifications of the proteins in his milder *Variolae vaccinae.* When his version of smallpox began to ravage the nonbelievers, it wouldn't be recognized by antibodies created by vaccination using old *Variolae vaccinae* strains. Strains that various governments might have on hand and attempt to use to save their people. Administered to believers, his own *Variolae vaccinae* strains would produce immunity to both the old form of smallpox and the new. Thus he could produce documentation of the success of his research into a new means for vaccination with his *Variolae vaccinae* and talk it up as a safer, better strain for vaccination. He could even justify growing up and freeze-drying large quantities of it. He'd just have to be certain it didn't actually get released to any governments.

He adjusted his scarf so that it covered the lower part of his face before he turned in to the burger joint. He stood and briefly appraised the menu before approaching and speaking to the pimply faced kid behind the counter. "Sorry, the PGR chip on my AI seems to have crapped out. Can I place my order here at the counter?"

The pimply kid behind the counter produced a surly looking nod. Adin stepped close to one of the microphones suspended above the counter to pick up requests from the employees and spoke quietly. Since all of the employees appeared to be busy and no other customers were at the counter, the first thing he did was to ask the AI to send a message to a number Adin had memorized. Once it acknowledged that request, he rattled off GPS coordinates as a simple string of numbers that ran right into a string of numbers for the date and time. He'd meet his contact at a spot one block south of that location, one hour before that time. Because he'd practiced reeling off the numbers, it took him well under a minute. Then he placed his order almost as rapidly and turned to find a seat.

Adin casually kept an eye on the worker bees behind the counter. When a large cluster of people entered the restaurant, passing between himself and the counter, he exited behind them without getting his food or paying. Paying would've left behind identifying numbers with which he could be tracked. A pit formed in his stomach over the fact that if someone *did* track the call to the restaurant, they could presumably go over the surveillance video and acquire Adin's face. He'd tried to keep his face turned away from the cameras he knew about, but even a side or overhead view might let them identify him.

He sternly reminded himself that such stores tended to record over the files from their cameras after a few days. After all, the employees tended to be unhappy if big brother kept a *permanent* record of their hijinks and misadventures, often erasing drives themselves if it wasn't scheduled.

***

NASA, Houston, Texas—D5R and NASA reported today that Phillip Zabrisk—the first person to have been transported by port when he was returned from Mars after an injury—has survived the experience without apparent ill effects. The results of extensive testing have not found a reduction of his intelligence, a feared consequence of porting that had been noted during animal testing.

Before you get your hopes up that you might soon be porting to exotic locations, please know that extensive preparations including an extended period under general anesthesia were required to achieve this result. It has been the conclusion of all investigators studying Mr. Zabrisk's outcome that, for the foreseeable future, porting of human beings should be reserved for emergency situations...

Adin watched uncomfortably as Ibn Sinar brought the hard-looking man into the room. Ostensibly, Adin was at this lawyer's office to write his will. Since the death of his son, he had no one to whom he wished to leave any of his worldly possessions. Therefore, the writing of his will was of virtually no consequence.

This lawyer had assured him that it was quite normal for a client and his attorney to have multiple meetings during the drafting of a will. Those meetings would provide a cover for Adin's meetings with the man who'd serve as Adin's conduit to the great jihad which Islam-Akbar was assembling around his virus.

The attorney bowed and left the room. Adin turned to the other man, "Hello, I am..."

The other man cut him off with a gesture, "Let us dispense with pleasantries. We are here on the business of jihad and should not waste time on other topics."

The man's gaze was intense. Adin'd committed himself to a holy war and told himself that he cared nothing for his own life but that it contribute to the elimination of nonbelievers. Nonetheless, he found himself swallowing nervously. *What if I am found wanting by this man?* he wondered as he nodded.

The man said, "You're sure that your virus will kill large numbers of people?"

Adin shrugged and spoke truth, "Fairly certain. It needs to be tested in cynomolgus macaques."

"Sinna what?"

"Monkeys. Cynomolgus macaques are used in a lot of laboratories and they're susceptible to smallpox. They're a pest in Southeast Asia so it shouldn't be hard to obtain some."

The man narrowed his eyes, "Why haven't you tested it yourself?"

"If I ordered some monkeys and started killing them with smallpox I'd be in prison. Islam-Akbar would have little use for me once I'd been locked up."

"So what, we gather some monkeys and inject them with this smallpox you've grown?"

Adin studied the man, wondering whether he was sophisticated enough to understand what needed to be done. "I'll explain what needs to be done in general. This plan can be modified depending on what materials you can get access to."

The man nodded slowly.

Adin continued, "You'll need two boats, twenty monkeys, and someone with some medical training. Both boats should have radio controlled explosive breaching charges. They go far out to sea with ten monkeys in each of two separate rooms on one of the boats. Everyone on board the boats and ten of the monkeys get vaccinated with the protective virus. Five days later all twenty monkeys get injected with the smallpox virus. Twelve days after that the ten monkeys that didn't get vaccinated should be dead. The other ten monkeys and all of the people should be fine. If so, the people return in the second boat and the explosive charge sinks the boat with the monkeys. If the people complain of getting sick, you sink both boats and I start over. This way you'll have proof of the effectiveness of the vaccine and the danger of the virus."

"And then you think we're going to go around the world injecting the virus into all the billions of nonbelievers?"

"Monkeys are much harder to kill with the virus than humans. Humans should catch it if we spray it into the air, then they should spread it from one to another by coughing and touching."

The man studied Adin for a few minutes, then he said, "This virus of yours, it's different from the smallpox virus that killed people in the past, yes?"

Adin nodded, "The original smallpox killed about thirty percent of people it infected. This one should kill a significantly higher percentage."

"And if it doesn't?"

Adin shrugged, "Then I'll need to change it."

"So, it needs to be tested in people?"

Adin nodded.

"Where're we going to do that?" He curled his lip, "We don't have a prison where we can do such experiments on the inmates."

Adin said, "Drop an aerosol sprayer from a helicopter onto North Sentinel Island in the Bay of Bengal. It's populated by the Sentinelese who've avoided contact with other peoples for hundreds, perhaps thousands of years. Since they generally come out and shoot arrows at any helicopters, a flyover a few weeks later should tell you whether there're any survivors."

The man seemed surprised to learn that there were

people so isolated, but then Adin himself had been surprised to learn of them. After a moment, he said, "And how do we check to be sure the vaccination provides protection?"

"If it works in monkeys, it should work in people."

"And if it doesn't?"

"If you want to be sure, you'll need to test it in some people. I'll leave that to you, but realize that if the smallpox gets out of your control before the day we've chosen to release it, someone may be able to create a vaccine quickly enough to make all our efforts pointless."

"Why can't they do that when we *do* release it?"

"When we release it, we'll do it using D5R's damnable ports. Before the release, you can place them by the thousands in the cities of the unbelievers, all around the world. We'll release the deadly virus by blowing it out of those ports as a highly concentrated aerosol, everywhere, all at once. I'm sure they *will* eventually generate a vaccine, but not until after hundreds of millions… and more likely billions are dead."

The man stared at Adin and this time *he* was the one who swallowed as if in fear. After a long pause, he continued, "And what'll we tell the believers when we're going around vaccinating them?"

Adin shook his head, "We won't tell them. You shouldn't tell anybody or there will be leaks. Your warriors will drop off ports all around the world without knowing why, or even knowing that they're fighting a battle. You could even give them a false story that you're using the ports to sample the air to determine whether the nonbelievers are fouling it. Months ahead of time we'll place the same kind of ports in the major cities of the faithful and, elsewhere, just in the mosques. They'll release the vaccine virus slowly in low concentrations so that it won't overwhelm anyone."

The man drew back, "But then it'll protect some of the nonbelievers... And some of the believers won't be protected by it!"

Adin shrugged again, "You're right, it won't be perfect. Some will sacrifice their lives in this great battle, *as in every other battle since the beginning of time*. Every war has unintended casualties *and* fails to kill all of the enemy, but the world will be a *vastly* different place afterward."

The man sat back thinking for a time. He leaned forward, "You say we'll release the vaccine months ahead of time?"

Adin nodded.

"Why? It's just more time for the great Satan to realize what we're doing and respond."

"The severity of an illness produced by exposure to a virus depends to a large degree on how many viral particles you're exposed to. If we expose people to just a few particles of the lethal smallpox version, many of them will survive. On the other hand, if we release the vaccine virus in high concentrations, even it will kill some people. If people start dying, the medical establishment will investigate and likely figure out what's happening. They may even be able to develop a vaccine to prevent our vaccination version that'll protect people against our smallpox version. Therefore, we must release the vaccine version in low concentrations over long periods of time so that people can develop immunity to it without becoming overtly sick. Even at this low concentration, some people will become ill. Health agencies will eventually begin to respond and, when they do, we must be prepared to release the great death immediately."

***

Feeling a rising sense of his own power, Adin sat down to wait for his next meeting with the man from Islam-Akbar. When he'd last met the man, Adin hadn't told him that Adin'd only worked out a *plan* for modifications to the two viruses and tested some of the steps. Now however, he'd actually successfully excised and replaced the genes for the virulence factors and the protein coat in both viruses. Growing the viruses in the immortalized HeLa line of human cells, he'd to his delight proven that a modified enzyme he'd inserted into their genomes rendered both viruses resistant to tecovirimat, cidofoviran and two other antiviral medications that were active against the pox viruses.

Finally, with what he thought of as a stroke of genius, he'd inserted a gene sequence into the vaccination virus. When this version of the cowpox virus infected human cells, it rendered them incapable of replicating the virus in the presence of the bovine thyroid hormone which was present in bovine serum. Since culture of the human cells in which the vaccinia virus was generally produced was usually done in bovine serum, this'd mean that they'd have to be grown in a different medium. However, if someone recognized that Islam-Akbar had released the vaccinia virus in Islamic areas to protect its own people and *they* tried to grow up that virus to protect *their* people, they'd almost certainly try to grow the virus in bovine serum. When it *didn't* grow, he hoped that it might take them weeks or even months to realize that bovine serum was the problem.

He'd vaccinated himself with modified cowpox virus. Doing so was dangerous, yes, but he'd decided that working with his highly malignant modified smallpox virus when he had no resistance to it was even more dangerous. The vaccination site had produced a pox scar on his inner thigh as expected.

He'd even named the two viruses.

The man from Islam-Akbar entered the room and said, "Are they ready?"

Adin nodded. "Do you have access to the monkeys and the boats?"

The man nodded and held out his hand.

Adin placed two vials, one wrapped in padding, in the man's palm. Pointing out the one in the padding, he said, "This one I call 'Vengeance.' If you break that vial, you and likely millions of others will die. I'd recommend that *if* you break it, you wash the area where it broke with Clorox, burn down the building, and kill yourself. He pointed to the other one, "This one's 'Guardian.' If you do loose Vengeance upon the world, before you kill yourself, tell anyone who *might* have been contaminated to vaccinate themselves with Guardian. Reaching in his pocket, Adin pulled out a folded sheet of paper and handed it to the man as well. "Here are the instructions, in the cipher we agreed upon."

The man simply nodded and left. Adin felt frustrated, having expected the man to be cowed by his dire instructions.

Now Adin must sit and do nothing for the remainder of the hour that his scheduled appointment with the attorney would've lasted. He leaned back and began to plan out how he and Islam-Akbar would replicate the viruses in the enormous quantities that'd be required.

***

Dinh had read the instructions that came with the two vials and collected the materials he'd need to mix up the preparations, even out at sea. He shook his head, wondering what the disease was that they were testing a vaccine for and why it was being tested on a boat, of all places. He shook his head, it didn't matter. The boat was pulling away from the dock so he drew up the solution to reconstitute the first vial.

~~~

Vaccinating the monkeys was difficult. First, he had to move from the main boat to the monkey boat. This was done in a small, outboard-powered inflatable boat that made Dihn nervous. Then the men assigned to handle the monkeys had to catch the animals so he could give them their injections. He was glad that the monkeys were all wearing different colored collars. The monkeys didn't like the injections, so they squealed and fought, bounding around their room. If he hadn't been able to check off the colors on his sheet, he'd never have been able to figure out which ones had already had their injections and which ones still needed them. He felt grateful that he only had to vaccinate the monkeys in one of the rooms.

Dinh's next problem arose when it came time to vaccinate the men on the boat. They didn't screech and run around like the monkeys, but two of them simply refused to have their injections. He didn't know how to handle this, eventually returning to the main boat. All but one of the sailors on the main boat accepted their vaccinations, though Dinh had a feeling that if they'd believed they *could* refuse, many of them would have.

Dinh found Markun out near the bow of the main boat. He'd heard gossip that their leader, fearsome as he'd appeared on land, had spent long hours throwing up after they first put out to sea. Dinh thought Markun still looked somewhat gray, though he wasn't vomiting, at least not any more. Dinh said, "We have a problem."

Markun produced a listless, unhappy look. "Besides these endless waves?"

Dinh shrugged, "I have some medication for seasickness if you'd like it?"

"Now you tell me?!" Markun growled angrily.

Dinh shrugged again, "I just learned you were sick."

"Yes, I'd like some medicine. What I'd really like is to go back to shore, but you've started the injections, right?"

"Yes, and the instructions plainly state that, once the injections have started, we're not to go back to shore for at least six weeks."

"And the Imam said we must follow the instructions on pain of death, yes, yes. You said there's another problem?"

Dinh sighed, "Yes, three of the sailors have refused to be vaccinated. I've told them they may become quite sick with whatever this disease is—they say they'll take the chance. I've told them the Imam's ordered that they take their vaccination—they say the Imam's not here to enforce his directive." He shrugged, "I don't know what to do. Should we have the other men hold them down?"

Markun shook his head wearily, "I'll call the Imam. If

Laurence E Dahners

he wants us to hold them down, that's what we'll do."

***

Dinh worried about his trembling hands as he prepared to mix the solution into the second vial. He'd never had a tremor before, but he'd been thinking about what they were doing out there on the ocean, injecting monkeys with a disease. At first he'd reasoned that perhaps it was a disease that had something to do with seasickness. But with days to think, he'd begun to worry that they were out on the sea in case the disease proved to be more dangerous than expected. If some of the men died, perhaps whoever wrote the instructions wanted it to happen far away.

The Imam hadn't insisted that they vaccinate the three sailors who refused. Dinh kept telling himself that that must mean the disease was bad, but not that bad.

The vaccinations had caused pustules at the injection sites. At first Dinh had thought that he'd failed in his sterile technique and caused some kind of infection at the injection sites, but when every person who had a vaccination got a pustule, he realized it might be an intended result of the injection. He desperately wanted to be able to look up diseases or vaccinations that caused pustules, but they didn't have any access to the Internet on the boats, and no medical books either.

However, the past five days had provided plenty of time for Dinh to worry.

Dinh managed to reconstitute the powder in the second vial without any incidents and drew up the solution in the row of twenty syringes, one for each monkey. He really wasn't looking forward to this next part. They'd have to capture the monkeys, wrap them in canvas like a straitjacket, hold their heads back and then he was supposed to inject the solution directly into their tracheas or windpipes. It'd make them cough he knew. He didn't want to have monkeys coughing this nasty stuff into his face. Per the instructions he'd brought surgical masks with him. He was not only putting them on himself and the animal handlers, but he was planning to put them over the monkeys' faces during the injections.

He shook his head. The monkeys were going to be hard to catch. They were going to be hard to wrap up in the canvas. It was going to be hard to hold their heads back and they'd fight having a mask put over their face. Despite all the diagrams that'd accompanied the carefully detailed instructions, Dinh wasn't confident that he'd be able to inject the monkeys' tracheas correctly. *This could be a disaster,* he thought.

***

Raleigh, North Carolina—Today the FBI reported the arrest of a Chinese national going by the name of Wang. Mr. Wang is alleged to have been funding an attempted kidnapping of Ell Donsaii to the tune of many millions of dollars. Apparently the kidnapping was unsuccessful, though the FBI did not reveal how they managed to thwart it.

The Peoples Republic of China has strongly denied that Wang is a Chinese citizen...

Dinh felt apprehensive as he rode the rubber boat

from the main boat over to the monkey boat. It'd been twelve days since he'd injected the monkeys with the material from the second vial. The sailors on the monkey boat had called on the radio this morning because Chung and Kiri, the two monkey boat sailors who'd refused the vaccination were sick. The man on the boat thought that because Dinh was a technician trained in medical procedures, that he'd know what to do. Dinh had tried to give generic advice such as hydration and Tylenol over the radio, but they'd insisted that Dinh come to examine the men. *As if I have any idea what to look for if I examine them?!*

The two men were in their cabin beds, complaining that they hurt everywhere. They'd gotten sick at their stomach and had been throwing up. Dinh stared at them, then abruptly left the cabin, having had no idea what to tell them. "I'm going to see if the monkeys are sick like you are," he called back over his shoulder as he closed the door.

The vaccinated monkeys seemed fine, tumbling over one another when he appeared at the door, apparently thinking he was bringing food. When he looked in the door at the unvaccinated monkeys they were sprawled listlessly about the room. A few turned their eyes or heads to look at him through the window in the door, but none of them got up. With a chill, he saw that several platters of their food lay on the floor untouched. He looked at the monkey sprawled on its back near the door. Beneath the thinner fur on the anterior part of its body he saw it had pustules. Hundreds of them... *Perhaps thousands*, he thought. They seemed to be everywhere.

"How long have they had the rash?" Dinh asked the sailor who'd been following him around the boat.

"Two days, maybe four?" the man said. "I might not've seen the rash when it first appeared. Are they *supposed* to get a rash?"

"I don't know," Dinh said, looking back in the window. He noticed the monkey near the door wasn't actually looking at him, just a spot near him.

He realized it wasn't blinking.

He looked at its chest.

A spike of fear shot through his gut.

It wasn't breathing either.

~~~

Dinh went back to talk to the two sick men. He opened the door, but couldn't bring himself to actually enter the room. "Do you have a fever?"

Chung shrugged listlessly, as if talking were too much effort.

"Do you feel hot?"

Kiri and Chung both nodded at that. Kiri rasped, "Do you have medicine for us?"

"Yes," Dinh said with sudden inspiration. "I'll be right back."

He went back to the galley and got three cups and a big jug. Speaking to the sailor who'd been following him around the boat, he said, "They need lots of water, salt, and sugar. The man helped him find the salt and sugar, then Dinh told him to add two tablespoons of sugar and a half a teaspoon of salt to each liter of water. The man couldn't figure out how to translate that for the big jug, so Dinh had to write down that he should put in twelve tablespoons of sugar and three teaspoons of salt each time he refilled the six liter jug.

Dinh got the Tylenol bottle out of his pocket and held it so his hand covered the label. Acting as if the pills were precious, he carefully counted thirty-two of them into the third cup. "They should take two of these pills four times a day and drink as much of the solution as they can."

The sailor nodded enthusiastically, happy to have something constructive to do. He headed back to their room. Dinh felt greatly relieved not to have to go talk to the sick men himself. Instead he went back to the stern and got in the inflatable rubber boat. The two sailors drove him back to the main boat.

"Markun!" Dinh said shaking the man awake. "We need to go back to shore. The monkeys are dying. The two men on the monkey boat who refused their vaccinations are very sick. We have to get them to the hospital or I think they'll die like the monkeys!"

Markun stared at him for a moment, then shrugged, "I'll call the Imam, but I think he'll say no."

"At least ask him what to do for them! I've given them Tylenol, and a sugar and salt solution that I used to make for my children when they were sick. That's *all* I know to do."

~~~

Markun found Dinh at the stern of the boat, wondering how long it'd take them to get back to land. "The Imam says you're doing exactly the right thing," he said.

"What?! I'm doing nothing! We must get them to a hospital!"

"The Imam says no. We must stay at sea." Markun held out a bottle, "Give them this medication. It might help, but the Imam says that they'll likely give their lives. They'll be heroes in our fight against the great

Satan."

Wide-eyed, Dinh stared at Markun as he took the bottle. Dinh was a Muslim and devout, but he wasn't the kind of radical Muslim who'd put on a suicide vest! He knew the sailors on the boats were also Muslims, but he didn't think they were even as devout as he was. *This Imam, whoever he is, he didn't give them a choice! He's not a leader! He's the kind who sends his people all unknowing to take risks for him!* Dinh turned away from Markun without saying a word, resolving that when he got back to land he was going to report this Imam to someone higher in the hierarchy.

He looked down at the bottle in his hand. It didn't say what the medication was, but it did have instructions on how often to take it.

***

Dinh felt like he was living a nightmare. Most of the unvaccinated monkeys were dead. None of the sailors would go in the room to check on them anymore, but they could see it through the door. The pills hadn't seemed to help Chung or Kiri. The two men had developed the rash of pustules the day Dinh had sent over the medication. Now Kiri was dead. Chung looked like he'd be dead soon.

The sailor on the main boat who'd refused vaccination had developed fevers and been confined to his cabin a couple of days ago. The rest of the sailors, despite the fact that they didn't feel sick, were in a panic. Dinh thought they were ready to mutiny.

This morning Markun had realized that the Captain had turned the ship back towards shore overnight. At gunpoint, Markun'd marched the captain to the stern of the boat, leaned him against the gunnel and shot him, letting his body fall over the side into the sea.

The sailors watched in wide-eyed horror, but when he'd waved his pistol about and asked them who wanted to be next, they'd shrunk away and returned to their tasks. The thoroughly cowed first mate had turned the boat back out to sea.

The men watched Dinh out of the corners of their eyes and he knew they blamed him. He wanted to tell them that he'd only been following orders, just like they had—but he didn't think it'd do any good. Dinh hadn't been sleeping, partly because of the nightmares, and partly because his door wouldn't lock. *They don't have to kill me in my sleep,* he reminded himself. *They could easily kill me while I'm awake*

As he wedged his sea bag in front of the door, he thought once again, *I'd be easier to kill if I were asleep...*

***

The next day, the monkey boat radioed over to say that Chung had died. All the monkeys were dead as well. The unvaccinated sailor on the main boat had the rash now...

Dinh heard a lot of shouting up on the deck and went up to see what was happening. At first he didn't understand and he looked around uncertainly. He saw one of the men pointing.

The monkey boat was churning back toward land. Dinh thought it was probably going as fast as it could...

Dinh moved back closer to the tiny bridge so that he could hear Markun shouting at them over the radio.

Apparently they weren't answering. When Markun stopped shouting, Dinh glanced back through the windows and saw Markun glaring out at the monkey boat as it approached the horizon. Markun glanced at Dinh, then back down as he did something with the radio. He lifted the microphone to his lips again, speaking more quietly.

He speaking to the Imam, Dinh thought, *which will bring no good.* Dinh pictured them chasing the monkey boat with the big boat. Assuming they could catch the monkey boat, Dinh had no idea how they'd stop it. He wondered with dread if the Imam might tell them to ram the smaller boat.

Looking back through the window, Dinh saw Markun had stopped speaking on the radio. Slumped and leaning forward on his arms with his head hanging, he appeared defeated. Moments later Markun exited the little bridge and went out to sit near the bow, staring out after the monkey boat.

Dinh went back down to his room, but ten minutes later shouts of consternation up on the deck brought him back up the stairs again. The men were agitated and shouting in several different languages. Markun stared sightlessly out toward the monkey boat, so Dinh turned to look as well. A column of smoke rose from where the monkey boat had been.

At first Dinh didn't understand, wondering whether the monkey boat was meeting a bigger ship that had a smokestack. Then with a cold chill he heard one of the men saying, "...and it just exploded..."

Dinh felt the engine speed increase and their own boat started surging through the waves in the direction of the column of smoke.

By the time the main boat arrived at the site of the

explosion, there was nothing left but bits of debris floating on the surface.

**

Dinh stumped up the stairs to check on their sick sailor. He'd been giving him hydration fluid and Tylenol as well as the medicine Markun had given him for the men on the other boat, but the man just kept looking worse. His pustules were so close together that they were touching in many areas. Dinh opened the door, saying, "Good morning," and turning on the light. "I brought you some more…" Dinh's words, intended to cheer the man, died in his throat.

The sailor's eyes stared motionlessly at the ceiling.

Dinh closed the door and turned to go tell Markun.

Markun's response was to say, "Good. We only have to stay out here a few more days. Once we're sure no one else's getting sick we can go back home."

When the explosion came Dinh was out near the bow, staring in the direction of his home. He found himself thrown high into the air. He flailed out to plunge clumsily into the water. By the time he'd flailed his way back to the surface, the boat, nearly broken in half, was engulfed in flames and about to slip beneath the waves. *Bombs in the fuel tanks,* he thought. *They really didn't want these boats to come back to shore.*

Though he swam poorly, he paddled in the direction of the boat's wreckage in hopes that some fragment of the boat might come back to the surface. Something he could cling to while hoping for rescue.

The fragments he found were too small to help.

Bioterror

He turned himself toward land. Or at least, where he thought it was. As he started to swim, he thought, *I'll never make it...*

***

Adin returned to the attorney's office. He and the attorney spoke briefly about the documents the attorney was drafting for him, then Adin once again waited for the man from Islam-Akbar.

When the man entered, his face told Adin that Adin now had the respect he was due. Adin said, "I assume the monkeys died?"

The man nodded, "And three of the sailors."

Adin drew back in alarm, "The vaccination didn't protect them?"

The man gave a little shrug, "They feared the needle and refused to be vaccinated."

"And you let them say no?!"

He shrugged again, "The Imam felt that it'd provide a test of the effectiveness of Vengeance."

Adin felt a little shiver run over him at the cold-bloodedness of such a decision. Then he reminded himself of his own decision to kill millions, possibly billions. "Okay," he said. "It did provide such a test, and a thorough one indeed. I assume that everyone not vaccinated died and everyone vaccinated survived?"

The man nodded. "They gave tecovirimat to the men when they became ill. It didn't seem to help."

"It shouldn't have helped, since the virus is designed to be resistant to such antiviral medications. But that's good to know. All ten of the unvaccinated monkeys died as well?"

The man nodded again, "And all of the vaccinated ones survived. The vaccinations caused a pustule though. Is your preparation contaminated or is that to be expected?"

Adin nodded, "It's a 'pock.' Those who died probably had hundreds of them, or 'pox,' correct?"

"Yes," the man said, looking thoughtfully down at the floor. He looked up again, "Do we still need to do the test on Sentinel Island?"

Adin pondered for a moment, "I recommend it, yes. That way we can be sure that an aerosol delivery system's effective. Admittedly, injecting it into the trachea of the monkeys and then having them spread it to the sailors, presumably by coughing it up as an aerosol, suggests that it'll work, but I think it's important that we be certain. I'd also choose another small, relatively-isolated island, perhaps Pitcairn or Little Diomede. There you could release Guardian as an aerosol to be sure that such a method will work to vaccinate our people against a release of Vengeance a month or two later."

The man gave a nod, then said, "We'll get to work delivering ports. We'll need a system for creating the aerosol that we'll be sending through them."

"I'd recommend the Mitiform Aerosolizer made by Plenum Therapeutics. It'll readily fit a one centimeter port and has a system for filling its reservoir in a closed fashion."

***

Research Triangle Park, North Carolina—D5R announced today that it has found life on the fourth planet circling the star Beta Canum Venaticorum (BC4). This is much more than the unicellular life found in the Alpha Centauri system. Huge dinosaur-like animals roam BC4 (see video link), though no evidence of intelligence to match the Teecees has been detected. This announcement, coming so soon after reports of the first successful human porting, may have you thinking that explorers will soon be wandering the surface of BC4, unfortunately the atmospheric pressure on BC4 is far too high for the survival of humans. One would have to visit the planet in something akin to a deep sea submersible and interact with the environment using mechanical arms...

This time, Adin was meeting the man from Islam-Akbar out in the woods. Adin felt uncomfortable since he rarely spent any time in nature.

He wore sneakers and nylon sweatpants—and a liberal dose of DEET. As directed he'd walked from where his car parked itself to the southwest corner of the lot at the national park. Then he'd walked 200 paces due west, following the compass on his AI. He'd been careful not to use any GPS tracking for this meeting, simply following directions he'd found handwritten on an advertising flyer tucked under his windshield wiper at work.

Adin looked around and caught a come-on wave from a man hiking a nearby path with a large backpack. Adin walked over to the same path and fell in a short distance behind the man, gradually catching up. Once he came alongside, he wasn't surprised to see the same man he'd been meeting in the lawyer's office. He said, "Should we know each other's names?"

The man shook his head and turned off the path.

After twisting and turning through the trees a little way, they came to a small clearing in the forest. Shrugging out of the backpack, the man pulled out one of the Mitiform Aerosolizers that Adin'd recommended and set it on a boulder. "So," he said, getting out a large soft IV fluid bag and quick connecting its tubing to the reservoir on the aerosolizer. "Next, I take the sealed syringe, uncap it, and insert the needle, right?" He pulled out a syringe with attached needle as he spoke.

Adin nodded.

The man carefully uncapped the needle and inserted it into the port on the bag, "I draw fluid up into the syringe and squirt it in and out of the bag several times so that all of the virus will be reconstituted and then pushed into the bag, yes?"

"Yes," Adin said, watching the powdered vaccination virus in the syringe vanish into the liquid. He could barely tell any change in the opacity of the fluid in the IV bag.

"Okay," the man said, reaching into his backpack and pulling out a power outlet—obviously port connected. Adin had wondered how he was going to power the aerosolizer and now felt like thumping himself on the side of the head. Ports had been getting more and more commonplace since they'd been invented them almost a decade ago, but it was still easy to forget all the things they might be used for. Self-amused, he thought back to when AIs had been new. *Back then you'd see someone apparently talking to himself and think perhaps he was crazy...*

Once the man plugged in the aerosolizer, he pulled out a port and held it over the aerosolizer's nozzle. He flipped the switch and the motor in the device began to hum. Just as Adin was wondering where the other end of the port was, the man said, "Do you see it?"

Adin looked around, assuming he was supposed to be seeing the other end of the port but wondering if the man was asking him about something else. He said, "No, what am I looking for?"

"Good," the man grunted. "If you were able to see the mist from the aerosolizer, the ports would be immediately drawing attention to themselves wherever we activated them. By adjusting the settings and using the finest nozzles, I've gotten this one to produce something approximating a vapor." The man stood up, "It's on that tree," he said, pointing.

Adin looked the direction the man pointed but still didn't see anything. "Which tree?"

The man stood, leaving the aerosolizer running and began walking closer. He pointed again, "Do you see it yet?"

Adin was quite close before he saw the small puff of vapor. "I see it," he said pointing. "Are you sure it's putting out enough?"

"It's putting out half of what you recommended," the man said with a shrug. "I figure we'll just run them twice as long. Better that, than people seeing them and investigating."

Adin said, "Let me get some samples." He got some syringes and a laser distance meter out of his pocket. As he walked closer to the vapor, he used a syringe to suck up a sample of the air at each of the distances he'd already written on them. He capped each one and put it back in his pocket until he'd done all ten. He turned, the man had stopped some distance away. "Are you afraid of it?"

The man shrugged indifferently, "You said that at high doses even the vaccination virus might make someone sick. I'm keeping my distance in the hopes that won't happen to me. I figured you could test me for antibodies in a week or so to see if I was close enough to be immunized."

Adin nodded, "That's a good idea. Before you move, let me measure your distance from the port."

Bioterror

Chapter Two

Kumar couldn't help thinking that it was essentially unbelievable that this guy also wanted to fly over North Sentinel Island. Admittedly, the island was pretty bizarre in the sense that no one ever went there. He'd talked to other helicopter pilots who'd flown over the beaches there and the natives pretty consistently came out to shoot at you with bows and arrows. The government had taken a non-interference attitude toward them since 2006 when some fishermen had been killed trying to land on the island. By law, no boats were supposed to approach within three miles. The rumors were that the islanders had eaten people that landed there prior to the 2006 incident. No one knew how many Sentinelese actually lived there, but they consistently came out and fiercely threatened anyone who flew over.

Kumar himself had never actually had anyone want to fly over there until about a month ago. Then he'd had a photographer show up and charter Kumar's helicopter to make a flight over the island. The guy'd claimed to be a nature photographer and been insistent on taking pictures with the door of the helicopter open. He ran a video camera constantly and took photos with several high end telescopic still cameras, one of which he'd fumbled and dropped onto the beach near a bunch of the savages. It'd apparently broken its lithium battery case because shortly after the natives gathered around it, it caught on fire. Kumar'd been surprised that a camera had a powerful enough battery to generate the clouds of smoke that billowed out of that one. As the helicopter lifted away, he'd seen the smoke practically envelop the islanders who'd gathered around the camera.

Now, after having made only that one flight to the island in his twelve years as a helicopter pilot flying the Andaman Islands, he was making a second flight barely a month later. This passenger claimed to be a naturalist interested in isolated populations. He'd come here to observe the most isolated population known on earth. He was also making videos, but at least this guy was happy shooting through the windows of the helicopter, none of that flying with the door open crap like the last guy. He just had one simple video camera and one fancy telephoto camera. Nothing like the amount of equipment the other guy'd been using.

"We should start seeing the islanders coming out on the beach pretty soon," Kumar said, speaking as if he had a lot of experience with their behavior. Actually, on his first flight the islanders had shown up on the beach, shaking spears and pointing arrows quite a bit sooner than this. He actually flew all the way in and hovered over the beach without seeing anyone. He started to worry that his passenger would want to land, which was definitely against the law. Besides, Kumar worried that if they landed and the guy got out, one of the natives might manage to shoot him with an arrow.

"Maybe none of them are near this beach," the guy said. "Why don't you just take me on a circuit of the island flying a little way off the beach? Surely some of them'll be close enough to the beach that they'll come out."

Kumar shrugged and swung the helicopter to the

right to begin following the beaches around the island. As they flew along without seeing a soul, Kumar slowly became concerned. "I don't know what's going on," he said, "the other time I was here they came out on the beach almost as soon as I arrived. Some of the older pilots who've been here before told me that they always do, as if they're really worried about outsiders."

Kumar's passenger made a noise that sounded like a chuckle, it was hard to tell in the headset. The man said, "Maybe we arrived on one of their national holidays?"

In the distance, Kumar thought he saw a couple of large pieces of driftwood on the beach. He skimmed in a little closer to get a better look as they went by. *Bodies!* he thought, slowing the helicopter so he wouldn't go by, but suddenly feeling like he shouldn't get too close. *They're bloated!* he thought, pulling away from the beach a little bit. He said, "Um, there's a couple of dead bodies."

"I see them," Kumar's passenger said. "Maybe they had a little war down there? They're supposed to be pretty combative."

After they finished their circuit of the island, the guy had Kumar fly up over the island. They made another circuit up pretty high, trying to look for any signs of huts the natives might be living in but not finding anything. The forest was pretty dense, so there could've been hundreds of people under the trees and they wouldn't have seen them. Finally the guy said, "Well, that's really disappointing. I guess we'd just as well go on back."

As they flew back toward Port Blair, Kumar had a thought. "Hey, you know, a guy I flew over here last month dropped a camera. I've heard that isolated people like these don't have any resistance to our modern diseases. I wonder if the islanders picked up

Laurence E Dahners

that camera and caught some kind of germs from it." As soon as he said it, he began to regret it. If this guy reported it to the police, Kumar could be in trouble for flying that close to the island. *Maybe for murder too?* he wondered.

Kumar's passenger gave a derisive laugh. "That's ridiculous!"

Somehow Kumar didn't think the guy was actually surprised. In fact, Kumar had a feeling that the guy'd already thought of that possibility but just didn't want Kumar to take it seriously.

After they'd landed, Kumar continued worrying. As he helped the man out of the cabin of the helicopter, he said, "Hey, remember we really aren't supposed to fly over that island. Please don't mention your flight, or the flight of the guy that dropped the camera either, okay?"

"Yeah," the guy said, "I don't want anyone to know about this little trip any more than you do." He picked up the suitcases with his equipment, then turned back to Kumar. "Hey, was that your last flight of the day?"

Kumar nodded, as he checked over the controls of the helicopter to confirm that he'd shut everything down. As he closed the door and locked it, his passenger said, "If you're driving into town anyway, could you drop me off?"

Kumar wiped the irritation off his face. Bad ratings could result in a drop in business, so he turned toward the man and put on a big smile. "Sure, if you don't mind waiting till I finish logging out. Where do you want to go?"

"I'm staying at the Sea Princess. Are there any bars near there?"

"Not the kind of bars you're probably used to, coming from the mainland. The Nico bar makes some pretty fancy drinks though, strong ones. Would you be interested in that?"

"That'd be great," the guy said.

As Kumar's car drove to the downtown area, the guy sat silently fidgeting in the passenger seat. Kumar had the distinct sense that the man felt nervous, though Kumar had no idea what he could be worried about. He'd paid for his trip in the helicopter before they flew, so he couldn't be worried about running out on his tab. Kumar'd implied that the ride into town would be free, so he couldn't be worried about stiffing him on that.

Kumar's car pulled up and pulled into a parking space near the Nico bar since things weren't crowded. He leaned forward and pointed to the bar. Kumar said, "Here you go, though I don't know what you're going to do with your suitcases at an establishment like that."

"Yeah, I should've thought of that." The man said as he got out, "I'll bet I can tip the barman to keep them somewhere for me. Let me just get them out of the back." The man pulled open the back door and leaned in to get the suitcases. He lifted one out and set it on the sidewalk. He climbed in after the second one. Kumar felt a sudden stinging pain in his shoulder and whirled his head. The guy had a needle and syringe in his hand. He held it down low and to the side so Kumar could barely see it out of the corner of his eye. Kumar knew the guy was trying to keep it out of the field of view of the cameras on Kumar's AI headband. Holding the syringe hidden behind his suitcase the man backed out of the car. "Sorry," he said, actually looking like he meant it.

"Heeyy!" Kumar said angrily, but his head was already starting to spin. As the guy closed the door of his car, Kumar tried to talk to his AI and get it to send for an ambulance. Unfortunately, his speech had become slurred and the AI couldn't understand him. Kumar's head began tilting out of his control. The last thing he saw was the man carrying his suitcases down the street, going *away* from the Nico bar.

***

AJ watched as the Kinrais family milled about in Raquel and Shan's house. After a pleasant few days spent there over Christmas, they were all getting ready to leave for their own homes later that morning. AJ'd been dating Morgan Kinrais for six years now. At first it'd been slow because he'd been so focused on his new job out at ETR. Things had been going very well on the job now for some time and for the past several years he and Morgan had been getting more and more serious. He thought they'd been getting along well but recently Morgan had been acting a little distant. He'd been out of town for his own family's Christmas celebration and really wanted to see her when he got back. He'd called her as soon as he arrived, worrying that she might be about to break up with him. He felt pleasantly surprised when she invited him out to Raquel's house for a big family breakfast before everyone left town. They were having waffles. Shan claimed to be cooking his "special" waffles, though as near as AJ could tell, they were just regular waffles with pecans in them. They might not actually be special, but they were very good and AJ thought a lot of the family were eating more of them than they should.

AJ'd been seated between Morgan and her nephew. Feeling nervous and wanting to engage with the family, he eyed Zage. The kid was pretty chubby so AJ'd been surprised when he only ate one section of waffle, and that one without syrup. AJ picked up another couple of sections of waffle himself, feeling guilty. He thought he should take off about fifteen pounds but knew that, eating his mother's cooking over Christmas, he'd probably put on a few instead. As he served himself he realized Zage probably couldn't reach the waffles. "Zage, would you like another section of waffle?"

Zage gave AJ a doleful look and dropped a guilt trip on him, "I'd really like one, but as you can see I'm obese and so I shouldn't."

AJ tried not to stare at the boy even though he felt astonished by his reply. Partly because a child had just turned down a treat, but mostly because the kid looked too young for the apparent maturity of his answer. After a moment, he firmed his resolve and said, "You're right, I shouldn't eat this waffle either... Hey, sticking to a diet's hard. How are you managing to do it?"

Zage sighed, "Determination so far. I don't have as much willpower as I'd like though, so I'm working on finding an easier way."

"Aren't we all," AJ said with a snort. "What's your strategy going to be?"

A few minutes later, AJ felt his brain reeling. The kid had just described several hypotheses regarding the obesity epidemic and possible causes for it that he was considering. The kid thought it might actually be a communicable disease and he had several disease agents in mind. He also had various strategies for treating them. To listen to the kid you'd have thought he worked in some kind of laboratory doing sophisticated microbiological and DNA research.

He glanced over at Morgan and saw she looked nonplussed as well. Turning back to Zage, he said, "Wow, that's really interesting. Where'd you learn all that?"

Suddenly Raquel appeared and plucked Zage out of his seat. "Hey munchkin, you know other people aren't as interested in obesity as you are. You need to get upstairs and brush your teeth. We need to be ready to say goodbye to everyone here pretty soon." She set him on his feet and pointed him toward the stairs.

Zage obediently trotted off toward the stairs, leaving AJ sitting there thinking that he actually *did* want to know more about what Zage had to say. Everyone else was getting up from the table and clearing away plates though, so he stood as well. Turning to Morgan, he said, "Since we both live in town, we should take the cleanup detail while all these other folks are getting packed up to go."

She gave him a smile that seemed both happy and sad as she started stacking plates, "That's a great idea. You're a good man Mr. Richards."

~~~

Morgan and AJ had filled the dishwasher. AJ was manually washing some of the large or delicate items in the sink while Morgan deftly wiped them down and set them on a drying rack. Shan Kinrais put them away and AJ couldn't help but think that it was pretty weird to have this month's Nobel Prize winner putting away dishes. Rationally, AJ knew Nobel Prize winners still had to put their pants on one leg at a time; it just seemed like they shouldn't be doing dishes.

His heart thumping a little, AJ snuck a couple of fingers into his pocket and back out into the bowl he was washing. He rinsed it under the faucet and handed it to Morgan. Reaching back into the water for the last dish, he watched Morgan out of the corner of his eyes. She'd frozen in place, staring into the bowl. He felt her eyes turned over to look at him. "AJ?"

"Didn't I get the ring clean?" he asked.

"AJ!"

He turned to her and knelt. "Morgan Kinrais, on this most happy morning, spent with your wonderful family, I'm hoping you'll consent to joining your family with mine." He shrugged, "And, maybe... starting our own little family?" She looked shocked. Staring up at her wide eyes, he felt his heart pounding and his body trembling. He'd been feeling a little distance from her; maybe she wouldn't want to do this? *I shouldn't have asked her... put her on the spot here with her family nearby. It's going to be really emotional and embarrassing if she says no! How could I have convinced myself it was okay to ask her to marry me just because she'd invited me to breakfast with her family?!*

Morgan reached out and thumped him on the forehead, then took a huge breath. "What in God's name took you so long?! After all these years I was getting ready to kick you to the curb for a lack of commitment!" She knelt as well to put her arms around him. With a sob she buried her face in the crook of his neck and said, "Of course I'll marry you... Even if getting a ring soaked in dishwater is about as unromantic as, as... anyone could possibly imagine!"

AJ pulled back to look into her eyes, "I'm so sorry! I thought it'd be... cute... or something..." He trailed off remorsefully and hopelessly. "I'm just not very good at romantic stuff I guess."

"You guess?" Morgan sniffed, "There's no *guessing* about that. You *suck* at it!" She pulled him in for another hug, "But I love you anyway."

AJ suddenly realized that Shan was standing there staring at them, a big grin on his face. Looking up at Shan, AJ said, "I proposed." He brightened, "And she's saying yes."

Shan snorted, "Swept her off her feet, didn't you Casanova?"

AJ felt a blush rising up into his cheeks. "I'm not the smoothest..." he mumbled.

"I'll say!" Shan reached out a hand, "Let me help you two love birds to your feet and then we'll go out and tell the rest of the family!"

~~~

By the time they got out into the big room it became evident that word had spread ahead of them. The women gathered to look at Morgan's ring and the men came over to congratulate AJ. But then AJ found himself facing Morgan's dad. Mr. Kinrais had a stern look on his face as he said, "You didn't ask for my permission!"

"Oh, I'm sorry..." AJ began, but then trailed off as Kinrais laughed.

"You don't need my permission, Morgan's a free woman!" He lowered an eyebrow, "And you'd *better* not forget it."

A whirl of confusion followed as everyone chattered excitedly about the engagement while busily packing up to leave. At some point AJ learned that he was getting married that summer out on D5R's island, and that he needed to line up three groomsmen. *When did Morgan plan this out?* he wondered.

At one point as AJ stood watching everyone, he

found himself next to Raquel. They talked a little about the wedding but when a pause came in their conversation, he asked, "Did you hear what Zage was saying about obesity?"

She nodded ruefully, "Yeah, not all of it. But I know the gist of what he said because he talks about it all the time. He's pretty upset about his weight problem."

"Did you hear him talking about vectors and transmission; bowel microflora; antigens and targeted vaccination...? I didn't even understand most of it."

Raquel's expression tightened a little bit and she pressed her lips together, merely nodding in response.

"He's only five, right?"

Raquel nodded.

AJ glanced over at Zage who was talking to Morgan's sister, Lane. "I hope you've got him in some kind of advanced classes. He seems like he's way ahead of what I'd expect a kindergartner to be."

Raquel turned to gaze at her son too, "Yeah, we've had him in advanced classes, but those don't let him socialize with kids his age. We've also got him in a regular class part of the day, but he hates it. He thinks it's a waste of his time."

***

Miki frowned as she looked at the three skin lesions. As a nurse, Miki was the only medical person on Little Diomede Island, so everyone who had anything wrong with them came to see her. Siluk was the tenth person to show up with these odd pustules on their skin. Ten people didn't sound like a lot, but on an island with only 90-100 people, they represented about ten percent of the population. Probably a lot more people had the lesions if you considered the fact that the islanders didn't like to seek care and it was the Christmas holidays. Not all the Inuit on the island were Christians, but quite a few were.

Miki'd spent time searching on the Internet for such lesions without finding anything she could confidently say matched what she was seeing. On the other hand, there were a lot of possibilities. Yesterday, she'd given in and called a dermatologist on the mainland. He'd looked at the lesions over video, but he hadn't been sure either. He'd suggested that since a lot of people were breaking out with them, it might be some kind of contagious infection spreading through their tiny population. He'd suggested scraping or biopsying some of the lesions and sending samples to the hospital in Anchorage.

Miki looked up at Siluk, "You're probably not going to like this, but I need to get a biopsy and send it to the mainland. You're not the only person with these things and we need to find out for sure what's causing them."

Siluk drew back, a worried look on his face, "Do I have to pay for this biopsy?"

"No, the health service will pay for it."

Siluk relaxed, "Okay then," he waved at the splotches. "Do whatever you want."

Siluk was tough and let Miki get deep scrapings from all three of his lesions. She put them in the three different types of tubes the doctor'd recommended. Packaging them up for the next flight to the mainland, she wondered if anything would come from them. Frequently, when they sent samples off to the mainland, the information that came back was useless.

Bioterror

***

It was New Year's Day, a day Zage's dad claimed was a national holiday set aside for watching football. Shan did have some of the games playing on the big screen in the house's main room, but he didn't really seem to be watching them very intently. Nonetheless, Zage had decided to go sit in the room his parents called the library to get away from the games. He could ignore the video, but the announcers' steady chatter tended to distract him.

The so-called library actually only had a few old print books. But it had plenty of screens to pull up information from the net. Zage's AI, Osprey, was getting better and better at making the HUD (Heads Up Display) in his contact look like it was displaying multiple screens, even though all it was really doing was building a virtual image of the screens. In whatever direction Zage was looking, the screens were shown in high resolution and lo-res placeholder screens showed in the area outside the center of his field of view. Zage suspected that, at the rate Osprey was improving, he wouldn't be using physical screens much longer, but for now he still liked having a bunch of screens where he could put up several different kinds of information at the same time.

His mother came in and sat down beside him on one of the big overstuffed chairs. She was done up as Raquel. Zage still found it hard to believe that his mother and Ell Donsaii were one and the same person, especially the way she managed to change her accent, appearance, and even the way she walked between her two identities. Even the color of her eyes had slowly changed in the recent past. Now they were different between her two identities. More brown for Raquel and a brilliant green for Ell. He'd asked her about it and she said that it was pretty easy because the new AI contacts also let light *out* of the eye. So she could just alter the color of the image of her iris in the processing unit before it exited. She said, "What're you working on?"

"I'm trying to learn more about antigens."

She looked curiously up at his screens, "And what're antigens?

Zage was still coming to grips with the fact that his heroine Ell Donsaii didn't actually know everything. He doubted he'd be able to stump her on physics, but there seemed to be a lot she didn't know about biology. "Um, an antigen's a location on a germ, or cancer cell, or even on an allergen. It's a site that antibodies can attach themselves to. Usually it's a peptide, which is a small protein; or a polysaccharide, which is a chain of sugar molecules. Sometimes it's a lipid."

His mother blinked, "Oh, and what're you trying to learn about them?"

"Well..." he said slowly, thinking about how to explain, "I'm hoping that Osprey and I can search the genome of a virus and predict what its antigens'll be."

Ell looked unseeingly off into the distance for a moment, then said, "So... you find the virus's genetic coding for peptides, polysaccharides and lipids, then compare those to human genetic coding. Wherever the codes are different, you could assume that that particular part of the virus is an antigen that the human immune system could attack?"

"Well yeah, but it isn't really that simple. If, say, a peptide's different in the virus or isn't present in humans, then it *could* be an antigen that antibodies would attack. But, if that peptide's in the center of the virus, antibodies'd only be able to find and attack it if the virus was already dead and broken apart. So we're trying to find sites that could be antigens *and* that should be on the exterior of the virus," Zage said, tilting his head curiously as he wondered whether his mother would understand.

Ell gave him an intent look, "And if you were able to identify such an antigen, then what?"

Ell's narrowed eyes gave Zage pause. He wondered whether there was some reason she might object to his plans. Tentatively, he said, "Um, you could vaccinate people or animals with that antigen and produce immunity to the virus…"

"Are you thinking about vaccinating yourself to human adenovirus 36?" she asked slowly.

Zage slowly shook his head, "No, I'm pretty sure I'm not infected with the adenovirus anymore. My immune system's already developed antibodies and gotten rid of HA-36. I just have some of its DNA inserted into some of my own cells. That DNA may be causing trouble, but it wouldn't help to vaccinate myself against some DNA."

"Why not?"

"That DNA's inside my cells where my immune system can't attack it."

Ell's eyes turned back up to the screens. After a moment, she said, "So, how're you going to recognize possible antigens from a study of a viral genome?"

"Osprey and I've been working on a program that figures out how proteins will fold when they form…"

"Fold?" Ell interrupted.

"Yeah, a protein is just a long chain of amino acids…"

"I know about amino acids."

"Well, imagine a really long chain of them, like an extremely long spaghetti noodle. Now imagine that somebody threw that long noodle on your plate. It's such a long noodle that it's an entire serving by itself, but just like spaghetti, it's all folded up so it'll fit on the plate." He looked over to see Ell nodding understandingly. "Antibodies can only attach to the outer part of your serving of spaghetti, so making antibodies to the parts of the amino acid chain that are in the middle of that serving of spaghetti isn't very helpful. But," he held up a finger to emphasize the point, "as opposed to spaghetti, the amino acid chain pretty much always folds the same way. The DNA sequence tells us what the amino acid sequence will be. The amino acid sequence determines how it folds. If we can predict how the amino acids of that protein will fold, we'll know which parts of the molecule are on the outer surface of the molecule and exposed to the immune system."

Ell looked like she suddenly comprehended so Zage continued, "Also, we're working on being able to determine which parts of which proteins and polysaccharides are likely to be located on the exterior of a virus. There were some programs out there that tried to do these things but they weren't very accurate. I've been able to make some suggestions and Osprey..." Zage paused and looked up at his mother. "Osprey's... pretty astonishing you know? I know you said he's supposed to be pretty high end, but, from what I can tell, AIs aren't *supposed* to be able to do a lot of the things that he can?"

Ell studied her son for a few seconds, then ventured, "Your dad's a pretty good programmer, you know?"

Zage gave her a disbelieving look, "I'm not talking about programming! I'm talking about raw computing power. I've looked at Osprey's hardware and it's really good, but it's not even the best available."

Ell snorted, "Okay, you've got me. Osprey's CPU's actually much better than its label would suggest, but he's got some hidden PGR chips that link his CPUs to CPUs located elsewhere. We constantly upgrade that hidden bank of CPUs with the latest hardware. Essentially, even though Osprey himself isn't the very latest generation supercomputer, he's PGR linked up to a very large stack of the very best, along with links to huge amounts of additional memory and high-speed data storage. He's even hooked up to some QPUs that can handle some of the problems they're really good at."

"QPUs?"

"Quantum processors. They can solve some staggeringly difficult computations. Someday they may do all computing, but for right now they're kind of a specialty chip."

"So, you're saying that the part of Osprey I can see's only part of a widely distributed supercomputer?"

Ell nodded, seeming a little surprised by his quick understanding. "Yeah, it'd be kind of crazy for you and I and your dad to each have our own distributed supercomputer, since we wouldn't keep them busy. Essentially when any of us asks a really big question, that person's AI gets access to as many of the computing resources as they need."

Zage tilted his head, "So you mean that if I'd asked a really complex question that required an enormous amount of computational power, it might reduce your access?"

His mother laughed and ruffled his hair, "No, I have to admit that my requests would take priority over yours. Your dad's too." She got a serious look again, "I'd like to talk to you about some safety issues."

"You mean you're going to take me on tours of more tunnels, or something?"

"Um, no. Let's start by talking about your request to go to college instead of kindergarten."

"Oh, great!" Zage said sitting up and looking much more enthusiastic. "Can I start this spring semester?"

Ell rolled her eyes. "Yes," she said resignedly, though he didn't think she was really all that upset. "You did... you did astonishingly well on that SAT you took back in December."

Trying not to look smug, Zage said, "I thought I knew a lot of the answers."

"Still, I'm not sure how you'd fit into a regular college curriculum. You already know a lot of the stuff they teach in standard classes."

Zage nodded, "I've looked over the classes for a lot of the undergraduate degrees. I think I know what they teach in a lot of them and I don't really need to know what they teach in most of the others."

Ell shook her head and sighed, giving Zage the impression she didn't really know what to do with him. "It'd probably be good for you to get what's called a 'broad education' in things other than those you're interested in, but I'm not going to push that right now. So, here's what I've been working on. I've gotten to know a Dr. Barnes over at Duke University. She's a DNA researcher who's working with D5R. I know her pretty well as Ell and I've told her that one of my friends, Raquel Kinrais, has a really smart kid who's skipping high school and going directly to college, mostly at the graduate level."

"You didn't tell her I'm skipping elementary school too?"

Ell shook her head as if she felt a little bit exasperated by the whole thing. "I thought that'd be a little much for her to take in at first. I suspect she's going to be a little freaked out when you show up and she realizes just how young you are, but by then it'll be a done deal."

Zage widened his eyes in mock horror, "So you want *me* to do the dirty work of telling her myself?"

Ell grinned, "I did all the dirty work of setting this up for you, the least you can do is be the one who has to tell her how old you actually are!" Ell paused for a moment, but when Zage didn't say anything in response, she continued, "Dr. Barnes suggested one senior level class and one graduate level class for you to take. I've enrolled you in those. The rest of your time'll be in her lab doing research. I'd suggest you start looking at the readings for the courses so you can try to catch up with things the instructors will expect you to already know if you're taking those classes."

Zage looked very excited, "Okay! What'll I be doing research on? Can it be something I want to study?"

Ell snorted, "It'll be what *she* wants you to work on. You'll have plenty of time to study what you're interested in *after* you've learned what she can teach you." Ell turned serious, "I want you to understand that Duke thinks of this as just a few classes you're going to be taking, not something that'll lead to a degree. I'm pretty sure they really think of this as just a favor they're going to be doing for Ell Donsaii and not at all as something they expect you to succeed at."

"Do I *need* a degree?"

Ell shrugged, "I guess not."

Zage leaned forward and gave her a big hug, "Thanks Mom, I really appreciate this."

She leaned back and said, "Unfortunately, we're still not done with the serious stuff. If you're going to be traveling over to Duke University to take classes and work in the lab, keeping you safe's going to be more difficult."

"Oh Mom, you worry too—"

"*Don't* tell me not to worry," Ell interrupted. "You just got kidnapped last month."

"Okay..." Zage said resignedly. "Do you have a plan?"

"Several plans. First of all, you remember how we introduced you to Steve and the security team that watches over us back in December, right?" At Zage's nod, Ell continued, "Steve's hiring more people and some of them will be following you wherever you go. Not into classrooms or the lab, but they'll be hanging around outside of them. Osprey'll be able to reach them if anything happens and they'll be close enough to help right away."

"Okay," Zage said. In view of the fact that his kidnapping had been kind of scary, having people like Steve hanging around nearby sounded good. More importantly, it wouldn't waste any of his own time.

"And, I want you to take some self-defense classes."

"You mean like karate?"

"Yeah, though Steve likes a mix of different martial arts, not just one. He signed you up with a school here in town and he'll be teaching you some things himself."

"Okay." Zage frowned, "is this going to take much time?"

"An hour a week at the class and as much additional time as Steve thinks he needs."

Dismayed, Zage said, "For how long?!"

Ell shook her head and grinned at Zage's distress, "For as long as it's needed, then a while longer. There'll be other young kids in these classes so I'm counting on that to be your chance to socialize with your own age group. The classes at Duke'll be your chance to socialize with college age people."

"Mom! I get along just fine with people!"

Ell laughed, "Only when I badger you to actually talk to them. I'm pretty sure if I left you alone you'd be a hermit in no time!"

Zage rolled his eyes, "Okay." He took a deep breath, then said, "I don't want you to think I'm ungrateful. I really do appreciate you setting this up for me."

"One more thing that you're not going to like…?"

Zage sighed, "What is it?"

"I want to install a one ended port in some of the fat below your belly button."

"One ended port?"

Ell explained one ended ports and how important it was that it be kept a secret. "So, if you'd had one when you were kidnapped, I could've sent you a high-end GPS antenna and tracker. Kind of whatever might happen to you, Allan would probably be able to deliver some devices or materials to help you out."

"It wouldn't help if someone was just trying to hurt me."

Ell gave him a level look, "I could shoot Tasers or drugs through the port at them."

"Oh…" Zage thought for a moment, "Is that legal?"

"If I need to do it to save my son's life, I don't care if it's legal."

"Oh… Is it going to hurt?"

Ell slowly nodded. "I can send in some anesthetic first, if you like?"

"Okay…" Zage said slowly. "Can we do it on Saturday?"

Ell blinked, then slowly said, "Yes... but waiting won't make it hurt any less. In my experience it's just as well to get these things over with."

"It's just that... I've been doing these new exercises that make my stomach sore. I don't think I want you shooting things into it when it's already hurting."

"Okay, Saturday," Ell put out her hand to shake on it.

Zage shook her hand, understanding it was a way to signify agreement but thinking it was a weird thing to do. I'll have to move my peptide injections from my stomach to my thighs for the next few days. Hopefully the bruises'll be gone by Saturday.

***

Ell sat down at the ETR (Extra Terrestrial Resources) meeting and to her astonishment realized that Phil Zabrisk sat several seats down from her. "Phil? What're you doing here?"

Phil just grinned at her, but Ben Stavos leaned forward and said, "We invited him. He's had an idea we think we should talk about here. That's why Gary's here too; this brainstorm requires huge quantities of graphene."

Ell glanced over to where Gary Pace sat. She'd noticed him before, but at the time she hadn't registered it as unusual. Gary didn't usually come to ETR meetings, but she saw him a lot, so his presence didn't stand out like Phil's did. "Okay, shall we talk about this new idea before we move on to our other business?"

Phil glanced around the table, "As quite a few of you know, Lindy Thompson's experiment with the inflatable graphene dome on Mars is working pretty well. The dome has water from Europa in the bottom of it. Its atmosphere's made of CO_2 from Venus and nitrogen from the atmosphere of Titan. She inoculated the water with cyanobacteria; the kind of organisms that are believed to have initially generated Earth's oxygen atmosphere. Heat and light comes from a solar parabolic mirror at the top of the dome. For a while the cyanobacteria looked pretty sick in that environment. This was probably partly because of all the radiation on Mars, but also because the CO_2 levels were so much higher than they've been on Earth for hundreds of millions of years. However, the cyanobacteria appear to have undergone a spontaneous mutation that made them more tolerant. Since then they've pretty much been cranking out the O_2. Our astronauts could actually live in the dome without spacesuits if it wasn't for the radiation."

There were some excited questions from several of the people at the table who weren't aware of what'd been happening, but once everyone was up to speed, Gary asked, "So what's your plan? Allosci's making another dome already. Are you wanting to us to make a bunch of them?"

Ben opened a hand toward Phil and, taking the cue, Phil said, "As I'm sure most of you realize, the endgame would be to terraform Mars, but moving enough carbon dioxide, nitrogen, and water to Mars to make the entire planet livable would take decades even if we made the *enormous* investments it'd require to open thousands of extremely large ports. Setting up a bunch of domes like Gary just suggested could provide environments with livable atmospheres but we'd still have the radiation problem..." He paused to let this sink in, "My idea was to cover the Valles Marineris with layers of graphene…"

Ell queried Allan to determine what the area of the Valles was, but Gary'd already interrupted Phil, "Oh my God! Making that dome was already pushing the limits of what we can do and it's only a kilometer in diameter! The Valles has to be *way* bigger."

Ell gave a little laugh, "650,000 square kilometers!"

Gary snorted, then laughed, "Yeah, that'd take us at least a few weeks." He turned to Phil, "Right now, the widest we can roll out sheet graphene is two meters. We can join the edges of the sheets with a slight overlap, which is what we did to make the dome, but it isn't trivial. I hope you can imagine that covering the Valles might even take *months*." He looked up into the air for a second of thought, then said, "Actually, it took us six months to make that one kilometer dome, but we should be able to scale up fairly easily to do one a month so… 650,000 months'd be…"

"About 5400 years," Ell said, "and that's ignoring the fact that a dome one kilometer in diameter isn't actually a square kilometer. I guess we'd *really* have to scale up, huh?"

"Maybe just part of the Valles," Phil said a little weakly.

Ell turned to him, "Why cover the Valles rather than just putting up domes? We could put up domes anywhere on Mars that we wanted. Not just the Valles."

"Well, one thing would be that you could make the graphene cover over the valley in a couple of layers with a meter of water between them. The water'd serve as protection from both radiation and small meteorites."

"Why not do that in a dome?"

Phil shrugged, "The water'd tend to run down into

the sides and leave the top of it uncovered."

Ell said, "You're going to have to have a cellular structure with each cell filled by its own port anyway. If you suspended your graphene layers across the Valles, the water'd all run to the center and leave the edges uncovered."

Phil shook his head, "The air pressure underneath it'd hold it up."

Ell narrowed her eyes for a moment's thought, then it was her turn to shake her head, "Even high altitude air pressure would be way too high. Against a vacuum, even the pressure at 10,000 feet would exert around eight metric tons per square meter, but your cubic meter of water only weighs one metric ton on Earth and 0.38 tons on Mars. Your membrane over the Valles would bulge up and the water'd all run to the sides. It isn't really a problem though, it just means you'd *have* to have a cellular structure to hold the water where you want it to be. And, you can do that in a regular dome like Lindy's…" She paused and thought for a moment, then said, "I think you've had a great idea, it's just that we've got to start small. The Valles is way smaller than all of Mars, but it's still ridiculously big."

"But a dome's so small!"

"Come on Phil! A one kilometer dome has nearly 200 acres under it. We could put up domes one at a time and connect them together into a city. Settlers could live on the surface of Mars—which I agree would be way cooler than living underground. A meter of water only absorbs about fifty percent of the light passing through it, so people'd even be able to see outside. Also, if a meteor took out one dome, it wouldn't take out everybody, just the people in that dome."

Phil gave her a hangdog look, "You're always

crushing my dreams!"

Ell snorted, "Don't make me hit you with my purse. We'll *get* to your dreams, just not this year."

Around the table quite a few people looked at one another, wondering what the "hit you with my purse" comment meant. Most of them had never seen Ell with a purse. Gary said, "If we're serious about doing this kind of thing, I better start trying to figure out how to scale up sheet graphene production."

Ell gave him a bright smile, "Great idea." She turned to Phil, "Since you're on the injured reserves, maybe you could put in some time trying to come up with a design for a Mars city we can build one dome at a time?"

Phil got a mulish expression, "I want you to port me back to Mars."

"Hah!" Ell said with a grin, "I knew getting ported here in the first place lowered your IQ, I just didn't know it came down this far."

"Come on, they've just finished testing my IQ twenty ways from Sunday. This's the perfect opportunity to ship me back out there and give me all those tests again to see how much of a problem it really is."

Ell lifted an eyebrow, "Wow! It took your IQ all the way down to 'guinea pig?'"

Phil snorted, "Yeah, so it wouldn't even be a 'human subject' experiment, right?"

Ell glanced around at the others, "Maybe we shouldn't make all these nice people listen to us bicker about this. How about if just you and I duke it out after the rest of the meeting's done?"

"Okay," Phil said, then continued with a sly look, "as long as you don't bring your purse."

Ben glanced back and forth between them, then

Bioterror

said, "What's the deal with the purse?"

"We could tell you… but then we'd have to kill you…"

***

Dr. Tigner looked up and saw Mary hovering outside her office door. "What is it Mary?"

"Those samples from the weird lesions on Little Diomede island?"

Tigner nodded.

"Um, they're growing out a virus. I've PCR'd it but it isn't matching anything in our database. I think we've got to send the sequence to CDC."

"Does the system say it's similar to anything in the database?"

"Um, the closest things are the orthopoxviruses, but it isn't really homologous to any of them."

Tigner'd heard of orthopoxviruses, but couldn't bring to mind exactly what they were so she spoke to her AI and looked over at a screen. A list of ten species popped up and her eyes scrolled down it, suddenly catching on smallpox. "Holy crap!" she breathed. Probably the most famous thing about Little Diomede Island was the fact that it was close enough for people on it to see Russia's Big Diomede Island. The Russians were well known to have created weaponized versions of smallpox back during the Cold War. They'd even had an accidental or possibly intentional release of it at Aralsk in 1971. *Everyone* infected with that agent had died! A weaponized version of smallpox would be similar to, but not homologous to, the orthopoxviruses. She raised her eyes to study Mary, "Has anybody but you worked with that sample?"

Mary shook her head, suddenly looking worried. She obviously hadn't looked up the orthopoxviruses until now, but must've seen smallpox on Tigner's screen. "Are you... are you thinking it might *be* smallpox?"

Tigner shook her head slowly while chewing her lip and thinking furiously. "No, it *isn't* smallpox, but if someone's created a modified version of smallpox, it might be even worse. Have you had any breaks in technique?"

Mary shook her head, looking uncertain, "No, not that I know of. But..."

Tigner knew what she meant, you could never be 100 percent sure that your sterile technique had been perfect. "Okay, I'm almost certainly overreacting, but I want you to go freeze down one sample with 'extreme biohazard' written all over it. Before you freeze it, thoroughly wipe it down with disinfectant. Any other small items that even *might* be contaminated—just drop them right into a tub of chlorine bleach. Wipe down your *entire* work area. Do anything else you can think of to disinfect the area. Send me the sequence and write down a list of *everybody* you've had contact with since you started working on it. Then stay there in your lab until I can get one of the infectious disease docs to find a place to isolate you. Meanwhile, I'll call the CDC and ask them what to do. Once I've done that I'll call out to Little Diomede and find out if the people with the lesions have gotten really sick or not. As soon as I confirm that they're okay, I'll let you know and we'll both breathe a big sigh of relief, but in the meantime we need to be taking all precautions, okay?"

Mary nodded, but the tears welling in her eyes told Tigner she wasn't really okay. She understood as well as anyone that the most important thing they could do was isolate her, and that was to protect everybody *else*, not her. If she had a weaponized version of smallpox in her system she was probably going to die.

Tigner wanted to go give Mary a hug, but that would be crazy. Instead she tried to give her a reassuring smile, "Hey, don't get too upset. There're some antivirals that kill smallpox now. If this's some kind of old Russian weapon, it was probably created back before they started coming up with all the antiviral agents we have nowadays. If it's bad juju, we'll get you treatment, don't worry."

Mary nodded and left her doorway, still looking terribly frightened.

As she should be, Tigner thought grimly.

Chapter Three

"Ueda-sensei?"

"Yes Mark?"

Mark indicated a chubby boy standing next to him, "This's our new student, Zage."

"Thank you Mark," Ueda said, thinking that the pudgy child looked just like the kind of kid who got beat up by his classmates. Probably his parents were hoping to stop the bullying by giving the boy confidence enough to protect himself. He looked back at Mark, "If you'll take him over, introduce him to the others and get started, I'll be over in a few minutes."

Mark was one of Ueda's junior senseis. Ueda didn't usually teach beginners himself, though he made an effort to participate briefly in their early classes to set the tone and to make them feel like they had the attention of a senior sensei.

~~~

By the time Ueda got over to the beginners' class they'd finished their stretching and were practicing basic kicks. As usual, most of them looked really clumsy, but then Ueda's eyes caught on the pudgy kid who'd just started that day. Although he was several lessons behind the others, he looked... much more coordinated. A kid as young as the boy appeared to be typically moved in an ungainly fashion, so the graceful way the child moved had Ueda narrowing his eyes and watching him for a couple of minutes. Finally, he gave a mental shrug. *That kid's taken lessons somewhere else,* he decided.

Then Mark saw Ueda standing to the side and called the class to attention so Ueda could make a few points...

***

The Imam narrowed his eyes. "You want to release a disease that you believe's going to kill millions, possibly *billions* of people?!"

Hamza curled his lip, "Infidels. Billions of *infidels*."

"And you believe that *Allah* wants us to kill *all* nonbelievers?"

Hamza shrugged, thinking, *I thought this Imam was weak.* He said, "It'll be the ultimate weapon in our Holy War. After all the centuries of treachery we'll finally get *revenge.*"

The Imam began shaking his head in disbelief, "I don't accept your idea that every nonbeliever's evil and should be killed. We *should* be bringing them into the faith. But, even if I *did* think that Allah wanted us to kill every nonbeliever, I can hardly believe that Allah would accept as his tool a weapon that might kill 10 to 40 percent of his believers as well." He stood and spat, "I stand in opposition to your misguided notions!" He turned and strode out of the room.

Hamza turned to the man next to him and sighed, "Not every Imam will make the right choice. I never thought that one had the courage for Islam Akbar." He jerked his head after the departing Imam, "Make it look like the Christians killed him."

The man got up and silently followed the Imam, eyes tracking the religious leader like a seeker weapon.

***

On the first day back after Christmas, Kimberly Binder looked out over her classroom full of gifted kindergartners. Something seemed a little bit off, so she scanned over the class again. *Ah, Zage Kinrais is missing.* She had her AI report it to the office, then called the class to order. She'd barely had time to regret the lack of his calming influence on the rest of the kids when she got a message back from the office telling her that he'd been withdrawn from the school.

At first Ms. Binder merely felt mild regret that she wouldn't have Zage in her class any more. But as the morning went on, she remembered how he'd had a two-day absence for a headache after being hit on the head before Christmas. At the time she'd wondered about it since even gifted children were sometimes subjects of abuse. Now she developed an uneasy concern that the two events might be related. She sent another message to the office, asking why he'd been withdrawn.

Shortly thereafter she got another message on her HUD, "Attending another school."

That eased her concern briefly, but then she wondered where they could've moved such a brilliant child. The Chapel Hill School for the Gifted where Kimberly taught was generally accepted to be the best school in the area for highly intelligent children. "What school?" she replied.

Bioterror

"Duke University."

I didn't know they had a facility for gifted children. Maybe it's for the kids of some of their faculty members? she wondered. Then she remembered talking to his folks on Meet the Parents day. The mother worked out at D5R and the father worked at UNC. *Even if Duke does have a facility for the children of their staff, it doesn't seem likely that Zage would be going there.*

She resolved to visit his home and make sure the boy was okay.

***

Mary looked around, warned by the pressure change when the door started to open. Even with two nurses assigned to her around the clock, she'd been living a lonely existence in the isolation room for almost 2 weeks now. The nurses didn't visit very often because of the requirement that they put on extreme isolation gear, a process that took a substantial amount of time. Putting the stuff on required an assistant, the reason that two nurses had to be assigned to her.

Everything they brought into her room was disposable, if possible. After it was used it was pushed through a little window into a heavy duty trashbag to be sealed up and incinerated. Big fans sucked air out of her room through filters designed to trap viral particles. That way when the door was opened, none of her possibly contaminated air blew out into the hallway because the air was flowing rapidly *into* the room. Technically, all these precautions were interesting, but personally, it felt unnerving. The fact that she didn't see anyone who wasn't dressed in something like a spacesuit made her feel abandoned and deserted—even though logically she knew it wasn't true.

Dr. Tigner'd called into the room a few times to tell her not to worry. The people on Little Diomede seemed healthy and Tigner expected the CDC to rescind their isolation order, but that'd been days ago.

Now Mary watched the door open wider, expecting to see Andrea, the nurse assigned to her during day shift. Instead, she saw Dr. Tigner and Mary's infectious disease specialist, Dr. Rosen, both with wide smiles on their faces. She liked Rosen because he'd put her on an antiviral agent which was known to be effective against orthopoxviruses. It'd made her a little sick, but as Dr. Rosen'd said, better a little sick than a lot dead.

The most astonishing thing was that neither Tigner nor Rosen were wearing isolation gear and they came waltzing into her room as if it were no big deal. "I'm off isolation?" she asked hopefully.

That question was answered when they each came over and gave her a big hug. Tigner said, "I hope you know that everyone at the hospital appreciates the hit you took to protect the rest of us. It turns out it wasn't needed, but it's a case of better safe than sorry."

Rosen nodded, "Yeah, everyone who had lesions over at Little Diomede seems to be fine and I've been telling those guys at CDC that we should let you out for days now. Hell, you never even got a lesion, so I don't think you were even exposed. Of course, Kelso and the other people at CDC wanted to play it safe, but *they* weren't the ones who were in isolation!"

Wanting to get out of the room, Mary nervously started packing up her kit, but then she turned to Rosen, "Have they decided what it is?"

He frowned, "Its sequence is closer to vaccinia than

it is to smallpox. The biggest difference is a mutation of the protein coat."

Uncertainly, Mary said, "Which one's vaccinia?"

"Cowpox," he said. "You may remember that's the virus they used to vaccinate people against smallpox. This version's more like the vaccination version than the original cowpox version."

"So, what're they thinking? That one of the geezers who got vaccinated for smallpox back in the old days is a carrier and his virus mutated or something?"

Rosen snorted, "Well, maybe. More likely it'd be some kind of animal carrier. Cowpox infects several natural animal reservoirs. Interestingly it grows better in some small animals like cats and rodents than it does in cows. So, it might've mutated in one of them..." He paused, thinking, "It's more worrisome to think that someone might've modified it intentionally."

"Why would anyone do that?!"

"Practice?" Rosen shrugged, "Some bioterrorist who wants to modify smallpox, but wanted to get his chops down on a safer virus?" He shook his head, "There's a lot of scary questions *that* brings to mind. Hopefully the people at CDC are chasing down all those possibilities."

***

As Nate walked into the first day of his senior level cell biology class, he was surprised to see a chubby little kid sitting in the front corner seat by the door. *What the hell?* he wondered. *Did one of the women fail to get a babysitter and just decide to bring her kid to class?!*

Realizing the kid was sitting all by himself, Nate thought, *Where the hell's his mother?* He never considered the possibility that the boy might be the offspring of one of the male students. Nate decided that as long as the kid didn't have a tantrum or otherwise screw up the class, it wasn't his problem.

After a few minutes, one of the girls who came into the class sat down next to the kid. At first Nate was relieved that the kid's mother was there, though he still thought it was pretty bad that she'd left him alone in the class for a while. Nate's attention drifted as he wondered whether any of his friends might be in this class. Since none of his buddies had come in yet, he let his eyes drift around, checking out the women in the class. Eventually his gaze returned to the kid's mother. He wondered what she'd been doing while she'd left the kid sitting there by himself. She seemed to be talking quietly with the boy and Nate got the impression she'd just asked the kid a question. She drew her head back as if she was surprised by his response. This time she spoke loudly enough that Nate heard her say, "Really?"

The kid nodded solemnly. He shrugged, "It's just because I want to learn though. Not for a degree or anything."

Nate had no idea what that might mean, but he didn't get to consider it for long because just then Dr. Marshall, their professor, came in.

Marshall did a double take when he saw the child. He looked at the girl sitting next to the kid and said, "Um, we can't have you bringing your child to class. It's not fair to the other students."

The girl said, "He's not *my* child." Although he was looking at her from the side a couple rows back, Nate had the impression that she got a little smirk on her face before she said, "He says he's a student in this class."

Dr. Marshall blinked in surprise then turned his eyes to the boy. Tilting his head, he said, "Where's your mom?"

The kid said, "She's at work. Someone'll pick me up later today."

Looking a little flustered, Marshall said, "But… but, who's going to watch you during class?"

"I will. I'm surprisingly mature. I won't cause any problems." The kid said, "I really am enrolled in this class. If you'll look up the class roster, you'll find my name, Zage Kinrais."

Dr. Marshall stared at the kid for a moment, then spoke to his AI. He glanced up at his HUD then back down at the kid. He cleared his throat, then said, "Are you related to Shannon Kinrais?"

The boy nodded while Nate wondered who the heck Shannon Kinrais was. He heard someone in the row behind him whisper something about a Nobel Prize. Nate knew some people in the triangle had gotten Nobel Prizes in December, but the only name he remembered was Ell Donsaii's.

Marshall said, "Are you just auditing this class?"

The boy shook his head, "No, taking it for credit, though I'm not actually working toward a degree at present."

Marshall frowned, "You don't have a HUD. Do you have an AI yet?"

The boy nodded, "My mom works out at D5R and she got me some of the new contacts with a HUD built-in."

"Well… welcome," Marshall said. He swept the room with his gaze and said, "Welcome to all of you." Marshall's eyes went back to the child one more time as if he had no idea what to do with him, but then he looked back at the class in general and said, "Let me lay out a few ground rules and tell you where we'll be going in this course..."

~~~

True to his word, the kid didn't cause any trouble during class. When class was over, Nate found it surprisingly annoying that three of the nice looking girls stopped to talk to the boy. *Oh well,* he thought, *the kid won't be around long.*

***

Adin was meeting with the man from Islam-Akbar again. The man said, "Your results so far have been perfect. In the tests on the boat, every unvaccinated monkey and man died and every vaccinated one survived. If anyone survived on Sentinel Island, the overflight didn't find them. Now you tell me that every blood sample we acquired from the people on Little Diomede shows that they have the antibodies." He smiled, "As do you and I." The man paused, then fervently said, "Allah Akbar! I believe we're ready to proceed, do you?"

Adin swallowed, suddenly shaken by the magnitude of what he was about to put into motion. But then he firmed up and nodded. "Have you rented the facility I suggested and recruited the technicians?"

The man nodded.

"And Ibn Sinar's set up the putative research

company under whose name we'll be ordering our supplies?"

"Yes, Harrell Health. We've already purchased most of the equipment and set up standing orders for most of the chemicals and culture media."

Adin stood and put out his hand, "I'll quit my job. We're ready.

"Ready to wield the world's mightiest sword…"

***

Carley was eating lunch with Alice and listening to her hold forth on just how unfair it was that Dr. Barnes wasn't letting them work with D5R's ET DNA. Rick, Dr. Barnes' other grad student was eating with them. He said, "Come on Alice, you heard her say she had to sign all kinds of agreements just to be allowed access herself. She's not *supposed* to let anyone else do anything with it."

Alice gave him a wide-eyed look, "They'd never know! Besides, she doesn't have to let us actually work with the DNA, she could just tell us what's going on."

Rick snorted, "They'd never know?! Come on! When've you ever been able to keep a secret?"

Alice rolled her eyes, "I can keep a secret!"

Rick turned to Carley, "What's Marvin's girlfriend's name?"

Carley winced a little, but quietly said, "Jim."

Rick turned back to Alice, "You outed him."

Alice folded her arms in front of her. "He didn't care," she said sullenly.

"He *did* care. He just says he doesn't care now, because there's no way he can put that secret back in the box."

Alice said, "I'd be able to keep whatever we learned about the DNA a secret," but Carley noticed she kept her eyes downcast.

Rick didn't let up, "You're really smart Alice, but if I were Dr. Barnes, and having word get out would lose me this opportunity, I wouldn't trust you with a secret either."

Alice's eyes flashed up to Rick, "Has she told you about it?!"

Rick gave her a sad smile, "No, she hasn't told me either. She made a commitment not to tell anyone and I think she's honoring her pledge." He shrugged, "I do think we'll learn about it before anyone else. As soon as they decide that ET DNA's not a threat to the world, we'll probably get to help Dr. Barnes work on it—long before anyone else gets to touch it."

Carley looked up and saw Dr. Barnes approaching their table. She laid a cautionary hand on Rick's arm as she brightly said, "Hi Dr. Barnes."

Barnes sat in the fourth chair at their little table but didn't pull out a lunch. She looked a little worried and Carley feared she had some bad news. Barnes said, "Hi guys. Um, I've got to get on over to the BSL, but I've been wanting to talk to all three of you together, so when I saw you..." She took a deep breath, "I have some strange news that I hope won't turn into a real problem."

Carley felt a sinking sensation in her stomach. *What if they've withdrawn one of her grants?* Carley didn't really understand how research was funded yet, but knew that if a professor lost a grant it could mean that a more junior grad student like Carley might be looking for a new position.

Barnes drew out a substantial pause as if she didn't know how to proceed, but finally she cleared her throat and said, "You know I've been working with the people over at D5R?"

Everyone nodded and Carley's heart beat a little faster. Maybe Barnes was about to let her grad students work with some of the ET DNA?

Barnes pursed her lips and looked down at the middle of the table. "Apparently, one of Donsaii's assistants has a boy who's somewhat of a prodigy. He's skipping high school and going directly to college." Barnes raised her eyes to look at the three of them and Carley wondered why a kid like that would affect them. Maybe Donsaii asked to have the kid's DNA analyzed to see what made him tick, or something dumb like that? Barnes said, "This boy's really interested in DNA and wants to work with it in a lab."

Alice, never one to hide her thoughts, said, "Oh my God! This kid's, what, thirteen?! And we're going to have to babysit the little geek in the lab?!"

Barnes looked chagrined. With a little shrug, she said, "Donsaii said if he causes any trouble, we just have to say the word and he'll be out of here. That said, the opportunity to work with extra-terrestrial DNA is *huge*. I know you guys haven't been allowed to work with it yet, but I'm hoping someday...? Also the funding D5R's providing's really generous. Hell, they're giving us unrestricted funding that adds up to fifty percent more than all three of my other grants. If I lose one of the grants, you guys'll still have jobs." Rick looked like he was about to interrupt, but Barnes waved him off and continued, "The kid must be pretty smart. I figure you can give him some rote tasks to work on, pipetting, centrifuging... Things he probably can't screw up. The rest of the time you can just let him watch you do what you do and it'll probably keep him happy."

Rick shook his head, "Donsaii's assistant had a genius level kid? Come on, we're in genetics. Where'd he get the genes for that?"

Barnes grinned, "Kid's name's Zage Kinrais. That make you think of anything?"

The three grad students looked at one another and all shrugged.

"His dad's name's Shannon Kinrais?" she said interrogatively with an eyebrow elevated. When the three of them still looked puzzled, she said, "Math professor at UNC who got Nobel prizes in physics and chemistry with Donsaii, just last month? You guys really need to keep up with current events in science."

They sat stunned for a minute. "Still," Rick said, "thirteen-year old boys get bored in a hurry. Then they get to be a huge pain in the ass. I not only was once a thirteen-year old boy myself, I have a younger brother." He shook his head and eyed Barnes, "And you *know* you're not going to want to tell Donsaii he's a problem."

Barnes shrugged, "He's registered as a student and he's also taking senior level Cell Biology and graduate level Molecular Genetics… "

Alice interrupted, "Wait! He's not only skipping high school but he's skipping all his undergraduate classes too?"

"Yeah," Barnes said with a little laugh. "And we all know how tough those courses are even if you've had all the prerequisites. I figure it won't take long for those classes to make him and his parents adjust their expectations. Most importantly, *we* won't have said no."

The three grad students glanced at one another, but

no one voiced any other objections. Carley thought that each of them was probably worried that they'd personally wind up doing most of the babysitting, but they could all understand how keeping Donsaii happy was important to the lab as a whole. When no further protests were forthcoming, Barnes stood, "Well, I've got to get to the BSL. He's supposed to show up at the lab sometime tomorrow. Be polite and notify me when he gets there so I can meet him. Don't be afraid to let me know if he starts causing any problems."

After Barnes walked away, the three grad students engaged in some prospective bitching, then split up. Alice and Rick had classes so Carley headed back to the lab to check on her DNA amplification. The polymerase chain reaction, or PCR, that she'd started before she left for lunch still hadn't finished, so she had her AI open her ongoing web search for her brother Eli. She still tried to spend 20 to 30 minutes a day searching for her brother, though more and more she felt like he'd slipped out of reach. The one Eli Bolin she'd found had proven to be quite elderly. There were 26,000+ people in the United States with the first name of Eli. She couldn't get access to any databases that'd let her search by Eli's birthdate, so she was having to pull people up one at a time and try to rule them out, a task which would take forever. So far she'd found one Eli with the correct birthdate, but when she'd contacted him, "he'd" turned out to be one of the very few girls given the name Eli.

Even worse, Carley feared that her brother's actual name might've been Elijah or Elisha or some even more obscure biblical name but that she just hadn't been aware of it as a child. From what she remembered of her parents, her father didn't seem like the type to use an obscure biblical name, but her mother might have.

Worse, what if, when he'd been adopted, they'd changed both of his names?

The thermal cycler chirped to tell her it'd finished the PCR and she turned to it with a sigh.

On her search? No luck, as usual.

***

Kimberly Binder knocked on the door of the house. It wasn't quite what she'd expected since she'd thought anyone who could afford to send their child to The School for the Gifted would display their wealth ostentatiously. Admittedly, it seemed to be situated on a pretty big lot, but it looked like a refurbished farmhouse.

Zage's handsome father opened the door and she gave him a little wave. "Hi, I'm Ms. Binder, Zage's teacher last semester at the school for the gifted, remember?"

"Yeah, hi," the man said, looking puzzled.

"I didn't get to say goodbye to Zage because I thought he'd be coming back for the spring semester. He was one of my favorite students, so I thought I'd drop by and tell him I'd miss him." She lowered her voice and gave a shy little shrug, "I thought about bringing him some cookies, but I know he's trying to lose weight."

"Come on in," the man said, still giving Kim an odd look. He led her through a little entry area, then turned left into a large room. It still seemed like an old farmhouse, though some of the furnishings seemed upscale. There were lots of large screens on the walls and Kimberly's eye caught on a brilliant white canvas splashed with blue paint. Her initial reaction was that some modern artist had simply splattered paint on a canvas and called it art. However, as Zage's dad called out the boy's name and stepped into another room to retrieve him, Kimberly found herself strangely attracted to the painting. By the time Zage and his dad came back into the room, she was standing close to the painting and staring at it enviously, trying to figure out just what made it so very striking. The man said, "Ms. Binder?" and she tore her eyes away.

"Hi Zage," she said, walking to him and bending down closer to his level, her eyes flashing over him. He had no visible bruises and certainly looked happy enough. "I was very sad to hear that you wouldn't be coming back to school this spring. You've been one of my favorite students."

"You were an excellent teacher," he said solemnly.

"The office said you're going to some program over at Duke?" She said, glancing questioningly up at his father. "Are you liking it?"

"Yeah!" he said, his face suddenly animated. "I'm learning some really cool stuff."

"Oh?" Kim said, suddenly very curious to learn how their program might differ from what she'd been teaching. "What're they teaching you there?"

"Cell Biology and Molecular Genetics."

"Um, that's interesting," she said, wondering if he even knew what the words meant. She could imagine a kindergarten class where they mentioned those concepts, but even that seemed a little extreme. She glanced up at his father who was biting his lip and looking as if he didn't know exactly what to say. "I hadn't heard about a Duke school for children. Is it for the children of the faculty there?" She gave him a little grin and a wink, "I thought you were on the faculty at UNC?"

Mr. Kinrais made a tiny wince, "I am. Um, Zage is..." Kinrais stopped uncertainly, then resumed, "He's wanted... more of a challenge. He's been learning on a college level for a while now." He glanced down at his son, "He's been bogging to actually attend a college. Duke's allowing him to study Genetics at a graduate level on a trial basis." He shrugged, "It's anyone's guess whether it'll work out, but so far he's very excited about it."

Kimberly suddenly remembered asking Zage to multiply two three-digit numbers and having him immediately give her the correct answer. *Oh!* she thought, *He really is a prodigy, isn't he?* She couldn't help but think it was ridiculous to expect the child to successfully skip grade school, high school, and college. She wondered whether skipping all that education might constitute abuse, but it certainly didn't comprise the kind of abuse she'd been worried about. She smiled down at him and said cheerfully, "Well, we're going to miss you. Maybe you'll drop by for a visit someday?"

As Kim said goodbye to the father and made her way out of the house, she found her eyes repeatedly tracking back to the brilliant blue painting.

***

Carter DeWitt got out of his car in front of ET Resources and saw AJ Richards' car pulling up behind him. As his car pulled away to find a parking spot, he waited a moment for AJ to get out of his vehicle. "Hey

AJ, how's engaged life treating you?"

"Pretty good! Morgan's whole family goes out to Colorado to go skiing for a week every February." He lifted an eyebrow, "I'm on the invitation list this year!"

"Oho, sucking up to the in-laws already, huh?"

"You betcha. Besides, my family lives in Colorado Springs, so we'll get together with them while we're out there too."

"Oh man, you're in trouble now you know," Carter said putting his hand on the younger man's shoulder.

AJ frowned, "Why's that?"

"You poor sod. All the women, from both sides of your new family, are going to be getting together and hashing out your wedding!" He shook his head as if dismayed, "They're going to be asking you questions, you know? Your real issue's whether or not you know how to answer them?"

"Um, honestly?"

"Oh! The horror! Didn't your dad ever teach you anything about this most important ritual?!"

AJ grinned at him, "Okay, I'll bite. How do I answer?"

"You say, 'Whatever you think dear.' No matter how she begs or pleads, you do *not* give an opinion. Any such opinions will, of course, turn out to be wrong and, worse than wrong, they'll be incorrect, wicked, sinful, unsuitable, improper, and just plain inappropriate. Years later you'll still be hearing about how you made her do some part of *her* wedding in such and such a way and how the fact that you wanted to do it that way broke her heart! 'Whatever you think dear,' or some variation of that sentiment's your only possible correct answer. *Do not* stray from it!"

AJ rolled his eyes and said, "Yes boss." As they walked together into the building, he slanted a look at

Carter out of the corner of his eyes and said, "It won't be hard, that's how I've learned to answer any questions here at work."

Carter gusted a long-suffering sigh, "If only you had, my boy, if only you had."

AJ said, "I've had an idea."

Carter stopped and turned to face him, "Let it out slowly, a little bit at a time. Some of your ideas explode on contact with reality."

"A few decades ago there was some talk about trying to improve traffic under some of the big cities like LA by running tunnels back and forth between some of the high demand areas. The advent of AI vehicle control lessened the need as citywide traffic optimization and the ability of vehicles to travel bumper to bumper at high speed let us move a lot more cars, faster and more densely on the same number of streets. But population density's continued to creep up and it's getting to be a real problem again."

"I know," Carter said, shaking his head. "They should outlaw personal vehicles in densely populated areas and make everyone take mass transit."

AJ shrugged, "I'd agree with you, if personal vehicles were still pollution-spewing, natural-resource consuming monsters, but they're not. In my opinion, if people want to take their personal vehicles despite horrible traffic, they should be able to. We're supposed to be living in a free country."

Carter tilted his head curiously as he thought back to what AJ'd said to begin with. "So, what, you want to use melting tunnelers to provide traffic bypass in high density areas?"

AJ nodded. "And runoff tunnels in cities prone to flooding. We'll have to be a lot more careful with the engineering, of course. There'll be a city on top of these tunnels so we'll need to melt some small test tunnels first, harvesting chunks of the walls and mechanically testing them to be sure they're strong enough. I'll bet a lot of the tunnels will actually need to be reinforced. Still, melting them'll be a lot cheaper than drilling holes with huge tunneling machines and the melt walls will provide some strength so the amount of reinforcement will be less."

Carter's eyes widened, "Oh! Would it be cost-effective to seal off sections of the tunnel and just grow some graphend on the walls?"

AJ shook his head, "We could ask Viveka, I guess. But I ran the numbers as best I could and I think it'll be cheaper to use concrete."

"Viveka?"

"Viveka Janu. She's the graphend guru out there at Allosci."

"I thought Dr. Pace was the guru?"

"He is, but when it comes to coating large objects, Viveka's the one. Pace married her. Some people say he only did it so she wouldn't get away."

***

Mark Amundsen stood on his back porch and looked out at the little water feature he and his wife had built in their yard. *I've got to get a job,* he thought once again, taking another sip of his coffee. Since Stockton fired him as Secretary of Defense, he'd refused to take a position that traded on his previous connections. Although he'd been paid well as Secretary, he hadn't been getting a salary large enough to put away a huge nest egg and he hadn't been a wealthy man before—so their cushion was thinning.

He'd taken some work as a consultant, of course, as long as he didn't think they were only hiring him for whatever influence he might still have in government. Consulting was paying most of the bills, but definitely not putting money in the bank. Once again, he wondered what he'd actually *like* to do. He'd enjoyed his life as a public servant and thought he was good at managing sprawling enterprises like the Department of Defense. However, it seemed unlikely that he'd be hired back while Stockton was president.

Maybe I need to sign up with some kind of headhunter firm. They could let some big corporations know I was available. He considered the fact that they'd probably want to shop his skills to various defense contractors. *I could just tell them not to,* he chuckled, *at least until we get a lot more desperate than we are now.*

His AI said, "You have a call from Ell Donsaii."

"I'll take it," he said, surprised at how emphatically he'd responded. "Dr. Donsaii, what can I do for you?"

"Hi Mr. Amundsen. I heard you're working as a consultant nowadays. Are you still... available?"

"Um, sure," Amundsen said, ineffably disappointed. His heart had leapt upon hearing who was calling. In the past, his contacts with Donsaii had seemed always to be filled with change... Changes that generally roiled history, almost always for the better. Her asking him to consult for her company seemed so disappointingly mundane in contrast.

"D5R's gotten... So huge and sprawling. You probably know I've been working as CEO, but my heart and my... my skills are better suited to being a CTO.

We'd like to find someone good at managing large enterprises to replace me as CEO. Someone ethical... Someone like you.

"My fondest hope's that you'd be willing to take it on yourself, but I'll understand completely if it isn't your cup of tea. If you aren't available, I'm hoping you might know someone... suitable?"

Amundsen groped out behind himself for the arm of his chair. He'd intended to settle into it, but found himself dropping into it with a thump while feeling a little lightheaded. "I'd, I'd be very interested. I think of D5R as one of the most positive forces for change in our world and I'd be proud to be involved any way I can. Can I come down to North Carolina and look around? Get a better handle on exactly what you need?"

"Oh! That'd be awesome!" Amundsen felt surprised at the excitement in her voice. Goosebumps ran down his spine at the thought of working with her full-time. She said, "My AI just did a handshake with yours, delivering e-vouchers for you and your wife's expenses on the trip. Can we have our plane pick you up tomorrow morning?"

Amundsen briefly wondered whether there was anything on his calendar for tomorrow morning. Nothing that can't be rescheduled, he decided. *I'll look at it after she hangs up.* "Tomorrow morning would be great. If you'll just send a message with what time and where, we'll be there."

Once Ell had hung up, Amundsen got shakily to his feet and made his way back into the house. "Mary?" he called out.

***

Carley felt a presence behind her and turned to look over her shoulder. Sure enough, a woman stood in the door of the lab, looking around curiously. A slender, pretty brunette, moderately tall at what Carley estimated to be about five-nine, she looked to be in her late twenties or early thirties. "Can I help you?" Carley asked, thinking that something about the woman was odd.

"Is this Dr. Barnes lab?"

"Uh-huh," Carley said, standing and moving toward the door. Suddenly, she saw that a boy stood beside the woman. He'd been hidden by the centrifuge.

"I'm Raquel Kinrais," the woman said, then indicated the boy, "and this's my son Zage. Zage's been enrolled at Duke in a special, non-degree seeking program and Dr. Barnes's been kind enough to agree to let him do research in her lab."

Flabbergasted, Carley found herself staring at the boy. *He looks like he's five! Six or seven tops!* Her eyes rose back to the woman, "Um, we've been told that... that, a boy was skipping high school and coming straight to college, but..." Her eyes dropped involuntarily back to the boy. Suddenly she realized that this was a political hot potato that she shouldn't even be commenting on. Nervously, she said, "Just a minute, let me contact Dr. Barnes." She spoke briefly to her AI and when Dr. Barnes voice came in her ear, she said, "Dr. Barnes, Zage Kinrais's here... with his mother. You wanted to be notified?"

Carley turned back to the mother and her child, "Dr. Barnes says she'll be here in about thirty minutes. Can you wait, or..." Carley realized she'd been about to offer to babysit the boy until Barnes got there, but if the boy needed babysitting this was going to be a much bigger nightmare than she'd dreamed of.

The woman said, "No problem, we'll be happy to wait. Do you mind if we look around the lab in the meantime?"

"Um, no…" Carley paused feeling torn between politeness and prudence. "Um, please don't… don't touch anything without asking though, okay?"

"Sure," the woman said, giving Carley a brilliant smile. She winked, "I'm hoping Zage can explain all this equipment to me."

Carley sat back down and turned to her screens, uncomfortably wondering whether it was okay for them to be wandering around the lab unsupervised. Surely his mother wouldn't let the child fool around with anything.

As Carley continued studying for her Population and Quantitative Genetics class, the mother and son duo wandered up and down the aisles of the lab murmuring to one another. Carley tried to avoid listening in. However, her abnormally acute hearing let her hear the boy launch into a description of their thermal cycler and how it was used to amplify minute quantities of DNA or RNA through the polymerase chain reaction. Listening to a child his age talk about highly sophisticated equipment as if he understood it was so astonishing; she found she just couldn't ignore his voice. To her utter disbelief, the next thing she heard was the boy describing the advantages and disadvantages of their particular model of thermal cycler! Since Carley'd always just thought of it as "the thermal cycler" without considering the possibility that they might want or need a better model, or be particularly happy with the model they had, this was an eye-opening experience for her.

He moved on to describing the uses of their robotic pipetter and why he'd have chosen a different model. He assessed their plate shaker as "perfectly adequate" since better models were exceedingly expensive and not a great deal better. He didn't like their centrifuge, but thought their freeze-drying system was state-of-the-art Their sonicator didn't perform as well as the model by Branson. He'd have chosen a homogenizer made by Benchmark Scientific. He didn't think their incubator was worth the extra money it'd cost.

This went on and on. Even their analytical balances were assessed. They were found wanting for an "alarming degree of inaccuracy if not frequently recalibrated." To Carley's dismay, his most disparaging comments were reserved for his evaluation of their DNA assembly modules which he said were a generation out of date. "…and the newer stuff isn't really all that expensive, so upgrading would be a good investment."

Can he possibly be that knowledgeable about the lab's equipment?! Would we really be a lot better off with the models he'd prefer?! Guiltily, she wondered, Should I have been trying to evaluate our equipment and figure out whether there was better stuff out there? It seemed crazy, she didn't even know whether Dr. Barnes could afford to get better stuff.

She sat, stewing, for several minutes. Worried that her professor was behind the times and that, therefore, what she was learning wasn't the cutting edge like she'd believed. Then, as if she'd been startled, she abruptly thought, *A few minutes ago I was worried that he was a five-year-old who needed babysitting! Now I'm suddenly concerned about his assessment of the equipment in our laboratory?! Get it together Carley! He can't really know, can he?*

Carley realized that neither of them had said anything for several minutes. When she glanced around at them, they were both staring off into space like zombies. *Oh. They have HUDs in their contacts.* Carley realized that the mother's lack of a headband had been what'd struck her as odd about the woman when they'd first arrived. Carley'd first heard about contact HUDs a couple of years ago, but they hadn't hit the mainstream as fast as she'd hoped. They were still quite expensive and the lenses themselves had to be fitted by an optometrist, then checked every so often. Only extreme early adopters and the wealthy seemed to be getting them so far.

Of course, if the mother works out at D5R, she probably gets a great deal on them.

Carley started studying again, but after a moment she decided to look up Zage Kinrais' name.

~~~

Carley turned around when she heard Dr. Barnes' voice. Barnes said, "Hello. Oh, hi Raquel. I hadn't realized that Zage was *your* son?"

The mother nodded. Dr. Barnes looked around the lab as if searching for someone, then turned back to Raquel, "Where is he?"

"Um, right here," the mother said, putting her hand on the little boy's shoulder.

Carley was both amused and a little freaked out by the shocked expression on Dr. Barnes' face. Barnes said, "But..." The pause went on for an extended period, then Barnes said, "Dr. Donsaii told me that your son was skipping high school and coming to college..." She looked at the boy and tilted her head curiously, "Just how old is he?"

Carley had the impression that the mother wanted to sigh, but she didn't. She said slowly, "He's five. Dr. Donsaii didn't tell you just how young he was for fear you'd reject him out of hand. I think if you'll give him a chance, you'll find he really can do the work." She glanced at her son, "He loves genetics so he's highly motivated."

Barnes looked askance at the boy, "Motivation can only go so far..."

"I think you'll find he's quite capable as well."

Addressing the child, Barnes said, "Have you been attending the Cell Biology and Molecular Genetics classes I suggested?"

The child merely nodded, a serious look on his face.

"And do you feel like you're understanding..." Barnes paused as if she suddenly had the feeling that that "understanding" would be impossible, but then continued, "That you're following what they're teaching?"

The boy nodded again.

"Can you tell me what the endoplasmic reticulum is?" she asked, obviously wondering whether he'd understood the early basics of cell structure in the cell biology course.

With a serious expression the child said, "A network of membranous tubules in the cytoplasm of eukaryotic cells which are contiguous with the nuclear membrane. Rough endoplasmic reticulum has ribosomes attached and is integral to protein synthesis. Smooth endoplasmic reticulum lacks ribosomes and is important for lipid synthesis and metabolism. Clinically, abnormalities in the XBP1 gene can lead to heightened endoplasmic reticulum stress response related to syndromes of increased inflammatory responses. Such responses have been confirmed to contribute to Alzheimer's disease in the brain and Crohn's disease in the bowel. The unfolded protein response…"

Barnes snorted and put up a halting hand. "All right, all right, you know what the endoplasmic reticulum is." She looked at the boy's mother, "You may be right. He may be capable of the work. I just can't help worrying that keeping up might be very stressful at a delicate time in his life…"

Zage said, "If it's too hard, I'll let you know. I want to do this because I think it'll be fun. If it isn't fun…" he gave them a grin, "I'll want to do something else."

Barnes stared at him for a moment, then broke out a smile of her own. "See that you do. As long as we're agreed on that, we should be able to find you something to do here in the lab. The first thing I have any of the grad students do is extract DNA from Baker's yeast, amplify it with PCR, use CRISPR to insert a fluorescence gene and a switching gene, then reinsert their modified DNA back in a yeast cell. I've written up a protocol for doing it that the students follow. It's my belief that running this protocol over and over until you get it right and your yeast glows is an experience that teaches you a lot about how things are done in a genetics lab. Do you feel up to taking that on?"

The boy nodded again, the serious look back on his face.

"Carley, could you give him a tour of the lab?"

"Um," Carley said, wondering how she could tell Dr. Barnes that the boy'd already toured the lab himself. She was saved when the boy's mother said brightly, "We've already been on a most excellent tour of the lab…" She glanced around, "Unless there're other rooms besides this one?" When Barnes shook her head, the mother continued, "Is there anything else he should do today?"

The boy said, "I could get started on that protocol…?"

Barnes said, "Oh no, let me send you the protocol and you can read over it tonight. Tomorrow you can come in, find your reagents and get started on it." Barnes glanced at Carley, "Carley, when will you, Alice or Rick be around tomorrow so you can answer questions for him?"

"I'm pretty sure that one of us'll be here almost all of tomorrow. We each have classes, but not all at the same time."

The boy said, "I don't want to bug them, I'm sure they all have their own things to do."

"Nonsense," Barnes said. "Each of them followed this protocol when they started in the lab and they all needed help from someone more senior to them. It's a long-standing tradition for seniors to help juniors. Besides," she glanced at Carley, "you never learn something quite as well as you do when you have to teach it to someone else."

After the boy and his mother made their goodbyes and left, Barnes turned to Carley and exhaled a long breath, "Holy crap! A *five*-year-old." She got a distant look in her eyes, "I'm not sure I know how to process this." She paused for a moment, looking thoughtful, then turned back to Carley, shaking her head, "What do you think? Don't pull any punches. If I have to tell them he can't work here, I'll just have to gird my loins and do it."

Carley blinked a couple of times, then said, "After

they first showed up, I did a search for his name—which is uncommon." At Barnes nod, she continued, "He's already listed as co-author on a publication about using ports to analyze gut microbiota by Turner and Jenkins at UNC."

Barnes got a pinched look, "Dilution of authorship's getting to be a real problem…"

Carley shook her head and interrupted, "I… I think he probably made significant contributions." She flushed a little bit, "The tour of the lab they took?"

Barnes nodded, "Thanks for that,"

Carley shook her head again, "I didn't take them around. Ms. Kinrais asked if *they* could look around, and I said, 'Sure, as long as you don't touch anything.' They walked through the lab and, I swear, they looked at every single instrument we have in here."

Barnes shrugged, "That's fine. If he's going to work here, he's going to see that stuff anyway…"

Carley interrupted again, "You don't understand. They were talking quietly, but I've got… really good hearing. They didn't just look at the equipment, that little boy told his mother what each thing was, what it could do, and how we use it to do the kind of things you do working with DNA." Barnes gave her an astonished look, but Carley lowered her voice as if telling an embarrassing secret and continued, "He also had opinions about almost every one of our instruments. Some were state-of-the-art, some were perfectly adequate; for some he thought we should've gotten a competitor's product, and some he felt were poor quality or out of date and really should be replaced!" She looked up into Dr. Barnes eyes, "I don't really know where you'd even get information comparing our instruments to whatever else's on the market! Does someone publish reviews?"

Barnes swallowed, then said, "Maybe someone does do reviews, but I haven't seen them." She glanced away, speaking quietly, "Sometimes you have to use what you've got because your grants won't buy all the newest toys..." She shook herself and turned back to Carley, giving her a weak grin, "Maybe he won't be a drain on our time and resources after all, huh?"

~~~

On their way home, Zage said, "I still don't think you needed to go with me."

His mom shrugged, "I know you want to do this college thing on your own. But they were freaked enough by your age that I think they might've sent you packing if I hadn't been there."

Zage folded his arms over his chest, "I think I could've dealt with it by myself."

Ell snorted softly, "Well, just think of it as humoring your worrywart of a mother then..."

Chapter Four

Mark Amundsen looked around the big research room at D5R. The room was filled with small clusters of bright-looking people animatedly working on obscure projects. They seemed to be using a lot of exotic looking equipment and he had the feeling that great things might be getting accomplished. It didn't, however, look very polished. It looked more industrial or something.

It wasn't nearly as glamorous as he'd expected. Ell had taken Amundsen and his wife out to a nice dinner the evening before; at which they hadn't talked any business. She told him that she wanted him to get a tour this morning without her so he'd feel free to talk to D5R's people and look at whatever he wanted.

A nice young lady named Bridget Spaulding was taking him around. She said, "Is there something in particular that you'd like to see?"

"Cutting edge research?"

Bridget shrugged, "This building's pretty much where they do all the research on new stuff. Manufacturing, port warehousing and control, allotrope synthesis, space energy and asteroid mining all happen at other facilities. Down there to the left's Quantum Biomed where they work out how to do biological interface stuff, like artificial arms, eyes, hearts, kidneys, lungs and pancreata."

"Pancreata?"

"Plural of pancreas."

"Oh... I understand how the artificial pancreas monitors blood sugar and administers insulin to control it, that's not so different from the external pumps people've been wearing for some time, it's just that it's done through implanted ports. I also have a vague idea how the arms and eyes work through their neural interfaces and that the artificial kidneys simply imitate dialysis without the person having to be hooked up to a big machine... And I'm pretty sure that the heart device just helps squeeze your own heart, right?"

Bridget nodded.

"But I don't understand how the artificial lung works. Is it something like the heart-lung machines they use in surgery?"

"Yeah, and that's the problem they're having as I understand it. They have to use blood thinners to keep the blood from clotting as it passes through the membranes to get oxygenated. Blood thinners are really dangerous, having a high mortality from bleeding into the brain and similar problems. Roger's working with some membrane chemists to come up with a membrane that'll exchange oxygen and carbon dioxide but won't stimulate clotting in the hopes it can be used without thinners. I don't know how it's going, but let me take you down where you can ask him yourself."

Soon Amundsen found himself talking to Roger Emmerit, an intense young man with an unruly shock of hair. They hadn't solved the clotting problem, but he was excited about several new possibilities they were getting ready to test.

Next Bridget took Amundsen down to talk to some people who were in the very early stages of working out a system of traffic tunnels that they hoped to put under large cities with the same type of melting tunnelers that were being used on Mars. They also expected that tunneling under bodies of water would now be cheaper than building bridges over them.

Amundsen felt like his head was spinning after just these two discussions. Bridget was talking about several other projects he could look at, but then she stopped and said, "Or we could go talk to Ell. She said to bring you by any time you felt like you were ready to talk to her."

"People here just call her Ell?" Amundsen said, feeling a little surprised that his tour guide was on a first name basis with the CEO.

Bridget shrugged and leaned closer as if speaking confidentially, "She's my roommate. If I had to call her Dr. Donsaii all the time it'd be kind of clumsy. I do it around outsiders, but she said you might be joining our team?"

Amundsen's eyes had widened, but he adjusted. *Roommate?!* he thought. *Don't they pay Donsaii enough for her to live by herself?* "I guess I am ready to talk to her, do you want to check with her to see if now's a good time?"

"No, it'll be fine." She waved a hand, "This way."

Amundsen followed her, expecting to go to a corner office with a great view of the verdant landscape outside. Instead, Bridget led him down an ordinary hallway to one of a row of offices that didn't even have windows. Inside, Ell was mounted on what Amundsen recognized as a waldo controller. When Bridget said, "Ell, Mr. Amundsen's here," she immediately told her AI to shut the waldo down, pulled off her 3-D goggles and dismounted with a big smile on her face.

Looking genuinely happy to see him again, she put out her hand for a shake. "What'd you think? Would you be interested in trying to herd this particular bunch of cats?"

He said, "I think so, yes. But there's still so much I don't know…" he trailed off hesitantly.

"Well, if you're at all interested we should get you around to see our other facilities. You've got to visit Portal Technology where the ports are manufactured and check out the huge port controller warehouses where we support the ports." She glanced at him, "Even though we *call* them warehouses, almost all of them are actually underground now to keep them safer from people with ill intent. That's especially true now that we can simply melt more tunneled space for them any time we need it." She glanced at a wall screen, then back at Amundsen, "Also, you should take a tour of ET Resources where they manage the asteroid mining, radioactives disposal, the solar parabolic mirrors, and the deep space cooling resources." She pointed up at the ceiling, "Since there's really no rush for you to make a decision, I think you should also take a ride up to the space habitats and look in on where Allotrope Science is manufacturing a lot of our carbon-based products."

"Um, I thought those were all separate companies, licensees of D5R's patents. Are you telling me they're all subsidiaries of D5R?"

She tilted her head, "Well, it's complicated, but, essentially the answer's yes."

"And none of them are listed on the stock exchange so… I'm assuming that everything's privately held?"

She nodded, "Everything's held by private investors, yes. We have a board and they vote their shares on important decisions, though they leave most of the day to day decisions to me."

"And if I were to decide to come on as CEO, they'd

make the final decision and I'd answer to them?"

"Yep," Ell said cheerfully and winked. "They'll like you, I promise." She tilted her head again, this time looking curious. "You look concerned?"

Amundsen shrugged and spoke slowly, "Well, so far I've only looked around the research facility. Admittedly, I thought I was looking at the biggest part of the company. Ms. Spaulding mentioned other facilities, but I mistakenly thought they were small outlying buildings where some space mining, allotrope synthesis and port manufacturing research was being done, rather than understanding that she was referring to entire companies that I simply didn't realize were subsidiaries." He shook himself a bit as if settling that knowledge into place, "In any case, I was little bit concerned about the lack of polish, or glitz, or whatever you might want to call it. You know, those shiny places companies show their investors to make them feel like they're investing in something substantial and cutting edge."

Ell just grinned, "Don't worry too much about that. Our investors are much more interested in results than sparkly bangles."

"I assume I'll be able to look at the financials?"

Ell nodded.

"And meet some of the major investors?"

"Sure. If you decide you want the job, we'll have a meet and greet."

***

Having checked with the house AI to make sure Ryan wasn't there, Ell bounded up the basement stairs into the house she shared with Bridget. As she made her way through the main room toward the front door, Mary from the security detail stood up out of one of the chairs. Realizing that Mary'd been waiting to talk to her, she stopped and said, "What's up?" She smiled, even though having one of her security team stop her for a chat was rarely good news.

Mary said, "You might be aware that I'm taking a self-defense course at Zage's dojo because it falls at the same time as his class?"

Ell winced, "Yeah, I know. The class you're in isn't very advanced and so it's probably pretty boring, huh?"

With a shrug, Mary said, "That's no big deal. It keeps me in shape and lets me watch over the munchkin without it seeming weird…" She paused, as if uncomfortable, but then forged ahead, "It's the watching him that we need to talk about."

A little prickle of dismay came over Ell, "You getting tired of babysitting?" She'd frequently worried that her security team must find it boring to follow her—and now her family—around. She really liked Mary and would be pretty sad if she wanted to leave.

"Oh, no!" Mary said, looking startled. "Um, I'm wanting to talk about his… his performance in the class. You know how you're faster than any human has a right to be?"

"Oh," Ell said, thinking about how Zage had seemed more coordinated than most babies when he'd started walking. On the other hand, he'd started walking very late so maybe he should've been more coordinated? Maybe he was really struggling in the class? "I guess, what are you trying to say?"

"I think you need to have a little talk with him. He's performing way above the level of the other kids, even the ones older than he is. He's doing way better than any kid his age has any right to. I don't think the other kids have realized it's so far out of the ordinary yet, but I'm seeing raised eyebrows among the instructors at the dojo." She paused for a second, then continued, "The thing is, I get the feeling he's completely disinterested and not even trying. If he were to start performing at the level he's capable of, there'll be a lot more than raised eyebrows. Next thing you know he's going to be in the news and the dojo's going to be trying to put him up for national competitions. That kind of stuff could blow his cover."

"Oh…" Ell said, feeling a different kind of dismay than she'd expected when Mary first started talking to her. "You think I should talk to him?"

Mary looked surprised, "It's not my place to tell you what to do. I just didn't want this to catch you unawares in case you *did* want to do something about it."

"Thanks… I think," Ell said thoughtfully. "Do you think he's learned enough to defend himself already?"

"Oh hell!" Mary said, "*I* wouldn't have wanted to take him on even before he started the class. All I have to do is consider what he did to that kidnapper on the stairs, then realize that the self-defense course has given him even more tools…" She gave a quick shake of her head, "That said, I think the class is good for him in a lot of ways. He seems to be losing some of his excess weight and I think he's made friends with a couple of the kids there. They may represent his only chance to interact with kids his own age, right?"

"Right… Well, I'll have to think about this some." *Has he really been losing weight and I haven't noticed?* "Thanks for letting me know."

"Good," Mary said, bouncing to her feet and heading for the back door. She said over her shoulder, "Enough chitchat, I'd better get back to work."

Ell sat, pondering the issue for a moment, then stood up to go. Behind her she heard Bridget's voice, "Hey Roomie, want me to make you an omelet?"

Ell turned and smiled at her friend, "Of course I do, but I already ate a big breakfast before I left home. If I don't get a move on I'm going to be late for my meeting."

Bridget looked at her hesitantly for a second, then said, "I'd like to put a bug in your ear—something to think about?"

Ell nodded, hoping that it wasn't going to be another bombshell.

Bridget said, "I'd kind of like to..." she hesitated again, then said in a rush, "I'd like to invite Ryan to stay the night a little more often. 'Cause, you know, when I stay over in that pit he lives in's just plain disgusting. I haven't managed to domesticate him yet."

Ell grinned at her, "I don't think the male species can *be* domesticated. If you don't think you can accept him as he is, you'd better be thinking about kicking him to the curb."

"I know..." Bridget said, looking at the floor for a long moment, but then her eyes came back up sparkling, "but, I do love him. And I like him even better here, where *I'm* in control of the degree of slovenliness."

Suddenly feeling bad, Ell said, "You're all grown up girl, you certainly don't have to ask my permission to bring your boyfriend home at night."

Bridget raised an eyebrow. "I have, occasionally. But, if I start having him over here... a lot, and *you're* never

here at night..."

"Oh! I should've thought of that, shouldn't I?" Ell paused, thinking.

Bridget said, "Maybe it'd be better if I moved out?" She gave a weak grin, "I can certainly afford it now, my boss pays me pretty well."

Ell raised her eyes to Bridget's, "I want you to do what you want to do. Move out if you'd like..." she wrinkled her nose, "though I'd advise against moving into Ryan's place unless you burn it down and rebuild first." She waited trough Bridget's snort of laughter, then continued, "But it's nice for my cover story if I have a roommate. And I certainly don't care if my roommate has a live-in-boyfriend. The only real issue's the fact that Ryan doesn't know that Raquel and I are the same person. If you and he are committed to one another, maybe it's time we told him?"

Bridget clapped her hands together excitedly, "Oh! That'd be great! But... Can *I* tell him?!"

Ell laughed, "Sure, it's okay with me as long as you let me know as soon as you do. And, of course, really impress him with the extreme need for secrecy. Now, I've really got to get to work."

***

Ell found Zage in the room of the house they called the library. It seemed like he'd been spending a lot of his time there lately. As usual, he had all the screens lit with various information, some of the big ones divided into several smaller windows. "Hey kid, what're you working on?"

He didn't look away from his screens, "Osprey and

I've worked out an algorithm for identifying a virus's antigens from its DNA sequence. I'm trying to confirm how consistent the algorithm is at predicting known antigens."

Ell studied her son, then reviewed, "And antigens are proteins, polysaccharides or sometimes lipids. They make up the sites that antibodies can attach themselves to, right?"

"Uh-huh, and we've made a couple of serendipitous observations that we think enable us to reliably predict how proteins fold after they're synthesized. That lets us know the 3-D structure. I've gotten pretty good at guessing from the structure what a protein does, therefore where it'll be located in the cell or virus, and how it'll be oriented once it's there. When the protein's incorporated into the surface of the cell, we can tell what parts of it are going to be external and then which sequences of amino acids are in that section." He glanced at Ell, "Those parts of the protein on the surface of the virus act as antigens that might be recognized by the immune system." He frowned as if he were trying to judge his mother's comprehension, "Antigens that're inside the virus aren't accessible to attack by the immune system until after the virus's already broken up and nonviable."

Ell avoided the impulse to say, "You already told me that." She was out of her depth in this area and it was better to have her son over-explain biology than make him reluctant to do so. Instead, she said, "So, how well's your algorithm working?"

"Um, I think pretty well." He looked at Ell again, "We don't have an endless number of viruses to which antibodies've successfully been made *and* where we know the viral genome." He chewed his lip, "In fact, we've only been able to find good information on thirty-nine of them so far, but the algorithm predicted the antigen correctly in thirty-eight." He frowned, "Of course, the algorithm also predicts other antigens that it says the immune system *should* be able to recognize. Those antigens might also work, or they might not, we only know for sure about the antigens to which antibodies have been successfully created so far. We don't have any data that'll tell us whether antibodies *could* be generated to the other antigens the algorithm predicts."

"Thirty-eight out of thirty-nine sounds awfully good. You're sure you're not a victim of observer bias?"

He gave her a thoughtful look, "That'd be if I, as the observer, felt so sure the algorithm *must* be right, that if it gave wrong answers I'd find an excuse for it, or fudge the answers, or otherwise correct for it, right?"

Ell nodded.

"I'm pretty sure I'm not," he said, a serious expression on his face. "We developed the algorithm on a different set of thirty viruses and their known antigens for which effective antibodies had been created. Then we tested them against these thirty-nine additional viruses. I had to help figure some of the folding, but I didn't have to correct anything, the algorithm came up with the thirty-eight on its own."

"That sounds pretty great. What're you thinking you're going to do with this algorithm?"

"Well, as I understand it, it's probably pretty valuable intellectual property. Do we need the money we might get from selling it?"

Ell slowly shook her head, feeling astonished that Zage had recognized the potential.

"It could be a *lot* of money?"

"We really don't need it kid. On the other hand, if you feel like you'd like to earn some of your own money, I'd understand. I could even introduce you to some pretty sharp patent people."

"I don't really need money, as long as you're willing to keep buying me whatever equipment I want for the bio-lab downstairs."

"We're happy to keep doing that. If you don't want to sell the algorithm for money, what do you think you're going to do with it?"

"I was thinking about setting up an anonymous website where people could put up viral genomes and get back sets of likely antigens that they could use for making antibodies, or maybe even vaccines." He eyed her, "Kind of like my own little charity."

Ell tilted her head curiously, "Anonymous?"

"Yeah, 'cause you don't want people to know who I am, right?"

"Right. Sounds like a good altruistic endeavor to undertake, though it's hard to know whether a website like that'll take off or not. I hope you won't be disappointed if it doesn't."

Zage shrugged, "I'd like to put it up and see what happens."

"I'd like to suggest you get your dad's advice on setting up the website? He's kind of a genius at those kinds of things. He could make sure the site doesn't get traced back to you."

"Oh, okay, I'll check it out with him when I've got it ready to go." He turned his eyes back to his screens.

Ell kept studying her precocious son and, after a minute, he turned back to her. "Is there something else? Something you're waiting for?"

Ell gave a little laugh, "Yeah, I've been talking to

Mary, you know from your security detail?"

Zage nodded.

"She's a little bit worried about…" Ell ran down, not quite knowing how to phrase it.

Zage's eyes'd been tracking back to his screens, but now he turned fully back to her, a curious look on his face. "What is it Mom?"

"You remember, after you were kidnapped, Steve talked to you briefly about how you're really quick?"

Zage nodded. "Does Mary think I've been moving too fast in martial arts?"

"Uh-huh. She says you do not only better than any of the other kids in your class, but you do better than kids who're quite a bit older than you. And she doesn't think you're even trying. Are you?"

"It's not really my kind of thing, you know? I could try harder I suppose, but it sounds like you'd rather I didn't?"

"Um, yeah. It'd be really good if you could tone it down. I used to do that. I'd watch other people do a sport so I'd know just how good regular people were and then I'd try to imitate the way they did things so I wouldn't stand out."

Zage gave her a surprised look. "Are you saying that *you're* good at sports? That I might've inherited this from you?"

"Um," she said trying not to laugh. Trust her son, absolutely and completely uninterested in sports, to be one of the few people on the planet who had no knowledge of her athletic abilities. To be completely aware of and looked up everything she'd done in science, yet never have made any effort to look at anything else about her. "Yeah, I'm…" she paused, considering whether to tell him what she'd been able to do in the past. She decided not to, instead continuing with, "I'm pretty good. So, if people thought you were really good, that might tip them off to considering the possibility that you might be related to me."

"Oh," Zage said staring at her like she'd just grown another ear.

"So, do you think you could start trying to watch what the other kids in your class are able to do and then trying to imitate their speed and coordination? And do the same for any other sports you might wind up participating in?"

He gave a decisive little nod, "Sure." He glanced at his screen a moment, then back at her, "Is that all?"

"One more thing. Have you noticed that when you're upset or angry or frightened that you seem to be able to move even faster?"

Zage thoughtfully looked up at her. "I've felt some pretty weird things. First my heart pounds, then it feels like my heartbeat gets slower. In fact, the whole world seems to get slower. But then, later, when I think back on it, it seems like actually *I* was moving faster?" He grimaced, "Like when I hit that kidnapper guy on the knuckles when I was escaping. To me it felt like I was moving at an ordinary speed and he was just slow somehow. But then when I hit his hand, it seemed to do a lot more damage than I expected. I've gone back and looked at the vid a couple of times trying to understand it, but I'm not sure I do. I even researched it on the net and I can't find any description of this kind of thing happening to other people."

Ell nodded, "The same thing seems to happen to me. I think you've inherited it, but I don't think it happens in anyone else. Maybe I have a mutation that I've passed on to you?"

Zage suddenly looked interested, "Oh that'd be a cool thing to study." His gaze drifted thoughtfully off into the distance.

Before he got too distracted by the genetics, Ell brought him back to the question at hand, "I call it the 'zone,' because it seems to be a little like something that happens to a lot of athletes. They say they're 'in the zone' when they're suddenly able to play their sport at a higher level than they usually do. I worked hard on being able to control the zone, so that I wouldn't go into it unintentionally and maybe accidentally hurt someone while playing sports or something like that. I also wanted to be able to go into the zone on purpose when I needed to be able to be faster than other people."

Zage gave her a surprised look, "Really?"

Ell gave him a careful nod. "Taking a few deep breaths and thinking calm thoughts when I feel the zone coming on seems to minimize the effect in me. For a while when I wanted to get myself into the zone I just thought panicked thoughts, but it didn't take long to develop the ability to get into it even while I was staying calm."

Zage searched her face as if he thought she was teasing him, but then, apparently deciding she was serious, said only, "Huh."

"Do you think you could try to work on controlling when you go into the zone too? Or at least on trying be able to recognize when you've accidentally gotten into it so that you can slow yourself down and keep from hurting people?"

"Sure," he said, then paused for a moment, then said, "Anything else?"

Ell smiled at his transparent desire to get back to

working on his antigens. She leaned forward and put her arms around him, "All except for this little hug I seem to need."

He put his arms around her in return, squeezing firmly. "Hugs are *good*."

~~~

After his mother left, Zage decided to take a moment away from his algorithm project and get Osprey to do a search for Ell Donsaii and sports. He stared at the results. Instead of what he'd expected— just a few links about how she'd played a sport or two and done well—there seemed to be tens of thousands.

"Olympics."

"Gymnastics world records."

"World's fastest human."

"World's greatest athlete."

"Lowest golf score in history, probably never to be broken."

He had a vague recollection of his father wanting him to watch the opening ceremonies of the Rome Olympics a few years back. First he looked up exactly what the Olympics were, since he didn't know. Then he watched the section of the opening ceremonies and saw his mother light the torch. Then he watched some gymnastics, and a foot race.

Prickles ran over his scalp, She isn't just good! She's by far the best in the world! How did I not know about this?!

***

Shan came downstairs in the morning and found Ell

already slicing a banana into a big bowl of cereal. Since she only slept a few hours a night, she'd probably already been up for a long time. He gave her a hug and went to find his own brand of cereal. She got out the milk, but paused before pouring any in her bowl. "Before I start shoveling this in my mouth, I'd like to put a bug in your ear about Zage."

Getting down a bowl, he said, "What's that?"

"He says he's come up with an algorithm for determining what parts of viral protein sequences will be found on the surface of the virus."

"And knowing that's important because?"

"The part of a protein that's on the outer surface can serve as an antigen for antibodies to lock onto when your immune system's trying to kill the virus."

"Hmm, sounds interesting."

"Where you come in is that he wants to set up a website where people can put up viral DNA sequences. Then he'll give them back the protein sequences that'll be found on the exterior of the virus. Knowing that sequence they can make vaccines for that antigen—and therefore that particular disease—or at least generate antibodies that they might use in research."

"Surely people already have ways to determine what proteins are on the outside of a virus, don't they?"

She shrugged, "He says that figuring out how the amino acid sequence of a peptide folds into the three-dimensional shape of the finished protein's pretty difficult. Apparently, if you knew what parts were on the outside of the virus, you could immunize people or animals to just that part of the virus, rather than having to try to immunize them to the entire virus. Obviously using an intact virus can make that person sick, but a killed virus might be broken up and therefore generate a lot of antibodies to proteins on the interior of the virus. Being immune to the inside of the virus doesn't produce immunity to the intact virus." She shrugged, "At least that's how I understand it."

Shan said, "Is he wanting to sell this service?"

Ell smiled, "He asked me if I wanted him to. Said it could be worth quite a bit of money." She shrugged, "I told him we didn't need the money so it'd be okay to give it away. He seemed pretty happy with that. Called it 'his own little charity.'"

"So why doesn't he just give away the algorithm itself?"

"I don't know. I guess I should've asked him, but I didn't think of it. You can ask him if you want, but I was hoping you could help him figure out how to set up a website to do what he wants. One that can't get traced back to him."

"I can do that, but why would anybody want to find him because of a website? Are you thinking this's going to be important?"

Ell shrugged, "You've got me. I suppose it might not ever get any traffic. But if it does turn out to be a big deal I'd be pretty sad if we hadn't taken precautions before he got started."

Shan nodded, "You're right about that. I'll talk to him tonight."

~~~

Shan found Zage in the library with almost all the screens lit up with stuff that, as usual, looked biological. "Hey kid. Your mom tells me you're wanting to set up a website that'll help people find viral antigens?"

Zage looked up and said, "Osprey and I've already programmed a website, mom just wants you to make sure it's secure so nobody can trace it back to me."

"No problem. Can I ask though, why you don't just sell or give away the algorithm? Then people could determine what part of the sequence will be on the external surface of the virus and could be an antigen all by themselves."

Zage frowned, "The algorithm's pretty good, but there're always a few sections where it can't predict the folding."

Shan studied his son, then said, "I don't understand. If the algorithm doesn't always work, how does putting up a website solve that problem?"

"Umm... *I* seem to be able to predict the folding pretty well." Zage shrugged, "I think it might be like the way mom solves really difficult math problems in her head?"

"What makes you think your mom solves math problems in her head?"

Zage tilted his head, "She always claims that Allan feeds her the answers, but I've watched her when she comes up with those kinds of answers. She doesn't move her eyes to see them on her HUD, or get the expression she normally gets when she's listening to her AI. I'm pretty sure she just solves them herself."

Shan mentally rolled his eyes as he nodded, "OK, you're right. She can solve astonishing problems in her head."

"Somehow," Zage said, "I guess because I've been thinking about this for a long time, the protein folding solutions just seem to come to me." He looked off to the side and got a curious look on his face, "I should ask mom if math answers just pop into her head like that. I mean, I can solve some pretty large math problems in my head, though I can't do the kind of things I've seen

Mom do. But when I'm solving them, it's not like I work through them, it's just like the answer's just suddenly there." He looked back at his dad, "Same thing with protein folding."

Shan stared at his son, thinking about how almost anyone who'd ever had arithmetic just felt like they *knew* that two plus two was four. He, of course, just "knew" the answers to a lot more complex math problems than that, but his real talent was his intuition for how math questions might be solved. He relied on computers to do the kind of computations that Ell could do in her head. He took a deep breath, realizing there was no way he was going to understand how the human brain worked in such a situation. Instead, he addressed the obvious problem. "If people start sending you a lot of viral sequences with questions about the resulting antigens, couldn't you wind up spending all your time trying to figure out how those proteins fold? I mean, if you did have an algorithm that'd do it, people could send you thousands of sequences and Osprey could solve them almost instantaneously, but if you're going to have to solve them yourself..."

"Oh, no," Zage interrupted, "Osprey can work out almost the entire 3-D structure. It's just that there's almost always a few sections he can't solve. He only shows me that part of the sequence and the 3-D model he's worked out so far." Zage shrugged, "The answer almost always feels instantaneous to me, not like it's a lot of work."

Shan said, "Well, there's a pretty good chance no one'll ever stumble across your website, in which case you won't get any queries and it certainly won't suck up any of your time. I guess you can wait to worry about what to do about *too many* requests if it actually happens."

Shan looked at Zage, "Let's get your website set up so it's isolated by a PGR link. Physically finding one end of a PGR link, gives you no clue as to where in the entire universe the other end of the link is. But, since PGRs come in pairs, in theory if someone found one side of the pair you'd bought, they might be able to trace the sale of the pair back to you. However, because there're so many people who want to have anonymous PGR links, brick-and-mortar electronic stores have big bins full of loose PGR pairs from which you can pick a pair at random after you've paid. That way, nobody knows who bought that particular pair. We don't have to do that though; your mom already has a bunch of anonymous PGR linked connections to the web. We'll just hook your website up through one of them. What's it called?"

"Gordito."

"Gordito? Where'd that come from?"

"It's Spanish for 'little fat boy.'"

Shan drew back and looked at Zage, "Are you referring to yourself? You look like you've been losing weight. I've been feeling pretty proud of you."

"Yeah," Zage shrugged, "My hope's that someone'll use the website to come up with a vaccine for Human Adenovirus 36. Maybe kids won't have to be gorditos in the future."

***

Nate snorted, the little fat kid who was in his cell biology class had three of the best looking women in the class sitting around him, looking like they were hanging on his every word. Nate studied the kid, thinking that the little tub of lard looked like he'd lost some weight. *But why're all the girls hanging around him?* he wondered. He thought back to how he'd been told that if you wanted to attract women, you should go take along a baby or a puppy. *Still, you'd think that, even if the fact of being a child might get him some attention for a while, these girls wouldn't still be sitting around him after weeks and talking to him like...* Nate decided he didn't know exactly what they were talking to him like. He didn't think there was any way it could be romantic with a boy that young. And at the kid's age, he couldn't possibly be able to carry on a conversation about something that young women would be interested in. *I guess he must incite their nurturing instincts,* Nate decided.

Then Dr. Marshall came in. The man had a habit of starting the class by choosing a student and asking them to explain to the rest of the class what one of the intracellular organelles did. Nate was dreading the day Marshall called on him, but had been trying to read ahead a little bit so he wouldn't be too embarrassed when his turn came. "Ribosomes," Marshall said, his gaze sweeping the class. He focused in on the kid and said, "Zage, do you feel up to telling us what ribosomes do?"

Nate found it a little irritating that Marshall asked the kid *if* he felt up to it. He certainly didn't let the older students off the hook if they "didn't feel up to it."

Undisturbed, the kid said, "Yes sir. A ribosome's a molecular machine that serves the cell as a translational apparatus for protein synthesis. It assembles polymeric protein molecules according to a sequence controlled by messenger RNA. Amino acids are carried to the ribosome by transfer RNA molecules which enter one part of the organelle and bind to the messenger RNA chain at the correct site, thus setting that particular amino acid into the sequence correctly. A different part of the ribosome then links the specified amino acids into the chain to form the peptide.

"A ribosome's made up of complexes of RNAs and proteins and is therefore called a ribonucleoprotein. It's divided into two subunits…"

Astonished on the one hand, but furious on the other, Nate stopped listening at that point, though the kid went on and on until Dr. Marshall finally raised his hand and brought him to a halt. Nate expected Marshall to go back over what the kid had described, making corrections like he did for the other students he called on. Instead, the professor apparently found the boy's description completely adequate, saying, "Thank you Zage. That was an excellent description of the process and I'm going to let it stand."

Marshall said, "I'm going to use the screens here to show you some cartoons that I hope might help you remember what Zage said by giving you visual images of how you might think of the ribosome zipping along messenger RNA and guiding the amino acid assembly."

Nate thought, *Crap! I'm going to have to go back over my AV record of what the kid said…*

Nate didn't consider the possibility that the child's extensive comprehension suggested he might be able to carry on a conversation the young women in the class might enjoy.

***

Ryan was getting ready to go home when Bridget said, "You can stay over if you want."

He paused, looking back over his shoulder at her. "What? What happened to your limit of once every seven times we go out?!"

"Well, I've decided that I kind of like being around you. Around you for more than just our dates. So, realizing that there's absolutely no way I could possibly move into that hovel you think is a home, I've been thinking that maybe you should move in here."

"Really? I've been thinking more and more about how great it'd be if we lived together..." he paused, frowning. "Wait, what about that old saw you've given me about how you don't want me running into Ell around the house here. That she doesn't want to have me here interrupting her privacy..." He gave Bridget a sly grin and lifted an eyebrow, "And what about your concern about how she just won't be able to hold herself back if she runs into this perfect specimen of manhood," he waved a hand up and down at himself, "walking down her hall in nothing but a towel."

"We don't have to worry."

"You can't be serious!" Ryan said, striking a pose. "How could she resist?"

"I *meant*," Bridget said in a tone of exasperated patience, "we don't have to worry about you running into her."

"What? Why? Is she moving out?"

"No, but if I tell you, you have to be sworn to the utmost secrecy, okay?"

Ryan shrugged, "Sure."

"I mean, cross your heart and hope to die kind of secrecy. The kind of thing you can't tell anyone. Not your best friend, not your mother... no one."

Ryan frowned, "Really? Is somebody going to take me out and shoot me if I blow the secret?"

"Probably not. But a whole lot of people you really care about would be really, really disappointed in you."

Ryan pondered this for a couple of seconds, then stuck out his little finger. "Okay. You want me to pinky swear?"

"No, if you promise me, that's good enough."

"Okay, what's the deal then?"

"Ell doesn't sleep here at night."

Ryan drew back, "Oh, come on! She comes home every night she's in town! I see her leaving in the mornings too." He rolled his eyes at Bridget, "I have on the few mornings you've let me sleep over, anyway."

"Yeah, but she doesn't *sleep* here."

Ryan's brows drew together, "What do you mean by that? Where does she sleep?"

Bridget shrugged, "Over at Shan's house."

"What?! Why in the world would she do that?!"

Bridget just sat staring at him for a minute, waiting for him to tumble to it by himself. When it seemed he just wasn't going to get it, she said quietly, "Because *Shan* made an honest woman out of her... Something I'm still hoping my man'll do for me."

Slowly, "An honest woman...? What does that mean?"

It was Bridget's turn to roll her eyes, "He *married* her, you dolt! 'Honest woman' is an old timey term for being married as opposed to... carrying on like we've been doing."

"But... *Shan's* married to Raquel..."

"Same girl."

Ryan just stared at her blankly for a minute, then a sudden thunderstruck expression appeared. "No! That's ridiculous. They look *way* too different."

"Come on Ryan. If there's anyone in the world who could use technology to instantaneously change the way they look, who'd it be?"

He closed his mouth, "You've got to be *shittin'* me! Wait..." A look of intense concentration came over his face.

"No," Bridget said, guessing at what he was thinking, "you *haven't* ever seen Ell and Raquel at the same time."

Ryan'd been standing this entire time. Now he suddenly sat, as if someone had cut a puppet's strings. "Wait, so when I asked Ell out and she told me she already had a boyfriend on the sly... that was Shan?!"

Bridget nodded slowly.

Ryan turned and for several long minutes he just stared out the window that faced towards Shan and Raquel's house. Then he turned back to Bridget and gave her a sly grin, "So, from the tone of this conversation, I've gotten the idea that you'd like to be an honest woman, instead of 'carrying on' like we have been?"

Bridget nodded slowly. Hoarsely, she said, "I'd like that very much."

Ryan dropped to one knee and took her hand in his, "I'd like that very much myself. I'd like to tell you that I planned this out well enough that I've got a ring in my pocket, but I don't." He winked at her, "I have ordered one though? Maybe, this way you can take a look at what I picked out and give it your stamp of approval before..."

Bridget threw herself forward, casting both arms around her man. "Yes! The answer's yes. I *will* marry you. I'm sure the ring you've picked out's fine, but I

Bioterror

would appreciate the opportunity to look at it."

Laurence E Dahners

Chapter Five

Reggie Barnes felt guilty as she approached her lab. She'd given Donsaii a solemn promise not to let anyone one else have access to the gene sequences from the Virgies. Because of this, she'd been doing all of the work on those genes herself. The fact that she'd also promised to carry out any work with the alien genes in the biosafety lab meant she hadn't been around her own lab to advise and help her grad students as much as she felt like she should've been.

In addition to not being around to help as much as she'd have liked to, she'd also felt bad about dumping Raquel Kinrais' kid on them. Child prodigy or not, he'd probably been sucking up a lot of their time as they tried to get him through the yeast autofluorescence project she made everyone do. As smart as he seemed to be, and even though he was pretty much following a recipe, it'd probably be weeks yet before he managed to complete the project successfully.

Of course, there was the possibility that even a genius wouldn't be able to perform a complex genetic modification like that at such a young age—in which case she'd have the unpleasant task of telling the child's mother *and* Ell Donsaii that she really couldn't have the kid in the lab. If he *did* correctly modify the yeast, then she'd have to try to think of some subproject on one of her grants he might be able to carry out. Choosing that subproject could be guided by how much of a struggle it was for him to do the yeast modification.

She reminded herself that since Donsaii was essentially supporting the kid by buying any supplies he needed and providing additional funding on top of that, at least he wasn't a financial drain on the lab. Nonetheless it'd still take some of her time, and probably a lot more of her grad students' time, trying to get him through any of the subprojects and provide him with a reasonable experience.

Pondering the situation for her grad students, she thought, *I've got to find a way to make it up to them. Maybe once I've convinced Donsaii that working with ET DNA sequences isn't really as dangerous as she thinks it might be, they can get involved in researching extraterrestrial DNA. After all, we're not working with the actual DNA, only the manually transcribed sequence, presumably for a single gene at a time.* She shook her head, *It's hard to imagine much risk in a sequence that's obviously far too short to form an entire organism.*

When she got back to the lab, she found Alice, Rick, and Carley there. She looked around, wondering if she couldn't see him because he was behind some equipment, "Isn't Zage here?

Carley shook her head, "No, he wasn't copied on the messages you sent about meeting this afternoon so I don't think he knew about it. He's gone skiing with his family this week, so he probably wouldn't have been able to be here anyway, but I think he'd have used his AI to join us virtually if he'd known. He's been wanting to talk to you. Do you want me to ask him if he can attend right now?"

"Oh," Reggie said, putting a quick query to her AI and seeing that she'd failed to list Zage under the "grad students" tag she used for sending out messages to the lab as a whole. "Sorry, I screwed up." Then she had a thought, "Maybe it was a fortuitous screw-up though. I've been worried about how much trouble he's been for you guys and it'll be easier for you to give me an honest opinion if he's not here listening."

They all gave her a curious look and Alice asked curiously, "Trouble?"

"Yeah, I don't want you guys feeling like you have to babysit him. I've been worrying that while I'm over working with the ET DNA, you guys've been spending hours, just handholding. Have you had to do big parts of his yeast fluorescence project for him?"

The three grad students looked at one another, then Rick turned to her and said, "My schedule coincides with his more than Alice or Carley's, so maybe I should take this one." He shrugged, "He really hasn't asked for any help. He checked in with me a couple of times to make sure he understood lab policy about how we do things here. I think he asked Carley a few of the same kinds of questions, right?" He turned to get Carley's confirmation and after Carley nodded, he continued, "I haven't even had to show him how to order stuff, his AI managed to handshake with the lab's AI and placed all his orders, no problem."

Reggie's heart sunk, "So all he's done so far is order reagents?"

Rick looked a little surprised, "Oh, no, he's had his fluorescent yeast for quite a while now. I'm not sure exactly how long, because he didn't make a big deal out of it like I did when I finally got it to work my first year... it's kind of embarrassing, actually."

Reggie blinked. "How many tries did it take him?" she asked, thinking back to how she'd had to start over several times on a similar project back when she'd been a grad student herself.

Rick looked at the other two grad students, then turned back to Reggie, "I'm pretty sure he got it to work the first time." He grinned, "At least he didn't do any cussing like when *I'm* trying to get an experiment to work." He shook his head, "The little guy's pretty amazing. It's like he's done this kind of stuff before, but he's just pleasantly tolerant of the fact that we're making him prove he can do it again."

"So, having him around hasn't been a big pain?"

All three of the grad students shook their heads. Carley diffidently said, "He's... actually been a big help to me."

Reggie frowned, "He has?!"

"Um, yeah," Carley said, looking kind of embarrassed. "I was having trouble with the X-200," she said naming one of their DNA assemblers. "He told me that my problem was pretty common with that module and that there's a workaround posted on the company's website."

"Oh crap!" Alice burst out. "The problem wasn't..." she put her head down and squinched her eyes shut as if steeling herself against the answer, "that sometimes the output DNA's denatured, was it?"

Carley gave a slow nod.

Rick looked like his head was about to explode. Alice threw her head back and moaned, "I thought *I* was doing something wrong!"

"Me too," Carley said quietly, "and I guess I was, since I hadn't thought to go on their website or ask anyone else about it myself."

At first Reggie didn't want to admit she'd had the same problem herself, then she realized she couldn't hide the issue since she really needed to get the workaround herself. She cleared her throat, "Maybe you could send me that workaround too?"

Her three students had the decency to look surprised that she'd been caught up by the same issue they had.

Reggie said, "It sounds like you think maybe he'd be ready to take on a piece of one of the grants?"

"Sure. He's welcome to my part of the protein folding grant!" Alice said. "I've been getting nowhere!"

Reggie felt a little disheartened to hear that. Using its DNA sequence to predict the final three-dimensional structure of a protein after it folded had been a problem since way back in the 1960s. There were a number of disease states, such as Alzheimer's, Parkinson's, and others that resulted from incorrect protein folding. The badly folded proteins often precipitated into clumps called amyloid rather than performing their intended functions. Clumps of amyloid in the brain were a hallmark of Alzheimer's and were even found in the islets of the pancreas in patients with type II diabetes. Understanding the causes of misfolding would be a huge step forward.

Reggie'd developed a hypothesis that folding could be computationally predicted if they generated large numbers of short, artificial sequences, determined how *those* folded, and developed "folding rules" based on those outcomes. She hoped to be able to determine why certain types of misfolding occurred, and perhaps develop therapies from that understanding. At the least, perhaps she could find peptide sequences that'd be found on the exterior of misfolded proteins and then design antibodies or enzymes capable of attacking or breaking down such misfolded proteins before they actually agglomerated.

Unfortunately, problems with the project were legion. The small segments they generated in the lab hoping to determine the rules frequently didn't seem to fold in the same fashion as that same sequence was known to fold in a full-sized protein. Alternatively, even if it did fold in the same fashion, it never folded in the incorrect fashion that sometimes occurred in large proteins when they *mis*folded. They hadn't even gotten to the point of working with chaperones, specialized proteins which were very important for the correct folding of some peptide sequences.

Reggie said, "Maybe instead of throwing him into the deep end of protein folding all by himself, we could have him work *with* you for a while, Alice. Sometimes just getting a fresh perspective can get you started down paths you hadn't considered."

Alice agreed readily enough, a certain sign that she was feeling really frustrated. They went on to discuss each of the grad student's projects and consider possible solutions for whatever obstacles they were encountering.

As Reggie left the meeting, her mind went back to the protein folding problem and her own frustrations with it. It may be a truism that young eyes often find solutions older eyes failed to consider… but I never thought I'd be hoping for help from eyes that were only five years old!

***

AJ felt a little bit weird, walking out onto a Colorado ski slope after years back in North Carolina. The prices still rocked him back and he had to keep reminding himself that he could actually afford it on the salary they were paying him out at D5R. The Kinrais family had been really nice to him and, to his surprise, he and Morgan had a room that Mr. Kinrais had reserved and paid for. AJ'd been thinking that perhaps Morgan's parents would be expecting them to sleep separately until after the wedding.

AJ'd decided to retire his old skis because his boots had developed cracks in their padding since he'd last used them. He'd rented some because he didn't know whether he'd be skiing often enough to make it worth buying another set. Just as he finished putting on his rentals, Raquel and Zage came up behind him with their own rental skis.

Raquel was pointing to the bunny slope and explaining to Zage how to put on his skis. AJ realized the kid apparently hadn't been skiing before, not surprising at age 5. Wanting to make conversation, he asked "This his first time?"

Raquel nodded. "I hope he likes it. It'd be good for him to have something else physical to do."

AJ thought it sounded like his mother thought the kid was kind of a couch potato. Learning to ski could be quite an ordeal if that was true. Trying to be encouraging, he said, "You look like you've been losing some weight Zage. You been sticking to your diet?"

Zage nodded, however he looked like he was a little uncomfortable with the conversation. His mother said, "He's been taking a martial arts class. Maybe that's helped burn off a few calories too."

AJ said, "If it's his first time skiing, maybe I could take him over to the bunny slope and get him started? When I was in high school, I used to work winter weekends teaching kids to ski." He looked at Raquel, "A lot of people think it's better if kids learn from someone who's not in their family."

Raquel looked a little conflicted, as if she might want to teach him herself, but also recognized the wisdom of having someone else do it. Then she glanced up at AJ and gave him a little grin, "I thought you were about to become part of our family?"

"Well, yeah, but it hasn't happened yet."

"Really, you should be skiing with your fiancée, shouldn't you?"

Morgan and AJ's sister Tina had come up behind him without his knowing it. Now Tina spoke past his shoulder, "You should let him teach Zage, Raquel. He was really good with kids back when he was teaching skiing."

Raquel leaned back down to speak to Zage at his level. "You okay having uncle AJ teach you how to ski?"

The kid didn't look thrilled, but he said, "Sure," and turned to give AJ an expectant look.

Before Raquel stood back up, she said something AJ didn't really understand, "Be sure to watch the other kids and see how *they're* doing, okay?"

Zage nodded and said, "Got it," as if it were an instruction he'd heard before.

AJ watched for a moment as Raquel, Morgan, Lane, and Tina moved off toward the lift, then he turned back to Zage, "Ready to try skiing?"

Zage nodded and started clumping his skis off toward the bunny slope. AJ couldn't help notice that, oddly, rather than watching his own skis like most beginning kids, Zage seemed to be watching the other little kids on the slope as he made his way over to the belt that'd carry him up the gentle incline. AJ felt a little surprised that he hadn't had to point the conveyor out to the kid, but after all, the kid seemed pretty smart. He'd probably figured it out by watching the kids who were out there ahead of him.

Zage shuffled onto the belt without any trouble and AJ shuffled on behind him. As they slowly rode up the bunny slope, AJ noticed the kid was still turning his head to watch the other kids out on the slope. Taking advantage of this, AJ pointed out how the kids were making their way down the slope and talked about what some of them were doing wrong.

When they got to the top, AJ moved up behind Zage, ready to grab his collar if he stumbled getting off the belt. However, Zage didn't have any trouble with it. Like he had when he was teaching classes, the first thing AJ did was show Zage that falling down didn't hurt. When AJ encouraged Zage to fall back on his butt himself, Zage did so. Somehow the kid made the fall look graceful. *He probably learned to fall in his martial arts class,* AJ thought.

They started off down the gentle slope, AJ skiing backwards in front of his pupil. With virtually no instruction, Zage made slow turns back and forth across the slope as they went down. He didn't fall. There was nothing really surprising about it, except AJ'd seen a lot of kids learn to ski and it usually took them several runs to look as smooth as Zage did. In fact, Zage seemed to ski just like most of the other kids, but looked like he was completely in control. There were no jerky staggering motions where he nearly lost his balance and then caught it again. When they got to the bottom, AJ decided it was silly to make another run on the bunny slope. "I don't think we need to have you do that again. You want to try going up on the lift?"

Zage glanced quickly up at him and AJ had the feeling that he looked a little apprehensive... or perhaps chagrined? "You think I'm ready?"

AJ nodded, "You bet. I've done this a million times. Kids who can ski as well as you do fine. We'll just go down one of the easiest slopes."

Riding up the lift, AJ noticed that Zage spent his time hanging over the edge of the chair watching the other skiers, though he mostly seemed to be focused on the other kids. Quite a few of the kids down below them were pretty good.

They got off the lift and started back down. Zage started out as if he were perfectly in control, but then fell down.

Gracefully.

AJ had the distinct feeling that Zage had fallen on purpose.

The rest of the run down the mountain followed the same script. Zage would ski smoothly, seeming to be perfectly in control, but then fall anyway. He never fell forwards, always softly back onto his buttocks. *Looks to me like the kid really is a little couch potato, intentionally performing badly in the hopes he can say he's tired and quit early.*

When they got to the bottom of the slope AJ said, "That was a good run for a beginner. Let's go down again, I'm sure you'll do a lot better."

As predicted, the kid *did* do a lot better on his second run. Way better. He only had two falls this run. Once again, AJ thought the two falls looked like they'd been staged for AJ's benefit.

On the third run, AJ decided to try the kid on an intermediate slope. He didn't mention that they were going to try a slope with a higher degree of difficulty, just steered Zage onto it, telling him that he thought he'd do even better this run. Zage didn't fall at all on the third run, though a couple of times AJ got the feeling he'd intentionally flailed his arm like he was trying to act like he'd almost fallen.

Even though AJ had the distinct feeling Zage was in no danger of falling and never had been.

I swear, I think he only fell on those first runs because he thought he was supposed to!

They went up again. AJ took him down another intermediate slope, this time leading the way and skiing pretty fast.

The kid kept up, essentially skiing in AJ's trail, copying every move! AJ skied harder, going as fast as the slope would take him. He hit an abrupt stop at the top of a short segment of black diamond slope. He turned to see what Zage'd do and found the kid slamming to a hard stop just like he had.

Perfectly!

There were no bobbles. No moments when it appeared as if he might lose control. Though AJ felt a little cross eyed, nonetheless, he calmly said, "You're doing just fine. It's not as hard as everyone makes it out to be, is it?"

Zage shook his head, "You're a great teacher." He looked down over the black diamond slope which was covered with moguls, "Wow, that's really bumpy."

Wondering just what the hell he was thinking, AJ said, "Yeah, the bumps make it a little harder. You want to try going down it?"

Zage studied his face, then said uncertainly, "You think that'd be okay?"

"Yeah, I'll just go down a little ways and you can follow me. If it's too hard, I'll just put you on my back and carry you down this section. I've done that for other kids in the past." Even though he hadn't been skiing for years, AJ felt sure he could make it down this short stretch of black diamond with a five-year-old on his back if he took it slow.

Zage looked over the edge, then shrugged, "Okay, I just do what you do, right?"

"Right," AJ said, then pushed off over the edge and traversed across the bumpy slope at a shallow enough angle to keep his speed down. When he stopped and turned to watch Zage, the kid was right behind him. "Um, if you'll wait a little to start skiing, then I can watch how you're doing and give you advice, okay?" At Zage's nod, he continued, "It looked like you did okay on that section. Shall we try going down a little faster?"

"Okay," the kid said with a shrug.

AJ went straighter down the mountain this time, using the moguls to control his speed with many quick turns. He didn't go very far before stopping and turning. This time, Zage was waiting until AJ waved for him to come on. AJ had the distinct feeling that Zage followed the exact same track AJ had on the moguls. At least as close as a small person on short skis possibly could. Despite the bumpy ride on the steep slope, Zage never looked like he was out of control.

And, of course, he *still* didn't fall.

AJ turned and gazed down the final section of the little run of black diamond, a bizarre feeling growing in him. *I'll bet if I went down the rest of the way as hard and fast as I could, the kid'd just copy me!* For a second, he was tempted, then reason returned, *And if the kid has a spectacular wipeout and breaks something, his parents'll never forgive me!*

AJ took the final section of the run in two pieces.

After all, getting too tired was a common cause of injury on the slopes. Zage made both of those sections look... easy. AJ didn't know what to think. You had to be a very good skier to make a black diamond run look easy. He knew the kid had some advantages due to his small size and low mass. Those factors would make skiing less difficult—but it was supposed to be his first day! He turned to Zage, "Okay, that's the last steep and bumpy section. Do you want to lead the way back down to the lodge? We can have some hot chocolate and catch your mom on one of her runs—tell her you've had your lesson and done just fine."

Zage looked up at him curiously, then said, "Okay, as long as it's a *small* hot chocolate." He pointed at the intermediate slope that made a pretty straight course on down to the lodge and said, "We go that way?"

AJ said, "Yep, or a different way if you want. All three of these slopes wind up at the lodge."

"Okay," Zage said heading off down the slope. He went fast and hard for an intermediate slope, but then stopped at the top of the next steep section.

When AJ caught up, he said, "You okay?"

Zage nodded, "I just don't have very good endurance. Is it okay if we keep stopping frequently, like you've been doing so far?"

"Um, sure," AJ said, thinking, I was stopping so I could teach you, not because I thought you needed a rest. He glanced back up the slope, How could someone who skis this well be tired after such a short run? Then he thought about how the kid used to be fat. He was still overweight. Maybe he just isn't in very good shape?

"I'm going again," the kid said, shooting down the steep section and out onto the flat below. He stopped before the next steep area. They went down the rest of the way to the lodge the same way, stopping at the top of each steep section for a rest before going on.

As they climbed the stairs into the lodge, AJ tried to assemble the kid's performance into a whole that he could comprehend. Could Zage actually have *been* skiing before? Could he have a *lot* of skiing experience? That'd jibe with his astonishing performance. But, if so, why was his mother having to explain to him how to put on skis and talking about taking him over to the bunny slope? Was there something about studying martial arts that gave him better balance than other kids? *"Better balance than other kids?!" If this's really his first day, he's got better balance than anyone I've ever seen!*

AJ had a sudden thought as they got in line for the hot chocolate. He'd had some kids who learned skiing very quickly in the past because they already knew how to skate. There were similarities between the two skills. Looking down at Zage, he said, "Are you a skater?"

Zage shook his head, he was looking out the window and now he pointed. "I think that's my mom, Aunt Morgan, and Aunt Lane. Oh, and that's probably your sister Tina too, right?"

AJ looked out the window and saw it was indeed the four women. It looked like they were coming into the lodge too. "I think you're right." AJ glanced around and said, "You want to take my coat and go sit at that empty table there? Spread my coat and your coat and our hats out on top of it to hold the table for when they get here. Then we'll all be able to sit together." He started shrugging out of his coat.

Zage looked up at him uncertainly, then back out at the table, then turned back to AJ and held up his hands for the coat, "Sure."

AJ had his coat off and Zage was tugging on it when

he started to worry that sending a five-year-old to hold down a table might not be appropriate. He didn't have much experience with kids and really had no idea. "Or, you can stay here with me and we'll just try to find a table when they get here."

Zage gave another tug on the coat, "No, I can do it, no problem."

"Okay, I'll be right here keeping an eye on you. Just yell if there's a problem." As the kid clumped off toward the table with AJ's enormous looking coat in his arms, AJ called after him, "Was this really your first day skiing? You're awfully good."

Zage gave AJ what he would've sworn was a stricken look over his shoulder. AJ thought it looked as if the boy felt embarrassed, as if skiing well was something to be ashamed of. But other than a shrug, Zage didn't respond to AJ's question. He got to the table and climbed up onto the bench, spreading AJ's coat out in the middle. Then he took off his own coat and spread it at one end and went to sit at the other end, putting his hat on the table there.

Feeling guilty for sending a five-year old out to save a table in a fairly large room moderately crowded with adults, AJ kept a careful eye on the kid. He sat there looking… surprisingly mature for a five-year-old. He didn't fidget or run around, or any of the other irritating things AJ might've expected a child Zage's age to do. *It's like the poor kid's grown up before his time,* AJ thought.

Then the four women entered the room. Zage jumped up on top of his bench, waving his arms and shouting, "Mom. Mom! Aunt Morgan, Aunt Lane!"

He looked like a kid again.

Rather than call across the room, AJ had his AI ask Morgan if she and the other women wanted any hot chocolate while he was at the counter. She responded, "Of course, big ones with whipped cream!"

When AJ got back over to the table with four big hot chocolates and two little ones, his family, old and new, were all excitedly talking. AJ sat down next to Raquel and said, "Wow! Your kid's an amazing skier!"

To his surprise, she didn't look happy to hear that. In fact, she darted a frustrated look at her son, who produced a palms-up shrug as if he was saying, "Sorry." Raquel turned back to AJ, saying, "That's great to hear. I hope he wasn't too much trouble?"

"Oh no! Not at all. Very polite and easy to teach." AJ narrowed his eyes, "In fact, we finished up the morning going down a heavily moguled black diamond, which I found pretty astonishing." He glanced at Zage who was watching his mother rather than AJ. "I asked him if he really hadn't ever been skiing before, and he just gave me a shrug. Can you tell me what the deal is? Because I'm having a really hard time believing he just started skiing this morning."

Raquel glanced at Morgan, Lane, and Tina who were still chattering excitedly about their runs. Her eyes came back to AJ and she leaned closer to him to speak quietly, "If you don't mind, I'd really like to talk to you about that tonight, not now, okay?"

What?! AJ thought. It makes no sense that this would be some kind of secret. So the kid's an amazing skier—we should be talking about getting him into some kind of training program so he can realize his potential, not treating it like it's something to be hidden! Still, Raquel was his sister-in-law to be. If she didn't want to talk about it here, it wasn't his place to argue with her. To Raquel, he said, "Sure, I just wanted to say…"

Laurence E Dahners

Raquel interrupted him with a hand on his forearm and an intense look, "Later... okay?"

"Okay," he said, feeling a little irritated. All this secrecy was way over the top.

Raquel gave him a big smile and turned to join the conversation amongst the rest of the people at the table. However, AJ was still thinking about what'd happened, so he didn't miss it when she turned away from the conversation a few minutes later and quietly addressed Zage. She said, "I *told* you to read up on skiing."

The kid gave her a hangdog look and said, "Sorry Mom."

She ruffled his hair and laughed, "Don't give me those puppy dog eyes! You know I can't stay mad at you when you look like that." Then, enigmatically, she said, "I can only hope *that's* the worst mistake you ever make."

Mistake?! AJ thought wonderingly. What kind of mistake did the kid make?! He skied beautifully; how in the world can that be a mistake!

***

That evening, while everyone was getting dressed to go out to dinner, Morgan turned to AJ. "Hey, Mr. Fiancé, I need to talk to you about something kind of serious."

AJ turned, his stomach dropping as he wondered if he'd done something wrong without realizing it. Morgan didn't look mad though. "What is it?" He asked.

"It's about Zage and his skiing."

"The kid's freaking amazing! Did you hear me trying

to tell Raquel about it?"

"Um, no, but Raquel talked to me about your conversation later." Morgan stared at him for a minute, not saying anything. At first, AJ thought she was searching for words, but when did she start to talk, he thought the pause might've been just to lend gravity to what she was about to say. "It's really... *really* important that you not talk about it, okay?"

"But... but why?! Raquel shouldn't be hiding this! She should be trying to get him training! Someone that's this good at age five could grow up to be an Olympic contender!"

Morgan took his hand as she spoke quietly, "My family keeps a secret for one of my uncles. Mom, dad, Shan, my sister, we all know about it, but none of us ever talk about it except to one another and even that's very seldom. It's a secret that'd be a disaster for my uncle if it got out, so, it's really important, and we go to great lengths to keep it to ourselves."

Puzzled, AJ said, "What is it?"

Morgan shook her head, "That's the deal. I can't tell you. I'd trust you with my life, but you really have no 'need to know,' so I'm not going to tell you. It's the kind of secret that we don't tell even family members just because they're curious. I can't imagine why you'll ever have a need to know, so I don't expect I'll ever be telling you." She tilted her head as if assessing his reaction, "Can you understand that?"

AJ shrugged, "Sure." He frowned, "But how could this secret have anything to do with Zage's skiing?"

Morgan shook her head, "It doesn't. This's a different secret from my Uncle's. And this's a secret that you probably *will* need to know someday. In fact, it'd have been good if you'd known it today, so I want to tell you about it now."

"Oh," AJ gave a nod, "okay."

"But, I'm wanting to make sure you understand that this's serious. *Really* serious. Not something you talk to your buddies about over a beer. I need you to know that if you let it slip out, I, and everyone else in the family are going to be very disappointed in you."

AJ shrugged, "Okay, I understand. I'll defend this secret against all comers, whatever happens."

"Okay, now imagine you were an amazing and famous athlete, and, because of that, you never got any privacy. People and paparazzi hounded you all the time, wanting you to do this and that and making various demands. Sometimes you're even attacked by people trying to *force* you to do things. Now, you have a child, who's also an amazing athlete..."

AJ studied Morgan, wondering what the hell she was trying to say.

"And you want that child to have a *normal* life..."

Someone knocked on the door. Morgan turned and called out, "Sorry, we're going to be a little late. We'll meet you at the restaurant."

A muffled "okay" came through the door and Morgan turned back to him.

AJ said bemusedly, "Are you trying to say that Shan's some kind of famous athlete?" Then he shook his head disbelievingly, "That can't be. He's famous, he's got a couple of Nobel Prizes for God's sake. But if he was a famous athlete too... I'm sure I'd know about it!"

Morgan gave him a sympathetic smile, "No, we're talking about Zage's mother."

"Raquel?" Then AJ shook his head, dismissing that as ridiculous, "Oh, wait, are they raising Zage for someone else?"

"Raq—Ell," Morgan said, separating the two syllables and emphasizing the second one.

"Shan and Raquel are raising Ell Donsaii's child?!" AJ said with a sudden rush of understanding.

"Nooo," Morgan said slowly, "Raquel and Ell are the same person."

AJ stared at his fiancée, uncomprehending.

"So, you can imagine that the world's most astonishing athlete might have a child who could learn to ski in one day, right? And since Ell's been kidnapped and attacked in various ways, you might understand how she'd want her son kept out of the kind of life she's led publicly. That she might be afraid some of those kinds of people might try to use her son as a lever to control her."

"But... They look so diff... they can't be the same person!"

Morgan gave him another sympathetic smile, "Not 'they,' dummy—'she,' looks so different. Some time, when you two are alone, you could ask her to change in front of you. It's pretty amazing."

~~~

As AJ and Morgan rode in their car on the way to the dinner, AJ suddenly said, "Wait, Ell was mad—"

Morgan interrupted him, putting a hand on his arm and saying, "*Never* call her Ell unless she's *done up* as Ell. You don't want to get in a bad habit and then someday give her secret away by accidentally calling her that in public."

AJ paused to think about that for a second, then nodded. "Raquel was mad at Zage for not reading about skiing before he came. Why was he supposed to read about it? He did just great without knowing anything before he started."

"Yeah, but he wasn't *supposed* to do great. He was supposed to watch the other kids and ski no better than the good ones. He was supposed to have read enough about skiing that if you tried to take him on an intermediate slope, he'd know that a beginner his age would have a hard time with it. And, if his *idiot* uncle tried to take him on a black diamond, he was *supposed* to know that he should be terrified and start calling the police because he was being subjected to child-abuse!" She grinned at him to soften the words.

AJ said, "But, but... it wasn't abuse. I could... could tell he'd be able to ski that slope."

Morgan snorted, "Yeah, I've no doubt. But he wasn't supposed to let you try it!" She got a dreamy look on her face, "I know what you mean though. I was with..." She stumbled a little bit, obviously having been about to say "Ell." Instead she continued by correcting herself to say, "*Raquel*, the first time she ever went skiing. She knew nothing about skiing and had no idea how well the average person could ski on their first day. You should've seen her go! I've *never* seen anybody ski that well. You know how she's the world's greatest gymnast, and sprinter, and golfer? I'm sure she could add greatest skier to that list if she wanted to." Morgan snorted, "When I confronted her about the fact that she was skiing far too well for somebody who was just starting out, she looked embarrassed, but then just told me a bald-faced lie about how she'd actually skied quite a bit!"

***

Bioterror

When they got to dinner, AJ found himself sitting across from Raquel. Try as he would, he couldn't seem to stop studying her face. She was tall, slender and graceful, those things matched the Ell Donsaii AJ knew of and had seen around D5R. But she walked differently, her skin was a shade darker and her face had a different shape. Even her eyes were a different color. He simply couldn't reconcile the two.

She gave him an amused smile and a wink, then said, "Thanks for taking Zage under your wing today. It looks like you understand the issues now?"

He gave her a wondering nod...

***

Mark Amundsen followed Bridget down the hall to Ell's office. He certainly could've found it by himself and felt a little bit surprised that, as informally as they did things at D5R, Bridget hadn't just told him to go on back. When they got back to her little office, they found her slouched back in her chair, eyes roaming from screen to screen. He realized that practically every bit of the wall surface of her office was covered with screens, all of them currently lit up with various charts, graphs, CAD drawings, three-dimensional images... and a weird image that looked kind of like a galaxy.

As soon as he came into view, she bounced up out of her chair and came around her little desk to greet him. "Hi Mr. Amundsen! I hope your wife likes the area?" She waved him into a chair and asked if Bridget could get him some coffee, which he politely declined.

"Please, call me Mark. You're the last person in the world who should be calling me 'Mr.'" He smiled and continued, "Mary's worried there won't be enough traffic congestion down here to live up to her standards. Otherwise she thinks the area's really great!"

"Do you feel like you've seen everything you need to see?"

"Yeah," he nodded slowly, "but there're still some big questions bothering me. When I ask your people about certain things, they just refer me back to you."

She gave him a wry glance, "I suspect I know what those things are and they either don't know the answers or rightfully didn't want to disclose them." She grinned and gave him a questioning look, "My due diligence people tell me we *really* want to hire you. Other than the things you got stonewalled about, are there any other reasons you wouldn't take the job?"

"Well, no, but I must admit that some of the things they've referred back to you make me pretty uncomfortable."

"Okay," she said leaning forward in her chair and fixing him with an intent gaze, "let's get down to the nitty-gritty. What's worrying you?"

"First of all, the Board of Directors. If I'm going to be answering to them, I'd kind of like to know who they are. Your people's responses to questions on this issue have varied from telling me that they're anonymous, to telling me that the board only interfaces with you, to telling me that they don't know for sure who they are!" He hesitated, then plunged ahead, "I expect the board to be tough, but some boards have people on them that're just plain hostile. I'd rather not be CEO if there're going to be some people on the board I can't work with." He lifted an eyebrow, "Nobody on your staff's even willing to show me the minutes for any of the board meetings. I can understand why they might feel that's privileged information, but it's the kind of thing that'd give me a feel for just how contentious things can get around here."

Ell nodded, "What else?"

Mark blinked. He'd expected an answer to the first question before being asked to pose another one. He shrugged and said, "The financials. The bookkeeping and numbers seem to be sound and to make sense—as far as I've been allowed to inspect them. There's this big area of the company that's completely transparent and makes a lot of sense, but then there's what I've been likening to a black hole off to one side. Parts of the company make huge excess profits; what doesn't get reinvested is siphoned off into the black hole. Other sections of the company, most notably the R&D section that's actually named D5R, and Quantum Biomed, run in the red almost all the time." He held up his fingers and made little air quotes, "The 'black hole' apparently just coughs up money to make up their deficits without anyone having to answer for it. I assume the investors have set aside some kind of capital reserve, but no one seems to know anything about it, or how much reserve there actually is. I find it a little frightening that no one seems to have any idea how much of a cushion the company has if some kind of disaster strikes."

Ell gave him another understanding nod, "Anything else major?" She shrugged, "Or minor but important?"

Wanting to roll his eyes at the way she'd just ignored his queries so far, instead Mark said, "Though you told me not to worry about it, I remain concerned that there aren't any nice offices or board rooms, or any exotic looking facilities we can use to impress board members or investors when they come to visit." He waved a hand around, "Your own office here, for instance. It's highly

Laurence E Dahners

functional, but as the CEO I'd expect you to have a nice large office with windows. Somewhere where you could entertain people with money. Personally, I'd be perfectly comfortable in an office like this one, but when people who think of themselves as big shots comes to visit, I'd want something a little more... impressive. Something that'd keep them from thinking we're running on our last nickel." He winked at her, "For instance, my reaction when I saw your office was that perhaps the company wouldn't be able to pay me even as well as I was compensated in the public sector." He shrugged, "To tell the truth, I'd be happy working here for less than the government paid me, but the fact that such a question came to mind when I walked in suggests our investors would have similar concerns whenever they come visit."

Ell grinned, "Anything else?"

He shook his head, "Nothing of significance."

She said, "You're comfortable that any further discussion of these issues still falls under our confidentiality agreement?"

He shrugged, "Of course."

She smiled, "You might feel like I've just been letting questions pile up one on top of the other, but I suspected all your questions would have essentially the same answer, 'Me.'"

Mark blinked and tilted his head curiously, "I don't understand."

She shrugged, and pointed at herself, "Board of Directors. There aren't any minutes for the board meetings since I'd just feel weird documenting my internal conversations. We actually have a *lot* of investors since most of the employees own little pieces of the company, but at present I own over ninety-five percent of D5R as a whole. For a couple of the subsidiaries, specifically ET Resources and Portal Technology, I only own eighty-six and eighty-two percent, but essentially my vote's the only one that matters."

She waved at herself again, "Black Hole and Capital Reserve…"

Amundsen interrupted, "Wait a minute! How… How can that be?!"

She shrugged, "You don't remember I invented PGR? We talked about it in the Oval Office back when President Teller gave me the Medal of Freedom. That was way back when I was still in the Air Force, but even then it was paying me over $2 billion a year in patent royalties."

Amundsen sat blinking in startlement. "I remember being stunned by how much it was paying you…" he said hesitantly, "but, you know how memory can be? I was remembering $2 *million* a year?"

Ell slowly shook her head. "It's one of the things that made me think of you for this job; that you're *supposed* to already be aware of this money."

"But… But how can it be so much?!"

"Even though D5R's a lot flashier and gets way more attention because the portals do so many really cool things, you have to recognize that PGR chips underpin essentially all the world's communications by now. The initial royalties were $2.1 billion a year, but they've worked their way up to $15 billion plus as of last year. And of course, if you've been looking at D5R as a whole and seen its numbers, you know it and its divisions are making some enormous profits of their own, which are almost all flowing directly to…" she waved at herself again.

Amundsen dropped his forehead onto his palm with a smack, then slowly shook his head, "I should've been able to figure this out..."

Cheerfully, Ell said, "Think of it in a positive light. I *am* the Board of Directors, so you don't have to worry about impressing them." She lifted an eyebrow, "Though, of course, you do need to keep me happy. But, thankfully, I'm not at all impressed with flashy board rooms or big offices. You're welcome to have one if you want, but if you're happy with something that's more functional, it'll fit better with the culture here. The capital reserves you were concerned about are essentially what I've saved up. Since I don't spend very much, that currently amounts to over $500 billion." She studied him for a second, "That's what *I've* saved up, separate from the value of D5R. Counting the subsidiaries, D5R's a two-trillion-dollar company. Or it was the last time I tried to figure it out. It's growing awfully fast." She tilted her head, "It's surprisingly easy to make money when you're selling products *everybody* wants."

As Amundsen sat there flabbergasted, she studied him for another minute, then said, "I was planning on offering you $5 million a year in salary. Bonuses won't depend on how much profit we make because I think focusing on profit is shortsighted. We're in it for the long haul. Bonuses depend on how happy the stockholders are," she waved at herself again. "Five million isn't much for the CEO of the world's wealthiest corporation. Obviously, we could *afford* to pay you a lot more, but I don't want the kind of CEO who wants to brag to everyone about the size of his salary or how big his golden parachute is... or is mostly concerned about getting big bonuses. I'm looking for someone who thinks what we do here's cool and wants to be a part of it. Someone who wants to make a difference in the world. Someone… who makes *my* life easier."

"I'll take it!"

Ell laughed, "You can think about it, talk it over with your wife and so on."

Amundsen chuckled, "No, Mary'd love to live here. It's a *lot* more money than I ever expected to be paid and a simpler job than I'd feared. I don't know why I couldn't figure out on my own how much you must be worth—in fact, I'm wondering why you're offering me the job in view of that glaring lack of insight. But if you're offering, I want to take you up on it before you figure out just how dumb I must be."

Ell put her hand out to shake.

Chapter Six

Alice looked up and saw Zage walking into the lab. "Hey Zage, how was your ski trip?"

He paused as if giving the question serious consideration. "It was pretty thought-provoking. I found it interesting to realize how much harder it is to breathe up at higher altitudes. Have you ever been skiing?"

Trust the kid to think that the most remarkable thing about skiing's how you get short of breath, Alice thought. She said, "I've been skiing, but only twice. We just went to Snowshoe, West Virginia." She gave him a wry wink, "Cheaper than flying out to Colorado, you know?"

He nodded, "My granddad really loves skiing in Colorado, so he pays for the whole family to go out there once a year. He thinks it's a nice way to get the family together for a little reunion."

Alice lifted an eyebrow, "Well, *he* must be rich."

"He had a business making household products. When ports first came out he got hooked up with an early license from Portal Technology and ET Resources to make portable heaters, coolers, camping toilets—all that kind of stuff."

"Oh! Smart move!"

Zage nodded, "I think he's done pretty well."

"Is he paying your tuition here at Duke?"

Zage shrugged, "Maybe? If he is, my parents haven't told me about it." He looked around, "Is Dr. Barnes here today?"

"Yeah. She'd like to talk to you and me together if that's okay. She has a project she'd like us to work on as a team."

"Oh, okay," he said seriously. "That'd be a good way for me to get started."

~~~

They were in her office and Reggie'd finished describing a number of the diseases which were attributed to misfolding of important proteins. Then she'd explained the issues with understanding protein folding. She'd already described in broad strokes her idea that they could predict folding of entire protein chains by developing rules based on the ways that relatively short, four-amino acid, tetrapeptides folded. Now she said, "Alice, can you tell Zage about some of the problems you've been having with the project so far?"

Alice took over and described how the relatively short peptides they'd been synthesizing so far didn't necessarily fold in the same manner that those particular amino acid sequences were known to fold within full-length proteins.

At this point, Reggie interjected, "I'm afraid that the peptide sequence near the folding point of interest is influenced by the amino acids that're nearby on the chain. The only solution I've been able to come up with so far is to work with longer peptides than we'd planned for. Maybe octapeptides...?"

Alice said, "Unfortunately, that makes the problem much more complex. If the folding at a site's influenced by amino acid sequences that're even a relatively short distance away, the number of factors influencing folding goes up a lot!" Getting a grumbly tone in her voice, she said, "Probably why it's an unsolved problem so far."

"I still think we've got to give it a shot…" Reggie said, trailing off thoughtfully.

There was a brief pause as Alice and Reggie marshaled their thoughts. Zage said, "There're twenty amino acids, so the number of possible sequences in a peptide are twenty to the power of the length of the peptide sequence. Twenty to the fourth power means that there're 160,000 possible sequences for your tetrapeptides. Even that isn't really doable, but if you start making octapeptides, twenty to the eighth power's over 25 billion possible peptides you'd have to synthesize before you could determine the folding of each sequence a single time."

Stunned, Reggie stared at him for a moment, wondering why she hadn't heard him query his AI for those answers. "Math's never been my strong suit," she said slowly. "I knew it'd be a lot of peptides, but I guess I should've asked my AI to do the math for me instead of just trusting my instincts on this one." She snorted and looked at Alice, "Seems like someone who does what I do for a living should have a better feel for this, but it turns out I didn't have any instinct at all for this one."

Alice said, "Geez, I thought it'd be a big number, but I was thinking thousands, not billions! I should've done the math too." She paused for a second, then turned back to Reggie, "I'm not coming up with any great ideas for how we might solve this problem. Do you have any suggestions Dr. Barnes?"

Disheartened, she shook her head. "I'm going to have to give it a lot of thought, see if I can come up with any other ideas." She took a deep breath, then said, "That still leaves us needing a project for Zage." She turned to Alice, "Could you use some help on your sequence sifting project?"

Alice smiled at Zage, "Sure. I'll ask Rick and Carley if they could use a hand with any of their projects too."

Alice started to get up, so Zage did too, but he said, "Have you tried putting your sequences up on the Gordito website?"

The two women turned to look at him, then at one another in puzzlement. Alice said, "Nooo, I haven't heard of it." She glanced again at Dr. Barnes, but Reggie shook her head.

Zage said, "It's a pretty new website. You feed it the DNA sequence from a virus and, it recognizes the protein sequences in the code. It determines how the protein sequences fold and forms a 3-D model that lets it recognize the protein's likely function. If the protein's going to be located on the exterior of the virus, it tells you which amino acid sequences are located on the most accessible surfaces of the protein." He shrugged, "The website was set up to help investigators recognize likely externally located peptide sequences that could serve as antigenic targets for immune responses, but it has to work out the folding to do that. Presumably it could answer folding questions for you if you needed them…" he kind of ran down, then rushed to finish, "even if you don't need to know about any antigenic sites."

Reggie found herself staring. A glance showed her that Alice was confounded as well. "That's… that's astonishing. If this website can do that, the people who've set it up have solved a protein folding problem that's been driving people crazy since the nineteen sixties! Why haven't we heard about it?!"

"Um, it's really new. I don't think it's seeing much traffic yet. I... I just got lucky... um, finding it." Reggie had the distinct impression that Zage was actually embarrassed about finding the website, though she couldn't imagine why he'd be nervous to admit that he'd found a site on the web that claimed to be able to do something most people thought was impossible. That was nothing to be ashamed of. Zage shrugged, "I just thought it might be worth a try."

"Do you know who set it up? Has anyone checked it to see whether the information it generates is any good? If it can do what you say, then my protein folding grant's essentially pointless and I should probably return the money to the NIH." She shook her head, "But whoever figured it out needs to tell the rest of the world how to do it. Science is supposed to be open."

"It seems to be an... anonymous site. Maybe it won't work for anything except recognizing viral protein antigens." He shrugged, "Maybe it doesn't even work for that, but even if it does, maybe it won't correctly predict the folding of other proteins. Do you want me," he hesitated, "or Alice and me to try to check it out?"

Reggie said, "First see if someone else's already validated it. If you can't find evidence that it's been confirmed to work *and* to be accurate, then we could talk about some methods we could use to try to validate it ourselves. That might be a good project for you. It's always important that anyone's scientific methods get checked out by others to confirm they work." She shook her head, "Really the first thing you should do's find the people that set up this website. They shouldn't be working in isolation. Think about it, even if their website works perfectly and is a boon to mankind, if the people that built it were to die and nobody knew where their server was to maintain it, the world could lose that resource. They need to be open about whatever it is they're doing."

"Oh," Zage said softly, looking as if he'd just been chastised for doing something wrong himself. "Okay."

Reggie gave kind of a dismissive wave and said, "Alice, why don't you and Zage have a look at this website. See if you can find the authors or at least someone who's checked it for accuracy. If not, run a few known sequences through it to see if it gets them right. If it isn't obviously bogus, let me know and I'll give it a quick once over myself."

~~~

Back in the lab Alice turned to Zage and said, "You want to try to track down whoever set up or is funding the Gordito website while I pick out a few sequences where we know the 3-D structure of the protein that we can send Gordito as a test?"

Zage shook his head, "I've already spent quite a bit of time trying to figure out who Gordito is. I haven't had any luck, so why don't you give that a shot while I pick out some sequences?"

With an indifferent shrug, Alice said, "Okay," and they split up to separate screens in the lab and had their AIs start looking.

~~~

About twenty minutes later, Alice came back over and said, "You're right. I can't find *anything* about whoever created that website. However, I did find a review of it on a site that reviews scientific web engines, you know, the kind of sites that compute or find science information for you? They said it correctly worked out known antigens for three different viruses."

"Oh, I didn't find that review when I did my search," Zage said. He felt kind of good, even though it told him that at least three of the viral genomes he'd worked through so far on Gordito had just been tests.

Alice said, "Yeah, but it made me realize an issue. What if this's no more than a search engine for viral antigens and perhaps for protein structures? This Gordito website hasn't accomplished anything that *we* haven't also done just by searching through databases. We have no idea whether Gordito actually calculates a structure or just reads the information out of somebody's paper."

Zage chewed his lip. "You're right. The only thing I can think to do is ask Dr. Barnes if she's got access to unpublished three-dimensional structures of any proteins. Or, maybe she has an in with someone here on campus who can determine the 3-D structure of a couple proteins that no one's ever studied?"

"That'd be a big favor to ask someone," Alice said. "Let's hope she's got unpublished structural data on a few proteins just laying around." She glanced up at the time, "I know you've got to go, so I'll ask her."

~~~

Zage was almost home when he got a message from Alice. "Dr. Barnes *did* have 3-D data on some proteins that've never been published. I'm putting the sequences for three of them up on the Gordito site. We'll know if the site's any good in the next few hours."

~~~

Zage realized from the tone of Alice's message that

she thought the Gordito site must be running a computer program that worked out the protein folding. He wondered if he should immediately try to start working on whatever sequences she submitted in the hopes he could turn them around quickly enough that she wouldn't be disappointed. After thinking about it for a little while, he decided he shouldn't establish the expectation that sequences might be turned around in a matter of minutes. That certainly wouldn't happen when he was asleep and he felt sure there'd be plenty of times when he was too busy to get to them right away.

Nonetheless, he felt very curious about what she'd submitted and whether he and Osprey *could* work out protein folding on non-viral proteins. He decided he'd work on it as soon as he'd spent some time throwing the ball for Tanner. However, even if he got it done quickly, he'd schedule the results to be put up sometime during the middle of the day tomorrow. That'd both set expectations that this could take a while, *and* imply that he had nothing to do with it if they came out while he was at school.

***

Ell was in her waldo controller running Virgwald. At present, Virgwald was talking to Striper, the older appearing Virgie with the black stripes who seemed to be a respected scientific adviser. Her AI, Allan, was translating for her as she tried to get Striper to explain how the Virgies disseminated DNA to every cell in their body. It apparently wasn't a very important problem for them, since they usually manipulated DNA in small parts of their body rather than trying to change it in every cell.

However, Ell wanted to know how she could insert the DNA for the Virgies' radiation resistance mechanisms that enabled them to do well in their high radiation environment. It wouldn't be very helpful for people on Morris to be protected from radiation damage in just some of their cells. Striper conveyed the idea that such a radiation resistance mechanism *should* be inserted in the first cell of an organism when it was being formed. That way, when that initial cell proliferated to form an entire organism, the mechanism would already be present in every cell in the body.

It'd been difficult, but Ell had managed to convey the idea that she, as Virgwald, hadn't had the radiation resistance mechanism inserted by her progenitor and would *really* like to have it done now.

Striper had seemed somewhat grumpy, complaining that modifying most of the cells in a certain region of the body was much easier than trying to modify all of the cells throughout the body. Ell'd managed to obliquely refer to the diagrams of the DNA molecule Virgwald had provided and the diagrams of the compound microscope-eye that Striper was growing in herself. Although Striper's microscope-eye was still developing, it was apparently already producing images that Striper found very exciting and several of her colleagues were starting to grow their own compound lens eyes. Ell thought one of them was trying to follow the diagram for a telescope.

Ell's strategy of mentioning Virgwald's gifts had apparently succeeded in making Striper feel guilty about her refusal to help with DNA dissemination. Striper had proceeded to draw a set of diagrams that appeared to show something that Ell thought looked like a virus being inserted into a cell. Apparently that cell would make thousands of copies of the virus releasing them through the cell membrane a few at a time. Those viral particles would then go out and infect more cells in a geometric process that appeared to Ell to be pretty much the same way she understood that viral diseases worked here on Earth. When she tried to ask Striper why such a virus wouldn't kill the host, Striper looked appalled, but Ell couldn't seem to understand Striper's explanation of why that wouldn't happen.

I'm going to have to show this video record to Dr. Barnes, maybe she can understand it. Striper managed to convey the idea that it'd take a while to collect and transcribe all the gene sequences necessary to create the virus. She asked hopefully if it'd be okay just to give Virgwald the virus itself and Virgwald had to reiterate his desire to only get the sequences, not the actual viral particles.

***

Zage felt nervous when Dr. Barnes came in the lab and started talking to Alice. Osprey's algorithm had generally had little difficulty with the protein sequences Dr. Barnes gave Alice. As usual, there were a number of places in the sequence where the algorithm didn't have a good answer for the folding but, as with the viral sequences, Zage immediately had a feeling for how the folding should go. When Osprey finished the 3-D model of each protein folded the way Zage thought it would, the completed model "looked right" to Zage.

But now, he was about to find out whether it just seemed right, or was actually correct and matched Dr. Barnes' known three-dimensional shape. He walked over closer so he could hear.

Alice was sounding a little disgusted, "I sent it in late yesterday afternoon, but the results didn't get put up until about 1:30 today. You'd think their computers would've spit it back out immediately, so now I'm worried some guy at Gordito just makes his best guess at the structure."

"Well, let's see," Dr. Barnes said. "Put the first one up on that big screen to the right."

Alice spoke to her AI and a couple of seconds later Zage saw the slowly rotating 3-D image of the first protein he and Osprey had predicted pop up on the right screen. As he watched it turning, he couldn't help but have the feeling—as he'd had many times before with protein structures—that it was somehow "right."

Barnes said in a mildly surprised tone, "Oh, that *looks* familiar. Let me put up the known structure." She spoke to her AI and a few seconds later a 3-D model popped up on the left screen.

Zage let out a breath—they were the same. To be sure, he tracked his eyes back and forth between them several times looking for minor discrepancies, but he didn't see any. He spoke quietly to Osprey and had him compare the Barnes model to what Osprey had from last night. Osprey didn't have to wait for the model to finish rotating, he said, "The data feeds are identical."

Barnes said, "Wow! They look the same to me. Do you see anything different?"

Alice shook her head, then, being graceful, turned to Zage, "How about you?"

Zage shook his head.

Bioterror

Barnes blew out a breath, "Let's see the others." She sounded mildly excited, yet somewhat disappointed. Zage felt pretty sure she'd been hoping to solve the protein folding problem herself. It would've been a real triumph after so many people had struggled with it for so many years.

Alice brought up the other two and it quickly became evident they were identical to the known structures as well. After studying them for a couple of minutes, Barnes said, "I think they're the same. You should have your AI compare the data for the images to be absolutely sure. Assuming they're as good as we think they are, you should test the Gordito site with the rest of those proteins I have the 3-D structures for. Then I think you could publish a brief "Note" documenting our comparison of the Gordito outcomes to actual 3-D imaging." She sighed, "Then, assuming you find what we expect, I'll have to try to figure out whether there's any way we can salvage the funding for that project or whether we'll have to return the money." She winked at Zage and spoke in a lower tone, "With the unrestricted money that D5R's granted us, we're really not short of cash, but it's really painful returning grant money. After going through all the work of applying for the grant, it kind of feels like it belongs to you."

***

Dr. Barnes plopped down in the chair next to Alice, "How did the Gordito website do on the rest of those proteins?"

Alice gave Barnes an awed look and a single shake of

her head, "Predicted all twenty-three perfectly. Pretty amazing."

Barnes heaved a sigh, "No *kidding* that's amazing. We need to know how they're doing it. Or, rather, the world needs to know. I don't suppose you've had any luck figuring out who's behind it?

Alice shook her head. Zage was approaching so she turned to him, "You haven't figured out who it is either, have you?"

Seeming reluctant somehow, Zage shook his head as well.

Barnes said, "I've been thinking about how to get them to come out of the shadows. I think one of the best things we could do's bring a little publicity to what they can do. You guys could write up a "Brief Note" for publication about how they accurately predicted protein folding for twenty-six known but unpublished proteins. That'd not only be a publication for your CVs, but would bring scientific attention to what they can do. In your discussion you could point out how this's something that *needs* to be public knowledge—perhaps that'd influence them some. You interested?"

Alice nodded, though she saw to her surprise that Zage was shaking his head. Both she and Dr. Barnes turned to look at him in surprise, "Why not?"

Looking serious, which admittedly he did most of the time, he said, "I'd rather start working on the misfolding issue in disease states like Alzheimer's."

"But writing up the Note would be pretty easy..."

Alice had no idea how dismayed Zage felt. In the first place, he didn't want to participate in an effort to bring publicity to Gordito, not only might it derail his mother's desire for him to remain anonymous, but it also felt like bragging, a trait his dad had taught him to dislike in others. Second, it seemed like his being part of a team that assessed whether or not his work on Gordito was valid or not seemed unethical. But he didn't know how to deflect Dr. Barnes and Alice from their belief that he should be a part of the publication. He crossed his arms, put on a stubborn look, and said, "I'd rather work on misfolding."

Alice put her hands up in surrender. "No problem, I'm happy to do it myself."

Dr. Barnes frowned at Zage, "How do you plan to tackle misfolding in Alzheimer's"

"I need to read more," Zage said thoughtfully, "but since certain genes are known to be associated with Alzheimer's, I thought it'd be good to find out which of those code for the proteins that misfold to become amyloid. Then we could submit the gene sequence for proteins that *aren't* associated with Alzheimer's, and for the sequences that *are* associated. Maybe the Gordito site'll recognize that the Alzheimer associated genes code for proteins that have a higher probability of misfolding?"

Barnes gave him a disbelieving look. "You think you can submit that as a question? 'Is this gene sequence more likely to misfold than that one?'"

"I think it's worth a try."

Still looking dubious, Barnes said, "If they can do stuff like that, I don't know why they wouldn't just do it themselves and claim credit for it. If they just haven't thought of it, it seems likely that once you suggest it, they *will* just do it." She shrugged, "Maybe they'll give you a footnote in their paper."

Still looking stubborn, Zage said, "I think it's worth a try."

Barnes shrugged, "Sure, go for it…"

She paused when Carley interrupted, "Dr. Barnes? Dr. Donsaii's here..."

They all looked around, and sure enough, Ell Donsaii was standing in the doorway of the lab! She gave a little wave, and they all stood up, though Zage did so belatedly. Alice glanced at him and thought he looked a little irritated—as if he were exasperated to have been interrupted by the world's most famous scientist!

Dr. Barnes said, "Dr. Donsaii! I didn't know you were coming! I'd have been happy to come out to D5R..."

Donsaii gave an offhanded shrug, "It's good to get out of my hole and see the world sometimes. I thought I'd understand things better if I saw what you actually do with DNA?"

"Sure," Dr. Barnes said, brightly. "First, if I may, let me introduce some of the grad students who do most of the work around here even if *someone*," she winked at Donsaii, "hasn't given me permission to let them work with ET DNA." She turned to indicate Carley who looked like she might not be breathing. "This's Carley Heune. She's in her first year of graduate work and doing an excellent job so far."

Donsaii stepped forward and shook Carley's trembling hand, "Carley. I wish you the best of luck with whatever you take on."

Barnes gestured to Alice, "Alice Norton. She's just started her third year as of January and is beginning to do some really serious research."

Donsaii stepped over to Alice and shook her hand as well, "Alice. Best of luck to you as well."

Barnes said, "Rick Klein, our most senior grad student's in one of his seminars." She indicated Zage with a wave of her hand, saying, "And, I suspect you've met Raquel Kinrais' son Zage?"

With a smile, Donsaii stepped forward and leaned down to shake Zage's hand, "Hello Zage." Standing back up she turned to the others, saying, "I mostly know Raquel, and of course, Zage's father Shannon, but I did meet Zage in Stockholm a few months ago."

Alice turned to stare at Zage, then realized that Donsaii must be referring to the Nobel Prize ceremony in December at which Donsaii and Zage's dad had won Nobel prizes in physics *and* chemistry for work they'd done together. Alice couldn't imagine that the kid would've been allowed into the ceremony, but perhaps Donsaii'd gone out to dinner with the Kinrais family while they were over there? In fact, she realized Zage didn't look nearly as flabbergasted by Donsaii's presence in the lab as Alice felt.

Dr. Barnes turned back to Alice and Zage. "So, I think we were essentially done anyway. Alice, you'll write up that Note. Zage, you submit some Alzheimer sequences to the Gordito site and see what happens." She turned back to Donsaii, effectively dismissing Alice and Zage as she conducted Ell toward the door. "Was there something in particular you wanted to see?"

After Donsaii exited, the room suddenly seemed much emptier. Alice turned back to her screens to begin drafting the Note. Zage had gotten up and started over toward the workstation where he spent most of his time when Carley said, "Alice, Zage? I'm having a little get together at my apartment Friday night, would you guys like to come?"

Zage immediately said, "Yes, what time?"

Alice had been gaping at Carley, astonished that she'd invite a five-year-old to a party with grad students who'd almost certainly be doing some drinking. By the time Carley'd said to come at 7:30, Alice had recovered enough to say, "Sure, can I bring something?"

"Chips, dips? Whatever you like, even that awful beer you think's so amazing," Carley said.

Apparently recognizing the protocol for such events, Zage asked, "What can I bring?"

Permission from your mommy! Alice thought, but Carley just said he should bring whatever he liked to snack on.

After Zage had made his way over to his workstation, Alice scooted next to Carley and heatedly whispered, "Are you out of your mind? Inviting a five-year-old to a party full of grads?"

Carley looked a little wistfully over toward Zage and said, "He's a lot more mature than some of the people that'll be there."

"Exactly!" Alice hissed. "How do you think his mother's going to take it when somebody has too much to drink and does something stupid in front of him?"

"Um," Carley said, glancing over at Zage again and looking a little chagrined, "I'm kind of counting on his mother either not letting him come or making him go home early. But I want to be nice to him. I was pretty lonely as a kid and I know he's got to be really lonely. There just aren't any kids like him that he could be friends with."

Alice arched an eyebrow, "You'd better be thinking about how some people *our* age would make *lousy* friends for someone his age."

"I am..." Carley turned back to Alice, "Maybe you can help me watch out for him?"

***

Bioterror

Ell had Reggie show her the biosafety lab, at least the parts of it that she could visualize without undergoing training. She also had a few questions about how some of the gene analysis and assembly steps were actually physically performed, things she apparently hadn't felt like she understood well enough from looking at diagrams and videos.

However, Reggie wasn't surprised to learn that Dr. Donsaii had another item on her agenda. During a break in the conversation, Donsaii said, "Can I show you a video?"

The vid had the bizarre-looking striped ET that Reggie'd been shown before. Ell explained that she was trying to get the Virgies' secret for inserting DNA into every cell in the body, something that'd be hugely advantageous for providing resistance to radiation and other mutagens in humans. "So here's some video of Striper trying to explain their process. I won't try to tell you what I think she's showing us because I'd rather get your unbiased opinion."

Reggie watched the alien diagram what for all the world looked like a viral replication system. She had the impression that Striper was trying to say that the outer surface of the virion was modified, possibly to make it non-antigenic, but she didn't really understand what the modification was. The virus was replicated by the cells, apparently without rupturing and thus killing the cells like many terrestrial viruses did. Striper appeared to be diagramming a geometric progression in the number of viral particles that could be created in such a fashion. She narrowed her eyes, "Aha!"

"What're you seeing?" Dr. Donsaii asked, stopping the video.

"Well, the first part seems to be pretty much a

straightforward viral replication system, though not one that's lethal to the host cells. But this section here... I think he's trying..."

"She's," Donsaii said.

Reggie looked at Donsaii for a second, then at the alien, "You know it's female?"

"We've decided to designate them all as female since any VIrgle can grow herself a uterus and generate a child whenever she wants. There don't seem to be any males involved in reproduction since they all 'design' their children by putting together a DNA sequence of their own choosing."

"Okaay," Reggie said slowly, feeling flummoxed by the idea. She looked back at the screen for a moment, then resumed, "I think *she's* trying to describe something like telomeres." She looked at Donsaii, wondering whether Donsaii knew what telomeres were.

Donsaii said, "Telomeres are things on the end of chromosomes that keep them from being copied forever, right? A big part of getting old because our cells eventually can't reproduce themselves anymore?"

Reggie nodded, "So, each chromosome has a telomere section at the end where the DNA repeats itself a number of times. Since, when you copy your DNA, you can't copy the entire chromosome all the way to the end, each time you make a copy it loses a little bit of the telomere section at the end. Eventually, the telomere section gets to be so short that the chromosome, and therefore the cell, can't be replicated." She glanced back at the vid, "I think Striper's trying to show us something similar in her viral construct. Viruses usually don't have any reason to stop replicating themselves, but this one's built with a mechanism that only lets it replicate a certain number of times and then forces it to stop. Presumably, it replicates enough times to make sufficient virions to infect all the cells in the host organism, but it doesn't just go on forever. That way it isn't like a viral disease that just keeps making viral particles until its host is dead."

"What keeps the host's immune system from wiping the virus out?"

"I think that's what Striper was trying to explain back at the beginning. I think the outer surface of the virus's altered so that your immune system doesn't react to it, but I'm not sure how it's done. Maybe, after we've seen the whole thing, we could go back to the beginning and watch that section again…?"

***

Abe Cohen settled into his seat and waited for LaQua Kelso to begin her presentation. As Director of the Center for Emerging Diseases he felt quite proud of his young protégé. Her last name might be Scottish, but the woman herself was very much African-American. Grown up poor in Mississippi, she'd excelled in school, obtained some very good scholarships, gotten into an MD-PhD program in med school, trained in infectious disease and come directly to the CDC after her fellowship. Abe'd been involved in her hiring and thought she was one of the best recruitments he'd ever participated in.

She'd been in on the evaluation of the first few cases of this new version of vaccinia when they'd popped up out on Little Diomede Island. When CDC'd started to get samples of the same virus from locations scattered all around the world, she'd been the obvious person to lead the team investigating the larger outbreak. From what he'd heard on the grapevine, she'd been doing a great job. Now she was about to bring the group up to speed.

She began by describing the outbreak on Little Diomede Island and pointing out its proximity to the Russian island of Big Diomede. She showed images of the characteristic lesions or "pocks" produced by the virus. Afflicted patients had developed anywhere from 1 to 13 lesions and they'd left behind scars typical of both smallpox and vaccination with the live vaccinia virus. A few people had felt mildly ill, but no one had gotten seriously sick.

The disease seemed to have burned itself out on Little Diomede. The patients who'd had it had all developed antibodies and then people simply seemed to stop getting it. After a period it'd seemed reasonable to believe that the micro epidemic had burned itself out without spreading to any other populations. Kelso described the lingering concern that it represented some kind of failed bio-weapon which had been created by the Russians and tested on Big Diomede. Although the natives of Little Diomede weren't terribly cooperative with questioning about it—each person claimed not to have island hopped themselves, but all of them suspected that someone else had—it seemed likely that, if there was an animal reservoir on Big Diomede, someone from Little Diomede might've visited Big Diomede and brought the disease back with them.

Kelso, of course, had wanted to sample some of the wildlife from Big Diomede, but, not surprisingly, no permission to do so had been forthcoming from the

Russians. In view of the fact that the disease didn't seem to be particularly dangerous, no one in Washington had been willing to expend political capital urging the Russians to change their minds and give her permission.

Kelso went on to describing the virus itself and the similarities and differences between it and the vaccinia vaccination virus.

Abe lifted a hand and Kelso acknowledged him. "This difference in the protein coat. Is it due to a snip (Single Nucleotide Polymorphism) or other relatively simple mutation that could've occurred naturally?"

Kelso shook her head, not uncertainly, but definitively. "No, it's intentional. Someone excised the entire section of DNA for several of vaccinia's surface proteins and replaced it. The substituted surface proteins are analogous to, but not exactly the same as those in the camel pox virus."

Curious, Abe prompted, "Camelpox?"

"One of the ten species in the Orthopoxvirus genus. Generally affects camels and can be spread camel to camel or carried by the camel tick. It kills about twenty-five percent of camels it infects. Camels do transmit it to humans, typically causing pustular eruptions on the hands. That, by the way, is the way cowpox was transmitted to humans and became the basis of the world's first vaccination programs. I'd like to make you aware that in 1995 Saddam Hussein admitted to having a biological weapons program based on camelpox. The idea was that, because of previous exposure, the local population would be largely immune if camelpox could be made into a lethal bioweapon. We don't know much about the program, but inserting sequences for camelpox proteins would've been difficult with 1990s technology. However, if they were capable, it seems like a reasonable weapons strategy. Most people in the world wouldn't have immunity to camelpox."

"But a lot of Arabs would," somebody grumbled.

Abe chose to ignore the comment as inflammatory and unhelpful. Instead, he said, "If it's a release, accidental or otherwise, of an Iraqi bio-weapon, why did it first show up on Little Diomede?"

Kelso shrugged, "As an accidental release of an Iraqi weapon, Little Diomede's so unlikely as to be absurd. As an intentional release, testing it on an isolated island sounds much more reasonable. But why create a bio-weapon based on the cowpox genome? It does occasionally kill someone, in fact, as I continue my report you're going to hear that we've documented some mortality, but it isn't exactly what most people think of when they think of a weaponized virus."

Abe said, "I'm sorry to have interrupted your presentation. Perhaps we should let you finish before we barge in with more questions."

LaQua nodded, and went on. "Since the Little Diomede incident, the virus has begun showing up all around the world, leading to the question of whether Little Diomede was actually the first incident or whether it was simply the first one recognized. However, we have not been able to find a location where anyone claims to have seen these types of lesions *prior* to the onset of the Little Diomede cases."

LaQua put up a map of the world, "Here we've highlighted in blue the areas where typical pustules have been reported and, in red, locations where they've been confirmed to come from the Diomede virus." She paused, giving people a moment to study the map, then continued, "As you can see, the greatest number of cases have been in northern and eastern Africa, the Middle East, and Polynesia. However, cases have been reported almost everywhere in the world…"

Dr. Rushdie suddenly interrupted, "They're targeting the Muslim world!" As everyone turned to stare at him, he looked around at them a little wildly. "If you pull up a map of the OIC, it'll be the same!"

"OIC?" LaQua said, a puzzled tone in her voice.

"Organization of Islamic Cooperation. It's a cooperative group of the Islamic countries of the world." His eyes went back to LaQua's map. "I'm pretty sure the maps'll be almost exactly the same!"

LaQua spoke to her AI and a moment later a map of the OIC popped up on the large screen next to the one she was using for her presentation. The similarities were obvious. Rushdie said, "Zoom in on Israel, I'll bet you'll see that in the Middle East, it alone isn't involved!"

Silence dominated for a moment as LaQua had her AI zoom in on Israel, then murmurs broke out as it became obvious that most of Israel hadn't been affected like the surrounding countries had. Rushdie said, "Those cases you see in Israel? Those're in the Palestinian areas. They aren't *just* targeting Islamic countries, they're targeting *Islam!*" His eyes went back to LaQua, "Show me the cases in the United States."

LaQua spoke to her AI and a map of the US appeared with scattered cases.

Rushdie said, "Zoom in on New York." When she did, he said, "That area in the northern part with all the cases? That's Hamilton County, where I grew up. It has the highest concentration of Muslims in New York, and I'm pretty sure that New York has more Muslims than the rest of the US."

Abe stared. The maps seemed pretty damning. Then LaQua said somewhat plaintively, "So, if someone's targeting Muslims with this disease—all around the world which would certainly indicate that it's an *enormous and concerted* effort—why're they attacking them with a disease that seldom makes anyone but the immunocompromised sick?" She turned to look at Rushdie questioningly, "The overall mortality's only about one in 10,000!" She shrugged, "As bioweapons go, it really isn't much of a threat."

Everyone turned back to the maps with puzzled looks on their faces.

To Abe's surprise—because Abe would've expected the man's Islamic faith to bias him against such an intuitive leap—it was Rushdie whose eyes widened with sudden comprehension. He said in a tone of immeasurable sadness, "It's a vaccine... Some misbegotten terrorists have released it among the Islamic world in the hopes of protecting those who follow Allah. At some point in the future, they plan to release a second, highly-lethal virus that'll afflict those who *haven't* been immunized by this one." Shaking his head in dismay, he said, "How could anyone..." He broke off with a rasping sob.

When Rushdie paused, no one seemed to know what to do or say. Finally Abe, wondering whether condolences would be considered appropriate coming from someone of the Jewish faith, leaned forward and put a hand on Rushdie's shoulder. "Every faith has its radicals my friend. It falls on us to try to set this right. You've made a mighty contribution to our understanding of what's happening. I hope that you'll make an even bigger contribution by lending your shoulder to stopping the turn of this wheel..."

Bioterror

Rushdie put his hand on top of Abe's on his own shoulder, saying, "Thanks, you can trust that I will." Then he turned his eyes to LaQua. "Do we know how the agent was delivered?"

She slowly shook her head. "Sampling finds viral particles in the air. Actually, we found more particles outdoors than we do inside around sick people. The people who're sick don't seem to be shedding much of the virus into the environment. Assuming that someone's dumping lyophilized virus here and there in the afflicted cities, it's surprising that there've been no reports of 'powders' blowing on the streets. People are pretty sensitive to that kind of stuff."

Someone in one of the upper rows behind them said, "Hey, they just convicted a guy in Philadelphia of murdering his wife by sending carbon monoxide through a port. You think these guys could be sending viral particles through ports?"

Abe felt an icicle form in his gut as he, Kelso, and Rushdie all turned to stare at one another in horror...

Chapter Seven

Zage got out of the car and started up the walkway to Carley's apartment building. His mother'd had conniptions when he'd told her that he wanted to go to a grad student party. At first she didn't want to let him go at all, then she'd decided he could go, but that she'd go with him! He'd pointed out that if one of her major concerns was about how he needed to learn to socialize, that if she wanted him to do so, she had to let him do it *without* his mother. Eventually she'd relented. She'd made some protests about how she wanted him to learn to socialize with kids his own age, but he'd retorted that he'd be happy to go to a party put on by one of the kids in his martial arts class if they invited him.

She might've begrudgingly accepted the idea of him going to this party, but she and Steve'd been in a dither about how to do it safely. Several members of the security team had been over at the apartment building early that morning to install surveillance devices. He hadn't been allowed to leave home until Steve had approved a condensed version of the video from the surveillance to make sure no one'd arrived at the complex that looked like they might be a threat.

Though Zage had arrived by himself in an AI piloted car, five members of the security team had arrived earlier, some of them parking near Carley's apartment and a couple of them pretending to be residents of the apartment complex who were sitting out by the pool drinking.

Zage shook his head. He still thought all of this was way over the top, but at least he wasn't showing up at Carley's door with four guards standing around him. He really liked Carley and wouldn't want her getting freaked out.

When he approached Carley's door, the door AI said, "Hello Zage Kinrais. Carley would like to apologize because she isn't quite ready. It'll be a couple of minutes."

In puzzlement, Zage checked the time on his HUD. It was 7:48, well after the invitation time of 7:30. His mother'd suggested that parties like this rarely started on time, so he'd shown up late, but he hadn't wanted to arrive too late because his mother insisted he leave by 9:30 at the latest. She felt like some crazy things might happen later on at the party, but hadn't wanted to explain to Zage what she thought they might be.

Not knowing what else to do, Zage leaned up against the wall next to the door, trying to look casual. In his ear, Jerry, one of the newer, younger members of the security detail who'd been sitting by the pool spoke, "Is there a problem?"

"The host isn't quite ready," Zage said, trying to sound calm despite his own nervousness.

Fortunately, before Jerry could quiz him any further, the door opened and Carley said, "Zage! I'm so sorry. Come on in."

She was still adjusting the cuffs on her blouse, so Zage assumed she must've been getting dressed when he arrived. Trying to produce a bland look, he stepped through the door saying, "No problem. I brought some bean dip, where can I put it?"

No one else arrived until five after eight, which was fortunate because Carley still seemed to have a lot of things to do to get ready. Zage made a concerted effort to help when he recognized things that he might do, however when he asked her whether there was anything else he could do, Carley didn't have any suggestions. "Just take it easy," she recommended. "Get yourself a soda out of the cooler there."

He'd been kind of hoping that he'd have a few minutes to talk to Carley about something besides their research, so when Carley finally paused, seeming to have things arranged to her satisfaction, he seized the moment, "Where'd you grow up?"

"Oh, here and there," she responded, not looking him in the eye.

Assuming that she might've moved around a lot, perhaps because her family was in the military, he said, "Where's your family live now?"

"They live in Cary, at least, my adopted parents do." She flashed him a sad smile, "I've lost track of my brother."

Zage hoped the shock didn't show on his face. A second later he put it together with what she spent a lot of her spare time in the lab doing. "Is that the 'Eli' you've been looking for?"

"Yes," she said looking surprised. "How did... Oh, you've probably seen some of the searches up on my screens, huh?"

Zage nodded. "You're not having much luck?" he said, then blinked. "Of course you're not, or you wouldn't still be looking. Are you doing database searches?"

She sighed, "Yeah, I've even paid for access to some of the commercial people finder databases, but none of them'll let me search for just a first name and a birthdate."

"You don't know his last name?"

She shook her head, "Our last name was Bolin, but mine got changed when the Heunes adopted me. I imagine the same thing happened with his."

"Um, my dad's really good with computer stuff, maybe he could…"

"Oh!" Carley looked mortified at the thought, "I couldn't ask him to do that! He's…" Carley ran down and waved her hand as if ushering the notion away.

Zage wasn't sure what she meant, but supposed that she thought Nobel Prize winners were so special that they never did ordinary things. He thought about asking for Eli's birthdate anyway, but decided she wouldn't want to give it to him. Instead, he said, "We're DNA scientists, have you thought of searching any of the DNA databases for someone that matches you well enough to be your brother?"

She'd gotten up to rearrange the napkins she'd laid out, but now she turned, head tilted as she considered him. "That's a great… No, wait, most of those databases are anonymized, so even if we found him, we still wouldn't know his name or contact info."

"No, but you might learn his approximate location, for instance it might confirm that he lives here in North Carolina." Zage shrugged, "Or, maybe it'd tell you that he lives in Wyoming. Either one'd narrow your search quite a bit."

"At least I'd know he's still alive," Carley said, a happily awed look on her face. "Maybe I could even get the database to send him *my* contact information."

The house AI interrupted then, "Rick Klein's at the door with a number of other people."

Laurence E Dahners

"Let him in!" Carley said excitedly, making Zage wonder if she was so happy not to have to talk to him. *Or, maybe she was just worried that no one else was coming to her party?*

Rick came in with four other grad students Zage didn't know. Alice showed up a minute or two later with several more of their friends and the party was soon in full swing.

Parties that Zage had attended so far in his life had usually been organized by one of the kids' mothers with various games and events happening in some regimented fashion. His mother'd tried to warn him that this'd be quite different from what he'd experienced so far, but he still felt surprised to see people just wandering around talking to one another. Most of them brought food like he had, but they also brought beer and wine. Zage thought they were drinking a lot more of the alcoholic beverages than they were eating from the food table. He wondered whether this was common at these kinds of parties. The music had been turned up loud enough that it was difficult to understand what people were saying and people were almost shouting to be heard over it. Three girls were dancing and laughing in one corner.

Zage was sitting by himself at one end of Carley's couch and trying to take it all in. He was wondering whether he should get up and walk around trying to talk to people himself. That's what everyone else seemed to be doing, but he wasn't sure what he'd talk to them about. Other than research, he feared he didn't have much in common with them. Especially because many of them seem to be consuming large quantities of either beer or wine. From his understanding of the biological effects of large amounts of alcohol, he felt surprised that some of them weren't throwing up or passing out. He reflected that many of them might have built up a significant tolerance if they drank this much on a frequent basis.

Trying to stop treating the students at the party like research subjects, instead he tried to eavesdrop on some of the nearby conversations in hopes of recognizing a topic to which he might contribute. Two of the guys standing near him were watching the girls dancing in the corner but arguing about the music. The shorter one disliked what was playing while the taller one thought the artist was a genius. Zage focused on the music for a minute and decided it sounded much like any other music he might hear playing in almost any location. Not bad, but not inspiring.

Somebody dropped onto the couch next to him and he looked to his left. It was Terry, one of the girls from his Molecular Genetics class. He was wondering whether to say something to her when she said, "Hi, cutie who're you? One of Carley's relatives?"

Zage could smell alcohol on her breath and wondered if she was already drunk or merely on her way. He shook his head slowly, "Hi Terry, I'm Zage Kinrais. I'm doing research with Carley in Dr. Barnes' lab. You and I take Molecular Genetics together."

She drew back and tilted her head as if she were having some difficulty seeing him. Sudden recognition dawned across her face and she said, "Oh! Yeah. I recognize you now. You're the little genius."

Zage thought her words parsed like a compliment, but might not be. Unsure how to react, he said, "I wouldn't say that. Everyone's good at something, I just happen to be good at science."

She snorted, then said, "Yeah, but there aren't any

other seven-year-olds taking molecular genetics, I'll guaran-damn-tee you that."

Zage didn't think he should correct her about his age and felt like there was a slightly ugly undertone to her words, so he didn't say anything more. After a few seconds, she shook her head, said she needed another beer and got up to wander away.

Zage didn't think she really needed another beer

He looked around the party and saw one of the guys putting his arm around Carley's shoulder. Zage thought the guy looked drunker than most. Carley shrank away a tiny bit, but the guy pulled her closer anyway. She did a neat pivot out from under his hand. From the movement of her lips, Zage thought she said "I need to go check on the beer."

She did go check on the cooler in the corner where the beer was on ice. Zage was thinking about getting up and going over to try talking to Carley or Alice, but at that moment Carley started walking his way. She sat down next to him, "Are you doing okay?"

Zage nodded thoughtfully, "I'm learning a lot about the effects of alcohol."

Carley stared at him for a second, but then seeing his eyes on the people at the party, she laughed, "I'll bet you are." She frowned at him, "Maybe you shouldn't have come, you might learn some things you're a little too young for."

He looked around the room, "I've always liked learning about anim— human behavior. This's an important part of it. One I haven't encountered before."

Carley laughed again, but then the guy who'd had his arm around her earlier appeared in front of them. He grabbed her hand and pulled her to her feet, saying,

"Let's dance!"

She pulled back, saying, "Hey!"

Zage thought she was about to refuse to go with the guy, but then she shrugged and let him tug her over to a corner where another couple was dancing.

Zage followed through with his previous plan, getting up and going over to stand near Alice. He hoped she'd talk to him, but she seemed to be pretty involved in a conversation with another student, one Zage thought looked handsome, though Zage didn't feel like he was very good at recognizing which men were attractive. As Zage stood there waiting, he watched Carley dancing with the guy in the corner. The music had slowed and both couples were dancing with their hands on each other. Zage found he didn't like the way the guy was pulling Carley closer to him, but reminded himself that it was up to her.

Then he noticed that she'd worked her forearms in between their bodies and seemed to be bracing them there to hold him away—working against the way the guy seemed to be pulling her toward him. Zage hadn't had any personal experience with the hormones and emotions that might be in play, but he had certainly learned about them back when he'd watched all those hundreds of nature documentaries. Most of the videos he'd watched hadn't really dealt with humans, so Zage felt unsure about whether the way the guy and Carley were interacting was normal for humans or not.

After a little thought, he wondered whether the question might not so much be whether it was "normal," but whether it was acceptable. He felt pretty sure that human males and females felt many of the same hormonally driven urges that he'd seen described in animals. However, they probably subordinated such urges to societal constraints. But, from what he'd read about the effects of alcohol on human behavior, it might liberate some of those urges from the normal limiting influences of the forebrain.

As if to put a point on Zage's concern, the guy slugged back the rest of his beer and tossed the can on the floor, thus freeing his hands to more fully participate in what appeared to be almost a wrestling match with Carley.

So, if this guy starts behaving in an unacceptable fashion, what's to stop him? Will Carley be able to? Will someone else step in? Should I be ready to help her?

He didn't know the answer, but decided that, as Carley's friend, he should be keeping a close eye on them and hold himself ready. *But, will I know if it's actually unacceptable and not just part of human mating rituals I've never observed?* Zage wondered. He glanced up at Alice, wondering whether he'd be able to tell from her expression if she thought what was happening was wrong or not, but Alice didn't seem to have noticed. She was pretty focused on the guy she was talking to.

Zage looked around for Rick, the only other person he knew at all well. Rick looked to be pretty intensely involved with a young woman he was talking to. Zage got up and went over to pick up the empty beer can the guy'd tossed on the floor. *This'd be a great opportunity to observe human mating rituals,* Zage thought, *if I wasn't worried about Carley.*

After throwing the can in the trash, Zage turned his eyes back to check on Carley. The guy was pulling her out the door of the apartment! *Is she feigning reluctance?* he wondered. *Or really trying to get away from him?* Zage leaned away from the wall and walked swiftly that direction, trying to get a look at Carley's face so he could see whether she really looked upset.

The guy had Carley out the door before Zage got a good look at her expression. He closed the door in front of Zage, but it opened readily enough when Zage tried it. The guy was pulling Carley around the corner and Zage was still in a quandary when he heard Carley say, "Let me go!" in an urgent tone.

Zage felt fairly confident that the tone of Carley's voice sounded stressed enough to indicate she truly meant the words. She wasn't just pretending reluctance; she really didn't want to go with the guy. Zage felt even more certain of his assessment when the guy said in a slightly slurred tone, "Oh come on! You know you want it!"

Zage started running toward the corner they'd just disappeared around while speaking to Osprey and asking him to send him a canister of pepper spray through the one ended port his mother had installed below his umbilicus. He held his hand in front of his abdomen, ready to catch it, worrying that he might fumble the catch because his abdomen was jerking back and forth with his stride. Then the port appeared with a tiny flash of light and the canister flew out into his hand, apparently moving relatively slowly. Zage caught it easily, realizing he'd dropped into the zone without feeling it coming on.

He shifted the canister into place in his hand by feel as he rounded the corner. Carley had one hand pushing on the guy's chest as she tried to wrench her wrist out of his grip with the other. Zage yelled, "Let her go!"

The guy shot a glance at Zage, saying, "Get out of here you little troll!"

As the guy turned back to his struggle with Carley,

he grabbed at the front of her shirt with his free hand.

It ripped, exposing her bra.

Zage had been going to shout another warning, that's what they taught him to do in self-defense class. But he thought if the guy was tearing her clothes, it'd definitely gone too far and needed to be stopped immediately. Besides, since he'd almost reached them, Zage would've had to stop running to shout the warning. Instead, he leapt upward, put one foot on the guy's butt, grabbed the guy's shirt collar for stabilization and reached around with the can of pepper spray to give the guy a quick shot in the face.

Zage kicked off the guy's hip and landed a couple of feet away as he watched to assess the spray's effect. The guy said, "What the...?" then let out an agonized bellow, letting go of Carley and dropping to his knees as he swiped desperately at his eyes with the sleeves of his shirt.

Carley crouched back away from him, clasping her torn blouse shut with both hands. An astonished look on her face, she said, "What happened?!"

Knowing he was in the zone, Zage moved and spoke very slowly. "Pepper spray." He wanted to focus Carley on something else besides what *he'd* just done, so he turned her attention on her own predicament, "Do you want me to try to get you another shirt? Or do you want to just hold that one closed while you're going back inside?"

She looked down at herself as if uncertain, then glanced at the side of the building. She stepped to it and tugged at the window, but it didn't budge. "This's the window to my room. Maybe you could go inside and unlatch it?" Then she looked apprehensively at the guy who'd been assaulting her. He'd pulled up the hem of his shirt and was wiping at his eyes with a clean area.

Zage looked at him also. Saying, "I'm pretty sure he won't be able to bother you for quite a while. I'll go unlatch the window. Would it be okay if I passed out a wet towel so he can wash his face?"

She nodded, and Zage turned on his heel to go back inside. As he turned the corner, he found Jerry standing in front of the door in his swimsuit. Jerry held a backpack in his left hand and his right hand was inside of it. Zage thought it might be holding the grip of a gun. Zage also saw several members of his security detail running toward the apartment from different directions. When Jerry saw Zage, he asked urgently, "What happened?! Allan said you called for pepper spray?"

Zage told Osprey to connect him to the entire security team, then said, "Everything's okay now. Please don't make yourself obvious. One of the guys at the party got drunk and ripped the hostess' blouse. I gave him a little shot of pepper spray. He's no longer a threat. I'm going back inside to open her window so she can get another blouse. Maybe one of you guys could go around the corner," Zage jerked a thumb in that direction, "and act like a helpful bystander. But if *all* of you show up like some kind of army, it's going to give away our secret!"

Zage went back into Carley's apartment and through her bedroom to open the window. The security team sent Linda, one of their new female members, around the corner to help Carley. Zage thought that was a good idea as she'd probably seemed less threatening than one of the guys. Once Zage had it open, Linda helped Carley climb in the window.

Zage quickly soaked a towel and passed it out the

window to Linda, then left Carley's room so she could change her blouse. As he exited her room, Zage ran into Alice who said, "Have you seen Carley? People are asking about her."

Zage nodded at her room, "She's changing her clothes. One of the guys tore her shirt."

Alice raised a hand to cover her mouth as her eyes widened, "What! Who...?"

Zage said, "I think she's okay, but she could probably use some support from a friend if you think you could?"

"Of course! But what happened?"

"One of the guys at the party seems to have lost control to some of his baser urges. I think he was drunk, so I suspect he was disinhibited. As you might expect, Carley's upset."

Alice drew back in startlement at this objective and somewhat clinical description of what she thought must have been a highly emotional altercation, but then she tracked back to the situation. "Have you called the police?"

Zage shook his head, "I thought that should be up to Carley, but I don't really know. There were some people outside helping her, they might've called the police already."

"Outside?!"

"Yes, it mostly happened outside. I just helped Carley climb in through her window because she didn't want to come back through the party and her torn clothing."

Shaking her head in dismay, Alice knocked on the door, "Carley? It's Alice. Can I help?"

There wasn't any answer, so Alice knocked again.

Zage touched Alice's wrist, "Alice? I promised my mom I'd leave the party by 9:30, and I'm a little late. If you can help Carley, is it okay if I go now?"

Alice nodded absently and Zage headed out the door. He felt conflicted, thinking that he should've stayed there longer in case Carley needed him. However, he knew that his mother'd be upset if he got involved in a big way with something that might bring a lot of attention. She'd already had him refuse a number of interviews about the little kid who was going to college.

He sighed, I'll apologize to Carley Monday, and blame leaving in the middle of her tragedy on my hyper-nervous mother. Hopefully she'll understand, and mom'll be happy too.

~~~

When Zage got home, his mother was waiting up for him. "Hi Mom," he said, hoping she wouldn't know what'd happened. He didn't expect that to be the case though.

She got up and stepped to him, kneeling and pulling him into a hug. "I'm very proud of you for helping Carley."

Having expected her to be angry, Zage felt pleasantly surprised. "Um, thanks."

She leaned back and gave him a look that he thought was somewhere between amused and frustrated. "However..." she snorted when he rolled his eyes, "I'm pretty sure you knew there was going to be a 'however,' didn't you?"

He nodded, "What did I think my security team was for? All I had to do was have Osprey call them and they'd have taken care of everything, right?"

Ell laughed, "How am I supposed to chastise you, when you beat me to it?!"

He shrugged, "I still think I did the right thing. That guy had already torn her clothes and the closest member of the team, Jerry, was quite a distance away at the pool."

She lifted an eyebrow, "Are you saying they should stay closer to you?"

"No!" he said shaking his head emphatically. "If you want to tell the world that I'm a target, all you need to do's start having a bunch of security start hovering around me!" He tried to give his mother a little more sympathetic look. "I think you've taken exactly the right strategy. You gave me the self-defense training and the single ended port to deliver weapons so I can protect myself briefly. That way a more loosely arranged team has a few moments to get there. *Don't* make the team obvious so they don't attract the very threats you're trying to protect me from." He took a breath, "It worked fine tonight. I was never in any danger, I only helped a friend."

"You *didn't* have to get involved," Ell said, sounding frustrated. "You could've called the team and they would've taken care of it."

"Mom," he said tilting his head and looking at her curiously, "Carley's my friend and I really like her. Someone had attacked her and was tearing her clothes. The team was minutes away. Would *you* have waited instead of helping one of *your* friends?"

His mother stared at him for a moment, looking frustrated, then her shoulders sagged. "No, I'd have done exactly the same thing you did... I hope. That was very nicely executed." She took a deep breath and let it out slowly, "Just... when these things happen in the future, and they almost certainly will, please think about your poor old mother and how terrified she's going to be on your behalf."

Zage grinned, "I'll keep it in mind."

~~~

When Zage got up to his room, he had Osprey call the Gordito site up onto his big screen. The large screen on his wall was recent enough that he still felt grateful that he had it. It'd been hard to talk his parents into letting him have it as they argued he should be sleeping when he was up in his room. But then he'd told them how he couldn't sleep very many hours a night. They'd looked at one another and his mother'd said with a sigh, "Neither can I. And it's pointless trying to lie there hoping you'll fall asleep." They'd only agreed to talk about it, but then when he'd gotten home the next day it'd already been installed.

Having the big screen was good because trying to work on the Gordito site using the HUD in his contacts would've been difficult. He stared, *Especially when it has this many requests!* he thought, somewhat dismayed.

Alice's Note had only gone up on the journal's website earlier that week. Somehow Zage had expected it'd take weeks to months before many people noticed the article. After all the website itself had been up for months with little if any traffic. He'd had a handful of queries he'd responded to yesterday, which he'd thought of as a big uptick. Now there were seventy-three more! *It's a good thing I don't need to sleep very much,* he thought. Then, *I wonder if this big bump's due to some kind of viral spread among scientists? I know that memes go viral in pop culture, but in science?*

Osprey'd already done the parts he could, so Zage had him throw up the first fold Osprey couldn't predict.

The answer seemed obvious so he fed it to Osprey and said, "Next."

As he went through fold after fold, it seemed to be getting easier and easier. He wondered if he was getting better at intuiting the folds or whether he was just getting sloppy. Caring less or something. He paused for a moment to wonder if there was a way for him to know. Realizing that some of the queries might be tests submitted by people who were dubious of his ability, he said, "Osprey, are the 3-D structures of any of these proteins known?"

Osprey replied, "The third submission and the fifty seventh are both known."

"Did I get the third one right?"

"Yes."

"Don't tell me which number I'm working on as I go through them, but after I do the fifty seventh one, stop me to let me know if I get it right too, okay?"

"Yes."

Zage kept working them and putting them back up.

***

When Zage got to the lab Monday, Alice was already there. She turned to look at him when he came in, so he walked over, "How's Carley? I felt really bad about leaving before I could be sure she was okay Friday night."

Alice said, "Okay, I think. She was a little freaked out at first, but about a half an hour later she was back hosting her party."

"Did the police take that guy in?"

"No, they came and downloaded the records off of

his AI. Carley's too. But she didn't want to press charges because he's a nice guy when he's sober. The police said that they'd keep the audio and video records of this incident and if he ever got in the same kind of trouble again he'd have hell to pay." Alice shook her head, "I think he'd better stay sober in the future."

Zage studied her, "Would you've pressed charges?"

She looked off into the distance for half a minute, then said with a shrug, "I don't know. I've always said I'd have no mercy on guys who act like that, but…"

Zage waited a minute for her to say something more, but when she didn't, he said, "Well, I'm really glad Carley seems to be okay."

Alice focused back on Zage, "Carley said you were there when it happened?"

Zage nodded.

"How'd that happen?"

"I'd been watching them dancing and it seemed like he was trying to pull her closer and Carley was fighting to get away. Then he took her by the wrist and dragged her out the door…" Zage shrugged, "so I followed."

Alice frowned, "Why didn't you get someone?!"

Zage grimaced, "I wasn't sure whether it was…" He gave her an embarrassed look, "I wasn't sure whether that was normal behavior at a college party."

With a startled and astonished look, Alice said, "You weren't sure…?! You thought maybe it was normal for guys to drag girls outside and rip their shirts off?"

Zage studied her for a moment, unsure whether she was serious. Deciding that she was, he said, "I'm only five Alice. I have no idea what college kids normally do at parties. Besides, he hadn't ripped her shirt yet when I followed them outside."

She got a blank look for a moment, then Alice

blinked and looked embarrassed. "Sorry. I guess you really wouldn't know what's normal. It's just that you're so smart about science that I always feel like..." she ran down as if she were trying to figure out exactly what she should say, but before she resumed speaking Carley came in the door of the lab.

Seeing Zage standing there, Carley dropped her bag and strode to him, dropping to one knee and throwing her arms around him in a smothering hug. After a moment she pulled back to reveal red rimmed eyes and wet cheeks. "Oh Zage! Thank you, thank you, thank you! Are you okay?"

"I'm fine, just worried about you."

"What happened to you? At first you were there, so calmly taking care of things. Helping me climb in my window and getting Matt that wet towel as if you handled things like that every day. But then you just disappeared! I was worried!"

"Sorry, you should have called me. I'd promised my mother I'd leave the party before 9:30 and I was already late." He shrugged, "She's a real worrywart."

Carley sniffed, "I did call your AI and asked it if you were okay. It said you were fine so I didn't think I should bother you."

"It'd never be a bother getting a call from you."

Carley gave him a curious look, "Did you see who sprayed Matt with the pepper spray? The guy that did it just reached around from behind, shot him in the face, then disappeared even faster than you did."

Surprised, Zage said nothing for a second as he contemplated the fact that he might not have been visible in either of their AIs' cameras when he reached around with the pepper spray. Then he tilted his head and said, "Sorry, I didn't get a good look at him."

Carley went back and picked up her bag, "Well, I owe you guys for all your help Friday night so, even though it doesn't seem nearly enough, I baked you some cookies." She pulled out a container and popped the lid.

Alice grinned and grabbed a couple, "Chocolate chip! My favorite!"

Zage gave them a wistful look as he shook his head, "I can't eat…"

Carley practically exploded as she interrupted him, "You're not going to tell me you still think you're fat? You *used* to be a little chubby, but you're not anymore."

Zage looked down at himself and blushed, "Maybe I could have a couple of cookies."

"You're dang right you could!"

***

Shan looked up as Zage came into the room. "Hey kid, what's up?"

Looking uncomfortable, Zage said, "It's the Gordito website."

"Really? Did someone break into it somehow?" Shan said, thinking that he couldn't imagine how that could actually be possible with all the safeguards they'd installed.

"Oh. No, it's just that it's getting so much traffic. If it keeps increasing I won't be able to keep up."

Shan frowned, "I thought it only took you about thirty seconds to work out the parts of the folding that Osprey's algorithm can't handle and then designate the best antigens?"

Zage sighed, "Yeah, but it turns out that there're a

whole lot more people interested in protein folding than ones who care about viral antigens. I'm getting hundreds of queries a day now and it looks like it'll be thousands pretty soon."

"Aha," Shan said with a big grin, "that's the problem with providing a free service. People are gonna take advantage. You just need to start charging."

Zage frowned, "But you guys said we don't need the money."

"Yeah, but you need the deterrent. You could make it a sliding-scale if you wanted."

"What's that?"

"The first one only costs a dollar, ten dollars each for the next five, $100 for the five after that..." Shan shrugged, "The way you're doing it now, they're going to submit any proteins they're even the least bit curious about. This way they'll pick the ones that they think really matter."

Zage gave him a curious look, "How do we know that subsequent submissions are from the same person?"

Shan lifted an eyebrow, "We can't tell that the *submissions* came from the same person, but we can tell whether the payments come from the same account. Unless these guys're willing to open up a new bank account for each protein they submit..."

"Oh... Okay, can you show me how?"

***

LaQua Kelso stepped into Abe's office looking disheartened. "Homeland Security's found ports hidden in American mosques. Our testing shows they're covered with the vaccinia type virus, as is the surrounding area. They're a type of port that come with sticky backs. You just pull off a tiny piece of paper and touch them to something and there they stick! It makes them really easy to hide. We've found them up high, in light fixtures and the like. My contact at Homeland thinks the people probably place them with some kind of extensible reacher-grabber that lets them just reach up and stick them into place when no one's looking."

Leaning back, Abe said thoughtfully, "Well, it's good to know the method they used for delivery."

As if she couldn't believe his calm response, LaQua said plaintively, "I'm sure they're planning to release the killer virus the same way. I can't imagine how we'd be able to stop them."

Abe pursed his lips, "First of all, you and Homeland should be talking to D5R. Maybe they've got some way to stop transmission of viral particles…"

"Oh, come on! How in the world would they do that?"

"I don't know, but over a lifetime I've learned never to assume that the other guy can't do something. It's at least worth asking." He took a deep breath, "Second, realize the bad guys presumably tested their first virus to be sure that it'll immunize against the second virus. We should be able to beat them at their game simply by producing their first virus in huge quantities and using it to immunize the population."

Dismayed, she shook her head, "You know some idiots are going to refuse to be immunized. They'll be hoping herd immunity'll protect them. Besides, they'd be absolutely correct if they complained that it's more dangerous than modern vaccines."

"First of all, herd immunity won't protect them from a virus that's being released into the air in large quantities. Second, the government could choose to force them to be immunized. Third," he shrugged, "it's a free country. I think idiots *should* be free to refuse immunization if they want—as long as the rest of us don't have to expend our resources trying to save them when they actually get the disease."

LaQua's distraught expression faded long enough for a brief chuckle, "I never figured you for a hardliner like that."

He sighed, "Unfortunately, my bark's way worse than my bite." He chewed his lip for a moment, "How're we coming on growing up the immunization virus? We probably should be starting to think about an immunization program for critical people."

She shook her head, "We're having trouble growing it. We can't seem to get the virus to replicate in culture for some bizarre reason. It grows fine in cats and rats and people, just not in culture. I have no idea how the people who're spreading the virus are growing it up. We're also trying to identify good antigens for a vaccine, but not having much luck so far."

"Have you thought of posting it to the Gordito site?"

"Really?! Come on. We don't even know who 'Gordito' is!"

Abe snorted, "Yeah, I know. And there're a hell of a lot of people who'd like to find out too. People who're a lot better than we are at tracking such things down." He shook his head, "But look at the results! Most people may be using it to get the 3-D structures of proteins, but it was *designed* to let you put up a viral genome and get back a list of likely antigenic peptides and recommended DNA sequences that you can clone in order to make those peptides! Usually, within a day! Whoever he is and however he came up with whatever algorithm he's using, he's some kind of genius. I don't think there's any harm in seeing what he comes up with."

"What *she* comes up with."

Abe frowned and narrowed his eyes, "Do you know something about Gordito…"

"No, just pointing out that while you probably see Gordito as some old Jewish guy," she grinned, "*I* see her as a young black woman… someone with a refined sense of style like me."

Abe snorted and smiled as he waved her away, "Okay, see what *she* comes up with."

~~~

Thirty minutes later LaQua leaned back in Abe's door. "Dang, we're a day late. Gordito just started charging."

"If it works, it doesn't matter how much it costs, we'll still think it's cheap."

LaQua said, "But it'll take a long time to run through billing and I don't think we should wait. We especially won't want to wait when the real bioweapon appears. How about if I pay for this one and you pay for the next one?"

"Okaay… Why do I think there's a catch?"

LaQua shrugged, "First one's a dollar, next five are ten dollars each." She turned on her heel and walked away calling back over her shoulder, "Send ten dollars to my account so we'll be ready, okay?"

Abe snorted and shook his head, *Suckered again…*

***

Allan, Ell's AI, spoke in her ear piece, "You have a call from Vivian."

"Put her through... Hey Vivian, trouble again?"

Vivian sounded depressed, "Yeah, I got a call from a Dr. Kelso at CDC. It's more port terrorism."

"CDC as in Centers for Disease Control?"

"Yeah, those guys. She says somebody's been using one centimeter ports to spread viral particles."

"Um... I haven't heard about any disease outbreaks in the news. At least nothing that sounded very serious..."

"Yeah, this's really scary. Apparently so far they've been sending through a mild virus that's related to one that used to be used to immunize people against smallpox. Kelso thinks they're trying to protect their own peoplse for when they release a virus similar to smallpox. Smallpox kills one in three people which is pretty bad, but, since they've modified the immunization virus, they've probably also modified the smallpox they're going to release. It may be even more deadly."

"Who're they trying to protect?"

"The immunization version's been released in mosques here in the United States. Same for other nations that have a mixture of religions. It's showing up pretty much throughout entire populations in countries that are mostly Islamic."

"If it doesn't make people sick, how do we know it's out there?"

"Chickenpox, cowpox, smallpox, they all produce pustules called pocks that leave scars. So, people seek medical attention for these pocks. And cowpox, which is what they used in the past to immunize people to smallpox and what this virus's related to, can make people really sick if they have weak immune systems or are kind of feeble. CDC estimates about one in 10,000 people are dying from it."

"So, is CDC going to start immunizing people for smallpox?"

"First thing I asked. Apparently they think immunization with standard cowpox like CDC knows how to make probably won't work because this new immunization virus's different enough that they think the old vaccination won't protect against the new smallpox version."

"They can't vaccinate people for the new one?"

Ell could hear the frustration in Vivian's voice, "A new version of smallpox hasn't been released yet, they're just guessing that it will be. But you can imagine it's hard to vaccinate people for a disease you're not sure exists and that you know nothing about."

Ell said, "But they know, presumably, that this new virus the terrorists are releasing will provide protection, right?"

"Yeah," Vivian sighed, "but the new virus is a lot more dangerous than standard vaccinations so a lot of people would object to getting it. At least they will until people start dying by the millions. Besides, CDC's having a hard time growing the new virus and nobody's sure why."

"So, they'd like us to do something to keep the virus from being spread through ports, right?"

"Uh-huh. And I've already pointed out to them that ports are only convenient. I'm sure the terrorists could find a way to spread the virus some other way."

"Do we have a way of preventing port transmission?"

Vivian said, "They're probably either blowing dry

viral particles through the ports, which would be like dust, or an aqueous aerosol of the particles. We don't have systems in place to detect those kinds of substances going through ports. If we could figure out a way to build in such systems, and would only affect future ports. Besides it'd make ports a lot more expensive which would make a lot of people unhappy."

"Well, if they found some of these ports that the vaccination virus was sent through we'll know when they started buying them. They've probably already bought all they need to spread the smallpox version. If they're only using one centimeter ports, we could just shut down all the one centimeter ports we've sold between the time we sold the vaccination ports and now."

"Ell! That's tens of thousands of ports! Maybe hundreds of thousands. All those people are going to file on our guarantees!"

"Vivian, we're talking millions and millions of deaths, right?"

There was a pause, then Vivian sighed, "Yeah. I'll get the information and we'll start figuring out which ports we'd need to shut down. Maybe CDC will figure out a better solution before we actually have to carry it out."

"If they're doing this worldwide, the bad guys almost certainly had to have bought ports in large quantities. You should be able to track sales well enough to only shut down ports sold in large lots. Homeland Security should be very interested in checking out anyone who's done that. Anyone who contacts you about the guarantee, complaining because a *few* ports've stopped working, isn't a bad guy, you can just reactivate their ports..."

Bioterror

Chapter Eight

Zage was working on queries to Gordito. Osprey said, "This next request's for viral antigens rather than protein folding."

"Which virus?" Zage asked, hoping as always that someone was trying to create a vaccine for an obesity virus.

"They haven't specified the name of the virus. Do you want me to analyze the genome to see if it's a known virus?"

"Yes," *of course,* Zage thought, though he didn't say it. Osprey's stunning computational abilities didn't enable him to intuit some things that humans thought obvious.

Osprey could however, analyze the genome almost instantaneously. "No published viral genomes completely match this virus. It has sections that're quite similar to vaccinia and others that're somewhat analogous to parts of the camel pox genome."

"What's vaccinia?"

"Vaccinia's a variant of the cowpox virus. Cowpox was used for immunization against smallpox and eventually versions of the vaccination virus that became somewhat different from native cowpox came to be called vaccinia."

"Find me stuff to read about vaccinia and camelpox," Zage said, thinking, *This doesn't sound like a natural virus. If someone constructed it, why?* He didn't want Gordito to help someone construct a bio-weapon. To Osprey, he said, "Go through the virus's entire genome and find any parts of it that aren't native to either vaccinia or camelpox. Those segments are probably also genes from other organisms, see if you can identify those genes as well."

By the time Zage had posed the second query, Osprey'd already found a large body of literature on vaccinia and camelpox. Zage started looking at it and sank into what he'd come to think of as a kind of fugue state. To try to understand what happened to him when he was in these episodes, he'd watched some security camera video of himself when it happened. While he was in a fugue, he gave nearly constant commands to Osprey to find and sort information while he glanced from screen to screen at information Osprey was putting up. He spent so little time looking at each screen it was hard to imagine that he took much in from any of them. However, when it was over, he'd feel like he was simply and suddenly much more knowledgeable about whatever topic he'd been studying. Like a psychiatric fugue, he'd barely remember the time he'd spent in the state. He thought of these episodes as similar to the "zone" that he and his mother got into for physical activities, but the fugues were for learning.

Coming out of even the relatively brief fugue it'd taken him to learn about the pox viruses, Zage said, "Show me your analysis of that viral genome and let's work out its folding."

Zage started working to understand what each segment of the viral genome coded for and where the proteins it coded for were located in the viral structure.

Zage shook his head, realizing that he'd gone into another brief fugue state just analyzing the virus. But, what he'd learned...!

Dreading what he might find out, he said, "Who submitted that viral genome?"

"A Dr. LaQua Kelso from CDC."

For a moment, Zage was relieved to realize that someone from the CDC'd submitted the viral genome. Someone who tried to prevent diseases, not someone who might be creating one. Then he recognized the fact that, if CDC was trying to understand this virus, someone else had probably already built it and spread it around! "Send Dr. Kelso a request for me to be able to speak to her."

"As Zage Kinrais?"

"No! Um, as Gordito. But first assemble everything you can find about Dr. Kelso so I can read about her before I wind up talking to her."

~~~

LaQua's AI said, "You have a call from a 'Gordito.'"

"I'll take it! But before you connect me are you able to identify the caller?"

"No, the origination point's disguised."

"Okay, connect me... Gordito?"

"Yes," she heard someone say in a synthetic voice, "I'm sorry to be using this vocal disguise but my privacy's very important to me."

"Oh, okay..."

"I'm calling about the viral genome you submitted for identification of antigens?"

"Yesss?" LaQua said drawing the word out because she was afraid Gordito was about to give her bad news.

"I assume you know that it's a synthetic virus and much of it's based on vaccinia?"

"Uh-huh."

"And that the code for much of the material on the exterior of the virus is a modification of external components of the camelpox virus?"

"Uh-huh."

"Um, and you've probably already considered that a virus based on vaccinia shouldn't be particularly lethal, but might've been created to serve as a vaccine against a lethal bio weapon, perhaps based on the smallpox virus?"

"Yes," LaQua said. On the one hand she wanted to tell this Gordito person not to teach his grandmother to suck eggs. She found it irritating being lectured about the virus when she'd sent him the genome for it. As if she knew nothing about it. On the other hand, *I only sent Gordito the genome a few hours ago! How in all the holy Hells has he figured all this out already!* However, LaQua swallowed those thoughts before they became comments. Instead she said, "Then you can understand why we're very concerned."

"Yes ma'am. I'm trying to help, really. I'm just trying to figure out what you already know."

"Ma'am?!" LaQua thought, having expected a pompous, arrogant, condescending attitude from this Gordito character. Someone who seemed to already know so much about a virus she'd *just* sent him. She suddenly realized that she'd gone into this conversation thinking of Gordito as a woman, but then quickly decided he was a man when he'd been asking her questions as if he thought she wouldn't know even the basics about the virus. *I guess I have my own biases and preconceived notions.* She said, "Do you think you'll be able to identify likely antigens?"

"Oh, yes ma'am. But, if you're thinking, like I am, that this represents some terrorists' live vaccine that they've prepared to protect their own people against a bioweapon they're planning to release, why aren't you just growing it up and using it as a vaccine?"

"Two problems," LaQua said. "First, it kills about one in 10,000 people, so it'll be hard to get people to accept vaccination with it. As you know, at least here in the United States there're large segments of the population who think even vaccines much safer than this one are too risky. Second…"

Gordito broke in, "Surely they realize it's much safer than an encounter with a smallpox based bio-weapon!"

LaQua chuckled morbidly, "Surely they will… *after* millions of people've already died from the bioweapon. A lot of people would conclude that the horse was already well out of the barn at that point. Besides, we can't get it to replicate except in very small quantities. I have a basic reluctance to going back to the old strategy of using pustules on one person to vaccinate the next person."

"Oh. You know the author inserted a genetic switch into the viral genome?"

"Um…" LaQua squinched her eyes shut in frustration, wondering why she hadn't considered the possibility. "No. What kind of switch?"

"It should shut down viral replication in the presence of bovine thyroid hormone. That'd make it difficult to replicate the virus in media containing bovine serum. Have you tried growing the supporting cell line for replication of the virus in porcine serum, or in serum free media?"

"No," LaQua said dryly, feeling thoroughly schooled, "we'll have to try that."

"If you'll log back onto the Gordito website, you'll find it has the gene sequences for a number of peptide antigens I think'll work for vaccination. There'll also be a sequence for a protein that should fold to expose all those antigens on a single molecule."

"Oh...!" LaQua said, stunned, "That'll... that'll be great. Thanks, I hope they work."

"Me too. Please let me know if they don't and I'll try again. This's what this site was established for."

***

Abe looked up. LaQua Kelso was standing in his doorway shaking her head. "You were only half right about Gordito," she said.

"He wasn't able to identify antigens for a vaccine?"

"Well, admittedly I'm not sure yet. *She's* identified sequences she says'll produce a vaccine. We're starting to fabricate them, but haven't tested them to see if they'll actually induce protective antibodies."

"Oh," he frowned, "so what part did I get half right?"

"It didn't take a day, it took less than half a day. Then, she didn't just post possible antigens, she figured out what it was, and who I was, then called me. She wanted to make sure I recognized that it was probably a synthetically created virus, intended to vaccinate people against an impending bio-weapon."

"She didn't think we'd have figured that out?" Abe said indignantly, using the feminine pronoun LaQua'd been using without even realizing it.

"Yeah, I found that a little irritating too, but I managed to restrain my hubris by focusing on the fact that she'd figured all that out in a few hours, not weeks like it took us. *And,* when I mentioned we were having trouble growing the virus, she told me that it had a genetic switch that kept the virus from replicating in the presence of bovine serum. Then she asked me if we'd tried growing it in serum free growth media, thus forcing me to admit, to my embarrassment, or that we hadn't." She turned to look out Abe's window, "And, of course, it *does* replicate in serum free media, and in media with porcine serum." Distantly, she said, "The girl's a genius and someone I really want to meet." She turned back to Abe, "You should be trying to hire her."

Abe sighed, "Maybe after we've got this potential bioweapon issue under control. Homeland Security's sending in a hired gun to take overall charge of dealing with this crisis. You and I'll both be reporting to him, which'll be irritating, but I'm hoping he can take over all the nonscientific grunt work and leave us to work on the best vaccination strategies. I'm raiding a bunch of other teams to increase the size of your team. We desperately need to be helping you deal with the medical issues. I'm bringing in a bunch of academic consultants Tuesday for a little mini conference in hopes of getting some genius ideas on how to vaccinate a reluctant population against a disease that we're not a hundred percent sure's actually out there. Hopefully, by then you'll have some numbers for me on how much of the vaccinia version of the virus you think you'll be able to have at what time points. I'm thinking we'll need to start a strategy of vaccinating critical personnel and first responders with the live virus pretty soon, even if eventually we use a safer, antigen-based vaccination for the remainder of the population. On Thursday I'm flying up to brief President Stockton on this threat and I'm hoping to have a good plan for dealing with it."

Kelso said, "Wow, so I'm not the only person

worrying about and working on this problem after all?"

Abe shook his head, "Pretty soon you'll only be one of thousands."

"A bit of good news. I talked to somebody over at Portal Technologies and she says they're going to shut down all the one centimeter ports sold in large lots from now back to three months before Little Diomede."

"Wow! How'd you talk them into doing that? Usually we have to threaten big corporations before they'll do *anything* that might cut into their profits."

LaQua shrugged, "The woman said 'Donsaii believes in doing the right thing.'"

"I guess there's plenty of evidence of her attitude on those issues…" Abe said, thinking of the comet and an infamous terrorist episode.

LaQua shook her head tiredly, "Closing the ports might slow them down a little bit, but there're plenty of other ways for them to spread a biowarfare virus."

"Yeah," Abe said, somewhat despondently. Then he firmed up his expression, "We'll just need to figure out how to get ahead of them with vaccination programs then."

***

Research Triangle Park, North Carolina—Portal Technologies announced today that they've shut down large numbers of one centimeter ports around the world because of concerns that they're about to be used for a bioterrorism event. Owners of ports that have become nonfunctional may contact Portal Technologies at its main website to request restoration of services. The company assures us that they will try to get those ports back in service as soon as safely possible...

"Vivian! You guys made an announcement that you're shutting down the ports for fear of impending bioterrorism?!"

"Ell, I'm so sorry. One of our bright young boys down in marketing decided that this was going to become a PR debacle and therefore a financial disaster. He thought he could mitigate the problem if he got out in front of it ASAP. By "ASAP," he meant 'even before vetting the idea with his superiors.'"

"Oh cripes! Homeland Security's already having conniptions and John Q Public's going to go berserk!"

"Can you think of anything we can do to mitigate?"

"No, the genie's already out of the bottle. I'm offering all of our resources to Homeland Security, but to be honest, I haven't thought of anything we can do." After a brief pause, Ell continued, "Get your people together and have them brainstorm. See if anyone can think of something we can do to shut this down."

"We've already shut down the ports we expect to be involved... Surely shutting down more ports won't help?"

"No, I don't think so either. I don't know of anything, but sometimes when you get a bunch of bright people together, someone comes up with a genius idea."

Usually you, Vivian thought, but said, "Will do."

~~~

Five minutes later, Vivian got another call from Ell, "I've thought of something else. Go through the GPS coordinates on those large lots of one-centimeter ports you've shut down. One end of the bioterrorists' ports are going to be scattered all around the world which doesn't do us much good, but the other ends should all be in one location. That'll be the location where they were manufacturing the virus and holding the ports so that they'd be ready to have the weapon blown through them. Get that location to Homeland Security and maybe they can stop this before it even gets started."

***

The man from Islam Akbar stormed into Adin's office. "Portal Technologies says they're shutting down the ports we were going to use for distribution!"

Frustration threatened to rise up in Adin's soul, but then he thought about all the things that had gone right so far with this project. It was about time for a stumble and this one wouldn't be too bad. "Have you tested a sample of our ports to make sure they've actually turned ours off?"

"Yes! They aren't working!"

Adin shrugged, "Be sure we test them all. If even a few work it'll make distribution of the virus easier. But, my friend, don't worry. There're many other ways to distribute the virus."

"How?!"

"In 1971 The Soviets exploded a small bomb with a little less than a pound of smallpox virus on a deserted island in the Aral Sea. Someone on a research ship that came within fifteen kilometers of the island caught the disease. She spread it to the city of Aralsk where only a highly aggressive vaccination program was able to stop its spread. And this was at a time when most of the population were already vaccinated. There's a good chance that if I sprayed a little of the virus out on the street today it'd soon spread *itself* all over the world." Adin leaned back in his chair and stared up at the ceiling. "Here's some ideas. We could put the virus in firecrackers, or AK-47 shells, or hacky-sacks, or all three. You distribute them around the world, getting people to fire the firecrackers, shoot the weapons, and play with the hacky-sacks. The epidemic won't spread as fast as it would've using the ports, but, it'll get around nonetheless."

"Sending such devices around the world will be expensive!"

Adin shrugged, "Changing the world costs money."

***

Homeland Security, Washington DC—Yesterday's announcement by Portal Technologies that it was shutting down thousands of one centimeter ports they believe might be used for bioterrorism has produced an absolute firestorm of panic. Demands for more information are coming from every quarter. Portal Technologies is referring all questions to Homeland Security and PR individuals at Homeland Security have not been forthcoming, claiming that providing more information will put the public at even higher risk. Experts polled by a number of news agencies have forwarded the possibilities that the purported bioweapon might involve dissemination of botulism, anthrax, smallpox, plague and various others. There is of course concern that these organisms, while dangerous enough in their own right, may have been modified with some of the new DNA techniques to make them even more dangerous or resistant to treatment.

If such agents were due to be delivered through ports all around the world as Portal Technologies' announcement suggested, this reporter, for one, thanks them for shutting down the ports—no matter the inconvenience to innocent owners and users of such one centimeter ports. However, it is obvious to even the most casual student of bioweapons that, while ports might make distribution convenient, terrorists could still distribute the weapon by other means.

Whether or not a bioweapon is ever released, the mere announcement has shaken the world's confidence. Injuries have already occurred as runs on surgical masks and HEPA filters have begun and fighting has been reported over the dwindling supplies...

Abe stepped into LaQua Kelso's section, finding the young woman looking harried but in control. When she spotted him, she stepped his way. Quietly, she asked "How're things going?"

"Well, that Portal Technologies announcement was a real cluster. I've never been so glad to have Homeland Security in overall charge of anything in my life. If all those reporters had descended on *us* we wouldn't even be able to get into our own parking lot!" He took a breath preparatory to continuing his rant, but then decided to get to business instead. "How're things here?"

"We've had some bumps adjusting to all the extra people you've given us, but they're really starting to make a difference. We've got a protocol set up that one of the commercial vendors will be able to use to churn out large quantities of the live vaccine using porcine serum culture techniques. Stupid me, I didn't realize we wouldn't be able to use that vaccine for Muslims. For that matter, a lot of the more kosher members of your own tribe wouldn't accept it either. We're having to set up to make some using goat serum and/or serum free media, but we won't be able to make sufficient volumes for everyone using those techniques."

"And," Abe said, "I assume by 'everyone' you're only referring to our list of critical personnel and first responders? Not everyone in the US?"

"Right. We're hoping to vaccinate the general populace with the Gordito antigen, assuming it works. Early testing in animals shows it generating strong antibody reactions. We're just now infecting some of the vaccinated animals with the vaccinia version to see if it protects them from it. Of course, we won't be able to be sure it'll protect them against the smallpox version since we haven't encountered it yet."

"Yeah…" Abe said, making the word into a long sigh. "Will you be able to produce the antigen in quantity?"

Kelso gave a little laugh, "Yes we will. That damned Gordito not only gave us the amino acid sequence for generating her 'protein folded to expose all of the relevant antigens,' but also gave us a suggested DNA sequence with tags attached for cell-free protein synthesis and subsequent purification of the output." Shaking her head, she looked Abe in the eye, "She did *all* that in just a few hours. Have you tried to hire her yet?"

Abe snorted, "I'll make the offer, just as soon as we know enough people have survived this bioweapon to make it worth having a CDC when it's all over." He smirked at her and said, "You know, I've been thinking. 'Gordito' is Spanish for little fat boy. If it was little fat *girl*, it'd be Gordita."

Kelso waved dismissively, "That's all just part of her plan to keep her anonymity." Then she frowned, "You think it's going to be that bad? That CDC might not survive?"

"It could be… I don't want to think it, but it could be. Getting Portal Technologies to shut down the ports we believe they were planning to use is going to give us a little breather, but we really don't have anybody immunized yet. If, this afternoon, someone shook a bag of lyophilized smallpox virus out the window of one of the skyscrapers here in downtown Atlanta, it'd fall on a completely unprepared population. Even if this engineered version *wasn't* more lethal than the original smallpox, hundreds of thousands of people would die." He looked around the room with hollow eyes, "If the people in this facility got sick and started dying before they could generate a response, millions more would die. We've got to start vaccinating each other."

LaQua put a hand on his shoulder, "You're right. We'll get started. Every day they give us, we're going to be more ready, but we also can't afford to have all of Earth's eggs in this one basket. We need to get this information out to other centers, not just here in the United States, but all over the world."

Abe said, "You're right. Assign one of your bright young people here to generate a file with what we know for distribution. They should update and distribute it again on a daily basis." Then, in an even more somber tone, he said, "We're going to have to tell the world what we're expecting. They need to know it's a variant of smallpox so they can be prepared. Have someone else, someone with clinical acumen, come up with a set of treatment recommendations to distribute to clinicians everywhere in case we have an epidemic before we have enough vaccine. Supportive care. How serum from people who were exposed to the vaccinia type virus and made antibodies might be able to cure people with active disease. How we're preparing both live and dead vaccinations, but that if we don't get there in time, how they might be able to use pustules from patients with vaccinia infections to vaccinate the rest of the population. If everything goes to hell, they might even want to use variolation, they should at least know how to do it."

"Variolation?! Isn't that where you take material from pustules on someone with *active smallpox* and use it to inoculate other people?!"

"Yeah… And it's *way* more dangerous than vaccination with vaccinia, but if there's an epidemic raging and no one available with active vaccinia, it's still a lot safer than catching smallpox the regular way."

"Oh my God…!"

***

Homeland Security, Washington DC—Anonymous sources at Homeland Security have revealed that the bioterrorism panic sweeping the world is based on the fact that the pustular eruptions which have been occurring in Islamic countries have been confirmed to be due to a modified form of the vaccinia virus. The original vaccinia (cowpox) virus was used to immunize people against smallpox back when smallpox was a major health threat.

Though no cases of smallpox have been reported as of yet, the concern is that an unknown Islamic terrorist group released modified vaccinia in Islamic countries and at mosques in countries with some Muslims in their population. The thought is that it was released with the intent that it would protect Muslims when a modified version of smallpox is released at some point in the near future.

Islamic groups worldwide have joined together in condemning and repudiating the presumed splinter group that has embarked on such a horrific plan...

Abe looked up at the sounds of argument out in the hall. He tried to return his attention to the document he'd been working on, but then closed his eyes as the argument approached his office. "Those rules, procedures, and certification standards were put forth for a *reason*, dammit!"

With that John Arquette walked into Abe's office without so much as a pause in the doorway. He was trailed by LaQua Kelso. "Abe? Are you aware of the fact that Dr. Kelso was about to begin vaccinations of our own personnel here at CDC—with a live virus that hasn't been fully tested! All indications are that it has a completely unacceptable risk profile!"

Abe sighed as he addressed the excessively punctilious Arquette, "Yes, John, I'm aware. Have you given thought to why we're proceeding without full testing?"

"Abe! We set up those protocols for very good reasons and only after extensive discussions!"

"John, we've weighed the risks versus the benefits. You're correct, this vaccination's significantly more dangerous than what we'd normally accept, but if it's capable of ameliorating the effects of a *biowarfare* version of smallpox, we think that benefit outweighs the risk. Remember, *you* do not have to get vaccinated, nor does anyone else. We're administering it entirely on a voluntary basis."

John stormed out of the office, calling behind him, "Well, I'm going to make sure those people are aware of the dangers before they volunteer to be your damned guinea pigs!"

Abe sagged, then looked up at LaQua, "I'm doing my damnedest not to hope that supercilious bastard catches the real disease when it comes out."

"I would never have considered that possibility," LaQua said with a wry grin as she turned to leave.

***

Atlanta, Centers for Disease Control—The CDC announced today that it has sent the gene sequence of modified vaccinia virus to similar agencies in other countries around the world. This with the intent that those agencies could develop their own live virus vaccination programs using the virus if they wish. They warn, however, that vaccination with that virus carries significantly greater risks than other modern vaccination programs. They have also sent a gene sequence for a protein that might be used for relatively safe vaccinations. Unfortunately, this protein has not been confirmed to be able to prevent the expected bioterrorism version of smallpox. It must be pointed out that we do not know if the live virus version of vaccinia can prevent the new smallpox either, but it is presumed that, since the putative terrorists ostensibly released it in an effort to protect the Muslim world, that they presumably tested it to be sure that it does provide protection. In addition, the CDC is distributing a set of recommendations for supportive clinical treatment of unvaccinated persons with smallpox. They're sending this to healthcare organizations and medical workers around the world. These recommendations are intended to attempt to ameliorate the presumably devastating effects of the disease in people who refuse or cannot get vaccinations.

The world is waiting in dread for the other shoe to drop...

Panic erupted on the streets of New York this morning when a woman dropped her bag of groceries and a white powder was noticed to have spilled out of it. The powder was swirling away from the bag on the breeze. In the subsequent frenzy and flight from the area, several people were injured, one being killed when she was apparently pushed in front of a moving vehicle. A hazmat team cleaned up the powder and it was subsequently determined to be ordinary white flour—as the woman had been proclaiming all along.

Employers are reporting large numbers of unexpected and unauthorized absences...

Runs on preserved foods and supplies of bottled water are plaguing local supermarkets...

Home Depot disclosed today that they are nearly out of plastic sheeting, caulk, tape of all kinds, air filters...

As happened to him occasionally, Adin was having second thoughts about what he'd done when the still unnamed man from Islam Akbar walked into Adin's office without knocking.

As the man always did—a constant source of irritation to Adin who felt like he should be accorded more respect.

The man walked over to Adin's window and lifted one of the blinds. He waved at the view, "We need to leave."

Adin looked out the small opening and saw the building next door swarming with people wearing Homeland Security jackets. It was the building where they'd stored all the ports that'd been destined to deliver the virus around the world before they were shut down. "What happened?" Adin asked.

The man shrugged, "I assume they tracked the damned ports somehow. It doesn't matter, I expect they'll be checking this building soon enough. We need to get out of here."

"But...!" Adin didn't finish the thought. He'd been going to complain that all their equipment would be lost, but they'd already made plenty of the virus. Shipments were on their way around the world. No one could stop his son's revenge now. "Okay," he said. He plucked a plastic bag off his desk and started for the door. Before he exited, he opened the bag and spilled the white powder in the hall...

~~~

Bob boosted Naomi up so she could look into the one of the high windows of the building next to the one where Portal Technology had told them to look for the ports. The Portal Tech guys had certainly been right about that. Naomi's team had found thousands and thousands of sequentially numbered ports in their original boxes in the building behind them. The ports had come from the banned list of ports sold in the months that the terrorists were thought to have been getting set up. Naomi'd been wondering how Portal

Technology knew where the ports were until she'd looked in this window. What she saw inside told her she had bigger fish to fry, "This's it!" she shouted. As agents looked her way and started to move toward her, she barked, "Don't get any closer without protective gear!"

***

Dallas, Texas—The Department of Homeland Security has confirmed that it investigated several buildings in an industrial complex in Dallas this morning. How they were tipped off is not known, but apparently they found a laboratory set up to grow viruses and capable of growing them in large quantities. They believe that they will know whether it is the purported terrorist version of smallpox by sometime tomorrow...

Zage climbed down off his chair and headed for the sink with his bowl. Ell said, "Um, I don't think you should go into Dr. Barnes' lab today..."

He turned to give her a mildly dismayed look, "Why not?"

Uncomfortably, she found she couldn't look him in the eye, "I'm worried about..."

When she ran down, he said, "The weaponized smallpox?"

Ell nodded.

"We don't have to worry, though it's probably going to be a big problem around the world."

"What do you mean, *we* don't have to worry?!"

"They sent me the viral genome last night. The antigens on its exterior are the same ones that're on the vaccinia virus that was released a while back. They'll be able to vaccinate people for it."

"*Who* sent *you* a genome for a bioweapon?!"

He tilted his head, "CDC sent *Gordito* the genome. They wanted him to tell them which antigens it'd have."

"CDC's trusting your algorithm for this?!"

Zage nodded.

"Why isn't CDC doing this in-house? Why in the world would they be sending it out to a website that's only been up a couple of months and is run by someone they don't even know?"

"Mom," Zage said in a calming tone, even though he looked a little frustrated, "they sent it here because Gordito can do stuff no one else can. That's why we're having to charge so much to reduce traffic on the site so I'm not overwhelmed."

"Oh my God! They have no idea they're talking to a five-year-old do they?"

He gave her a surprised look, "Of course not. If they did," he lifted an eyebrow and gave her a little grin, "they'd probably be skeptical of the results."

"Do you… do you know if they're checking… or whatever they do… your results to make sure they're correct?"

"*Lots* of people have checked Gordito's results. The consensus is that his results are astonishingly reliable."

"But… this one result is… *incredibly* important! What if you got this one wrong?"

"I didn't. Mom, I *knew* this one really mattered. I checked and rechecked. Besides, the guys that made these two viruses obviously intended the first one to be a vaccination for the second one. They almost certainly vaccinated their own workers with the first one to protect them while they were growing up the second one. Not only did I find that the two sets of antigens are the same, but all reasonable expectations *were* that they'd be the same."

"Who's your contact there? I should call them and…"

Zage had approached her by now, and at this point he climbed up into her lap. "And what Mom? Call into doubt some perfectly good and completely trustworthy information they've been relying on at a time when they're deep into crisis mode?"

She drew back and looked him deep in the eyes, "And you're absolutely sure that your analysis of this genome was completely correct? Sure enough that we should trust the welfare of the world to your results?"

He kept his eyes on hers as he nodded slowly and seriously. "Do you think we should all be vaccinated?"

She looked off over his shoulder, "Yeah, but so far I understand they're only vaccinating critical people and first responders. The rest of us have to wait until they have more vaccine available."

"I'm making some in the basement…" Zage said.

He'd leaned back as if he expected an explosion and he got one. "Zage! You're growing a virus in our basement?!"

"I should've said, 'in our basement laboratory.' It's not like I'm working in some dank corner, you know? Besides, I'm not actually growing a virus, I'm using that cell free protein synthesis set-up you bought me to make a protein that has the antigens on it."

Ell snorted, "*What* kind of 'protein synthesis set-up' did we buy you?"

"It's 'cell free.' Instead of using bacteria, or yeast, or mammalian mammary glands to manufacture your protein, you do CFPS in a test tube or vat. You have to have the components of a cell, or the so-called 'cell machinery' in the vat, then you supply chemicals to act as energy sources, amino acids to be chained together into the proteins, and the DNA template for the protein you want to generate. Since I'd already worked out the DNA sequence for a protein with all the antigens on it, including appropriate purification tags for the CDC, it felt crazy not to make some of our own in case they didn't get us vaccinated before the epidemic struck."

Ell blinked, "And you're sure it's safe?"

"It's just a small protein. It's easily sterilized by filtration."

Ell rolled her eyes, "I've heard *that* argument before. Something about a peptide you wanted to inject yourself with, just to help you lose weight."

A guilty look flashed over Zage's face, "Um, yeah…"

"Don't you feel better about yourself now that you've proven you can lose the weight with diet and exercise?"

He stared at her for a minute, then slowly shook his head, "Not really."

"Well, *I'm* proud of you!"

"So, you're saying that even if this weaponized smallpox was out there killing almost a hundred percent of people, and the government hadn't been able to vaccinate everybody, you'd rather die than get *my* vaccine?"

She studied him for a moment, then said, "Well, you've got me there. In that situation, I'd be delighted that you'd made some vaccine in the basement." She winked at him, "Did you make enough for the rest of the family?"

"Oh. Yeah, it doesn't take much. Our CFPS setup can make enough for a half million doses a day."

"It can?!"

"Um, yeah. Each dose's pretty small. Besides, when I

picked out the set-up, I decided it wasn't all that much more to get an industrial version that could turn out proteins in quantity."

Ell snorted, "And, you just assumed, correctly it turns out, that I wouldn't realize you were buying something far bigger than you needed?"

Zage shrugged, turning his eyes downward as if he were embarrassed, but Ell didn't think he really was. "How many have you made?"

"Um, it's been running for more than a week now."

"You've made over four million doses?!"

"Well… there'd be some wastage. You couldn't actually treat that many people."

"Why so many?!"

"In case the government doesn't make enough. If that happens, this could be really important for a whole lot of people. If they're able to make plenty of vaccine, we'll have wasted some money, but," he gave her a searching look, "you said you had lots of money, right?"

"Yeah," she looked out the window, swallowed, then patted him on the shoulder, "keep cranking it out kid."

***

Homeland Security, Washington DC— Francis Dorchester, spokeswoman at Homeland Security, disclosed that the buildings the agency cordoned off in Dallas yesterday were, in fact, growing a modified version of smallpox. Upon early testing, this virus appears to be almost exactly the type of bio-weapon that the Centers for Disease Control were expecting— based on the vaccination virus which had been released earlier. It is too early yet to know whether the mortality rate of infection with this modified bio-terrorism version of the virus will be higher than the commonly quoted thirty percent mortality for wild-type smallpox.

Only a few—apparently lower-level—personnel were captured at the site in Dallas, but upon questioning they have apparently confirmed that the despised Islamic terrorist organization Islam Akbar was the driving force behind the industrial production of the virus. They claim that the mastermind who constructed the modified smallpox was a virologist by the name of Adin Farsq who was not captured in yesterday's raid. Unfortunately, testing has also demonstrated that substantial amounts of white powder found in the hallways of the building were freeze-dried viral particles. The people who entered the building to investigate, as well as the personnel captured on site, are being quarantined in that building, though many experts have pointed out that it's probably too little, too late.

Though earlier reports suggested that the terrorists planned to release their bioweaponized smallpox through one centimeter ports, it appears that Portal Technology's quick action in shutting down ports of that size sold over the past few months has successfully shut down that strategy. Thousands and thousands of those ports—all nonfunctional—were found at the site in Dallas. It is believed that Islam Akbar subsequently converted to a strategy of physical distribution of the virus. Homeland Security is working with major shipping companies to try to determine addresses to which packages may have been distributed here in the United States and around the world. Anyone aware of other means by which the virus might have been distributed— for instance, anyone who was asked to take a package with them to another country—is asked to come forward immediately.

Because it frequently takes 10-14 days for the first symptoms of smallpox to occur after exposure, this bio-weapon may already have been released against the public and people may already be infected and simply in the incubation phase. A UPS driver was just admitted and isolated in a hospital in Dallas with a pustular eruption compatible with smallpox. This man reports that he accidentally dropped a package he picked up from the Dallas facility in question nine days ago. Dallas County Health and Human Services is currently finding all of his contacts, as well as his contacts' contacts and bringing them in for vaccination and isolation as well.

In view of the events described above, Homeland Security and the Centers for Disease Control have recommended an intense and aggressive worldwide vaccination program. Unfortunately, there are not yet sufficient quantities of either the live—and somewhat dangerous—vaccination based on cowpox, or the protein-based, non-living vaccination based on the live virus. At present, plans are to vaccinate exposed persons and isolate them in order to protect the unvaccinated remainder of the population. CDC and the government do confirm that they're in the midst of gearing up industrial programs to produce more of both of the vaccines in quantity.

CDC has confirmed that neither of the vaccines have been proven to prevent the new version of smallpox. However, it is presumed that the terrorists confirmed that the live virus does prevent the disease as they have been distributing it amongst Islamic groups that they wished to protect. Experts believe that the protein-based vaccine "should work" and is safer than the live *virus, especially for those whose general health or immune system is weakened. It'll be used preferentially in those types of individuals.*

It is important to note that the actions of the Islam Akbar splinter group do not by any means represent the thoughts, beliefs, or intentions of any but that one very small and radical minority of Islam...

Abe entered the room and looked around for LaQua Kelso. He saw her near the far corner, having an apparently heated discussion with one of the older staff. He made his way over, wondering what this argument was about. As he arrived, she was saying, "... the antibodies it generates in both rats and mice bind to the smallpox virus."

Abe now recognized she was talking to Norm Atwater, one of CDC's highly respected vaccine experts. Atwater said, "The fact that it binds *in vitro* doesn't mean that it's going to stop the virus *in vivo.*"

LaQua rolled her eyes, "We don't know that vaccination with the live virus is going to protect people either!"

"No, but we can assume that the terrorists tested it and that it does!"

"Dr. Atwater," she said exasperatedly, "we're growing the live virus as fast as we can. We've sent it out to every facility that can grow it, and they're growing as much of it as they can as well. We've essentially taken over every facility that we believe can grow the virus and we have them working full time. But we're in the midst of a crisis here! We don't have enough! We need something that we can mass manufacture, the way we can produce the antigen using CFPS. Facilities that can make a protein seldom overlap with facilities that can grow the virus and even if they do, the two processes don't use the same equipment. We're *not* making less of the live viral vaccine in order to make more of the antigen!"

Atwater turned to Abe for support, "This antigen… she's basing it on a sequence provided by that damned Gordito website. The site's only been up a few months. It's completely unproven and no one even knows who it is! Yet we're basing a nationwide vaccination program on it?!"

LaQua said, "Gordita. I don't know how you can say it's unproven. Multiple investigators have vetted her protein folding results!"

"*Her* results? Do you know something about this person?"

Kelso shook her head, "Let's just say I have a feeling." She winked, "Call it a *woman's* intuition if you want." Her smile vanished, "The fact remains that a lot of people have tested the site and it's right almost every time."

Atwater shook his head, "There's been multiple tests of Gordito's ability to predict protein folding, yes. There have *not* been multiple tests of its ability to predict viral antigens…"

Abe interrupted, "Norm, do you have an antigen we can use instead?"

Norm gave him a wide-eyed look, "No, we've just started working on it! You should *know* this isn't something that can be turned out overnight on demand!"

Abe put a hand on his shoulder, "But, Norm, we *need* results yesterday… Which, I must point out, Gordito gave us. Nothing about this keeps you from continuing to work on producing an inactivated viral vaccine, or your own form of antigen vaccine. If the Gordito vaccine fails to work we'll be ecstatic to have whatever you come up with waiting in the wings, but the fact that you're working on it doesn't keep us from manufacturing the Gordito version and hoping that it works. Because, Norm, I can guarantee your vaccine's too late. Hell, the Gordito vaccine's too late. Thousands, and probably millions of people are gonna die and you, my friend, should be in your lab working on your own vaccine rather than standing here hassling Dr. Kelso."

Atwater looked to Abe, frustration all over his face, but then his shoulders suddenly sagged and he turned, "You're right. I'll get back to work so we'll be ready when Gordito gets egg all over his face."

Abe turned to Kelso who was watching Atwater walk away with fury in her eyes. "LaQua," Abe said softly, "try to remember that he's on our team, trying in his own way to do the very best he can. In times like these you've got to expect people to have strong feelings."

LaQua rolled her eyes, "All right, 'Mr. Reasonable.' I'm just gonna tell myself he's *not* disrespecting me as a African-American woman."

"Nope," Abe said, "just disrespecting you for trusting one of those damn newfangled websites." He gave an exaggerated roll of his own eyes and sighed, "These young people today, always looking for the easy way out…"

Laurence E Dahners

Chapter Nine

Dallas, Texas—Tom Milner has died of fulminant smallpox. He was, the Dallas UPS driver who dropped a package mailed from Islam Akbar's viral production site and was admitted to hospital three days ago with a pustular eruption. In an alarming note, his illness did not respond to several antiviral agents which had been proven to work against ordinary smallpox. This has led to the concern that modified smallpox also contains changes that makes it resistant to antiviral medications. His wife and two young children had also been isolated at the hospital and have now developed similar pustular lesions. Vaccination of personnel at the hospital and all of the Milner's contacts is well underway...

All across the nation people are staying home from work. This problem is at its worst in healthcare facilities where workers rightly feel that their risk of contracting modified smallpox is higher than at other jobs. The CDC is apparently sending vaccines to healthcare institutions first since the people there work on the very front line of our defense from this terrorist attack.

Senator Gerald Munro of Tennessee has accused the Surgeon General of malfeasance for allowing dissemination of information about the bioterrorism epidemic to the general public and thus eliciting panic. He says, "It's akin to having shouted fire in a crowded theater. So far more people in this great country have died from panicked responses to the news of this supposed bioterrorism threat than have died from the disease in question…" Senator Munro is certainly correct, as the UPS driver in Dallas Texas is the only person to die of modified smallpox so far, but it is highly unlikely he will remain the only one. Although this reporter certainly hopes that Senator Munro's observation remains correct, that seems decidedly improbable.

UPS, USPS, Fed-Ex and other major shippers have been cooperating with the government in tracking down shipments made from the Dallas site where the terrorists were growing up the virus. Homeland Security reports that they believe they have tracked down over ninety percent of the shipments and sequestered them. A minority of shipments had already been delivered. Homeland Security, the FBI, and the police here in the United States, as well as similar organizations in other countries, are working day and night to find the people to whom the shipments were delivered and retrieve the packages. This is certainly good news, though it seems unlikely that all of the packages will be located…

The CDC is recommending a layered approach to the containment of any viral release episodes. A primary layer will involve cordoning off the immediate area where the exposure occurred, to include all persons who may have been exposed. A secondary layer will surround the primary layer and will include people, buildings, and vehicles which are not *thought to have been exposed. This secondary layer will be at least one kilometer wide surrounding the primary layer. At least initially, they recommend that all highways, trains, waterways, and airports in and out of the involved cities be closed until it's certain that the exposure has been adequately contained. President Stockton has issued a directive that the police, the military, and the National Guard be* assigned responsibility for maintaining the cordons and closing down the means of transportation. In a prepared statement she said, "In this crisis of unprecedented dimension, extraordinary means must be used to prevent dissemination of the disease in order to give the Centers for Disease Control sufficient time to vaccinate every single citizen of the United States." It's rumored that she has threatened to shut down every highway, every train, and every airfield in the United States if the virus gets out of control…

Protests have already erupted against the "grievous abridgment of personal freedom" represented by Stockton's mandatory containment and immunization programs but the protests have been limited in scope and there is little doubt that the vast majority of the population agrees with her policy.

Dallas has become the first city to be isolated under the CDC's layered containment guidelines.…

In alarming news, children who'd been given free firecrackers by a man in Buffalo, New York set them off in the streets last night. The firecrackers were quickly noticed to be generating puffs of white powder. Preliminary investigations of unexploded firecrackers have found them to be filled with viral particles. As yet the virus has not been confirmed to be the bioterrorism version of smallpox, but of course all suspicions are pointing in that direction. Homeland Security and the CDC have initiated the layered containment and vaccination program in Buffalo, making it the second city in the United States to be subjected to the draconian policy. There have been reports of children being given such firecrackers in Durban, South Africa, Budapest, Hungary, Mumbai, India and Busan, South Korea. However, it is not clear yet whether they *contained powder and, if so, whether the powder was viral in nature. Those countries are apparently undertaking various isolation programs of their own, but it is unknown how successful they will be. Also unknown is the status of their own vaccination programs and whether the United States or other countries in the developed world will be willing to share any of the limited quantities of vaccine they may have with countries that are not fortunate to have a healthcare industry capable of manufacturing their own vaccines...*

LaQua Kelso's AI said, "You have a call from Gordito."

She put up a hand, cutting off the person who was talking to her, and said, "I'll take it... Hello, Gordito?"

"Yes ma'am," the synthetic voice said. "I wanted to offer a suggestion that you release the live vaccination virus through the ports that were confiscated in Dallas. That way you could begin to immunize the same populations that Islam Akbar had intended to attack."

LaQua's eyes widened at the audacity of such a proposal. She said haltingly, "I agree that... such a policy might be the best... strategy for dealing with this crisis. But there's no way we'd be allowed to undertake such an airborne immunization program without the permission of the people who were unknowingly being administered the vaccine. It'd never get past the legal people."

"But... you could save millions of lives!" Gordito protested with an almost childlike frustration.

LaQua wondered whether Gordito was actually just some lonely soul with a computer. An immature genius, perhaps living in her mother's basement, seeing solutions to problems that no one else could, but completely unaware of the basic realities of modern social contracts. "I agree completely. If it were up to me, I'd do it, but it's not. Sorry."

"But…" Gordito said. Even through the flat affect of the voice synthesizer LaQua got the impression that a tantrum was impending. Then, suddenly Gordito continued in a completely reasonable tone, "Okay. If you can't, you can't. I wanted to tell you that the website has another gene sequence for you that improves synthesis rates of the antigen vaccine approximately ten-fold. That's assuming you're using CFPS?"

"Um, we are, but how do you know that improves efficiency ten-fold?"

"Well, it does in my CFPS set-up. Because the protein's pretty small, this modification just makes a long chain of identical antigen molecules that separate at low pH."

LaQua blinked a couple of times as she tried to picture a chain of the antigen proteins, each connected to the one before it with some pH sensitive molecule. She wasn't sure that synthesis of one large chain of the molecule would be faster than a number of small ones. "You have a CFPS set-up?"

"Yeah, I've made up quite a bit of the antigen vaccine. If I sent it to you, would CDC be able to use it?"

"Sure," LaQua said, trying to picture how she'd get it tested to be sure it was safe and efficacious, but not wanting to turn away any vaccine that might help people in this crisis. If he only delivered a couple of hundred doses, it might not be worth testing it. But if he had thousands of doses… "Aren't you worried that we'll figure out who you are from the shipping records?"

"Um, I'll have to work that out. When I do, I'll have it delivered to your attention, okay?"

"Okay."

***

When Zage came in to dinner he said, "Mom, I'd... or, I should say Gordito, would like to deliver some vaccine to the CDC. Can you think of a way to do that without revealing Gordito's identity?"

She turned and rested her chin on her hand as she fixed him with a musing gaze. After about thirty seconds of examining his features, she said, "You would, huh?"

He nodded, a serious expression on his face.

"And you think they're just going to accept a vaccine from an unknown entity, no questions asked?"

"Well, no. I'd hope they'd do some testing. Ensure its sterility and confirm that it binds to the appropriate antibodies etcetera before they put it to use."

"And you don't think they could better utilize their time making more of their own vaccine than testing whatever you deliver?"

He tilted his head, "The main limitation to vaccine manufacturing's the availability of protein synthesis equipment. I'm sure they're using all of their own equipment at capacity as well as farming it out to commercial establishments. I've recently sent them a modified gene sequence for the antigen that should improve their production efficiency significantly, but I still think it'd well be worth their time to do a little testing on the stuff I send them."

"Oh yeah," she said thoughtfully, "you have several million doses, right?"

"It's almost up to 40 million now. I improved the efficiency several days ago. I've just been confirming that the new product's as good as the original." He said quietly, "That'd be enough to treat the 27 million people in Durban, Budapest, Mumbai, and Busan. Otherwise, I think they're all going to die because I don't think anyone's going to feel they have vaccine to spare... Then they'll spread it to the rest of the world."

"Do you want to deliver it to those locations directly?"

"I don't think they'll take it from us. I think it's got to go through CDC."

She stared at him for a minute, then shook her head. "Where in the heck are you keeping 40 million doses? They're, what, half a cc each? That it be 20,000 liters! I'm pretty sure you don't have a tanker truck hidden away somewhere in the basement."

He gave her a surprised look, "Vaccines *are* often administered in half cc injections. But each injection only contains about fifteen micrograms of the protein. That means that enough of the freeze-dried protein to make up 40 million doses only weighs about 600 grams."

Ell snorted, "Well, I suppose it's probably worthwhile doing the testing for 40 million doses. We'd be delivering it to the CDC in Atlanta?"

Zage nodded, "Care of Dr. LaQua Kelso. I've told her it's coming. I thought about delivering it to her home, but I'm worried she might be sleeping over at the center during the crisis, so I'm thinking we should deliver it to the main entrance with her name on it."

"You picture somebody just walking up to the desk

there and handing over a big bag full of white powder, saying, 'special delivery for Dr. Kelso'?"

"Yeah, I thought that might be a problem so I've got it vacuum sealed in a nontransparent black plastic bag with a label carefully describing what it is." He gave her an almost beseeching look, "Could one of the security guys deliver it?"

Ell pursed her lips, trying hard to suppress a hysterical desire to laugh at what her five-year-old son had wrought. *40 million doses!* "I'll talk to them. How big is it?"

"Just a minute," he said, jumping out of his chair and trotting into the living room. A moment later, he came back with a black plastic object about the size of a small loaf of bread and set it on the table next to her. She hefted it and thought it weighed a little more than a pound.

***

Alice suddenly sat up, drawing Rick and Zage's attention. Rick said, "What's up?"

Alice said, "I was just checking the Gordito site. It's published the DNA sequence and methodology for making the smallpox antigens! Claims it's the same vaccine the CDC's manufacturing!"

Rick frowned, "How'd Gordito get it?"

Alice lifted an eyebrow, "I'll bet Gordito *gave them* the sequence."

Rick looked surprised for a second, then apparently accepted her thesis, "How's it manufactured?"

"Cell free protein synthesis."

Rick's eyes turned towards their CFPS set-up, "We

could be making it here?"

Zage said, "I noticed the recipe on the Gordito website last night. The site says it's putting it up in view of the vaccine shortage. The idea's that anyone with the right equipment could start making vaccine."

Rick stood up, "I'll go talk to Dr. Barnes. We should start making as much as we can!" As he started for the door he glanced at Alice, "Can you look over the methodology to see if we've got what we need here to start cranking it out?"

Zage said, "We've got everything we need. I ordered more and started the CFPS making a batch early this morning."

Alice and Rick turned to stare at him, "You started a batch without Dr. Barnes permission? Or letting her look over your set-up? That stuff's expensive, you know?!"

Zage shrugged unconcernedly, "I figured it's better to ask forgiveness than permission. Besides, I'm pretty sure my mom can get Dr. Donsaii to donate money to support a vaccine production program."

Rick turned to Alice, "Why don't you check his work while I go talk to Dr. Barnes. I'm pretty sure she'll be okay with it, but not if we run out a bad batch."

Alice had been eyeing Zage speculatively, "I'll check it, but I suspect Zage's set-up'll be fine." She got up and headed toward the CFPS.

~~~

A few minutes later, Dr. Barnes and Rick came into the lab, Barnes looking excited. For the past few weeks pretty much everyone'd been going around looking like they had a sentence hanging over their heads. Alice had a feeling that the mere possibility they themselves could do something to ameliorate the bioterrorism disaster had perked her up. Barnes looked at Alice, "You checked his set-up?"

Alice nodded.

"Let me look it over too," she said turning towards the CFPS equipment. "Did you find any problems?"

"No…" Alice said. "I started over there too, but as Zage pointed out, if you really want to check his work, you need to start over at the DNA synthesis and PCR set-ups to make sure he programmed in the right DNA and chained it up correctly."

Barnes stopped in her tracks and turned toward the DNA set-up, "Oh, yeah, if they just sent us the sequence it's obvious we'd have to start by making the DNA. Can you walk me through what he did?"

As Alice took Dr. Barnes through the steps Zage had been using, she had the surreal experience of correcting her professor each time Barnes thought she recognized a mistake or had an idea for a better method. Several of them were mistakes or ideas that Alice had considered when she looked it over. Zage had already pointed out where Alice misunderstood or why her idea wouldn't actually work. Alice was able to explain those to Dr. Barnes, but Dr. Barnes had a couple of ideas Alice hadn't thought of. Zage came over and explained why the way he'd done it was better than what Barnes wanted to try. *This's just freaking bizarre,* Alice thought. *Like I'm in some alternative reality. A place where a five-year-old schools professors on their own specialty…*

Then Barnes sat down, looking at the vaccine protocol on the big screen and occasionally glancing at the various pieces of equipment. Speaking as if to herself, she hoarsely whispered, "Sweet mother of Mary, that's elegant methodology. That Gordito's… just *blindingly* brilliant..." Leaning back in her chair, she shook her head, "Someone's got to find him or her..."

***

Dallas, Texas—The wife and children of Tom Milner, the first person to die of modified smallpox, have also now succumbed to the disease. Unfortunately, like Milner, they also did not respond to the antiviral medications which scientists had hoped would be effective against ordinary smallpox. However, in what appears to be good news, the classmates and teachers of the Milner children, all of whom were vaccinated after Mr. Milner first became ill, have either shown no evidence of the disease, or have become ill, but only mildly so. This suggests that the vaccines will successfully ameliorate the disease in people who've been recently exposed but haven't developed symptoms. The health-care workers who cared for Mr. Milner and were vaccinated within days have also remained healthy, though a few developed some pustules. CDC reports that both the live virus and the protein vaccine seem to have been effective.

Unfortunately, three contacts of the Milners who refused vaccination are now in the throes of the disease and it does not appear that they're going to survive. In light of this, President Stockton has authorized forcible administration of the vaccine to exposed individuals, though there are certain to be legal challenges to this policy.

Homeland Security reports that they are relatively confident that they have successfully isolated and vaccinated all individuals in the primary layer of containment due to the firecracker incident in Buffalo, New York. The city remains on lockdown while everyone in the secondary layer is vaccinated. The mayor reports that adequate food and other supplies have been donated and delivered to the city. "No shortages have occurred, and any sense of isolation is much reduced by the pervasive availability of electronic communications. Nonetheless, the people of Buffalo look forward to being able to rejoin their families and return to workplaces outside of the isolation zones…"

Although isolation and vaccination programs appear to have been fairly successful in Dallas and Buffalo, similar programs in Durban, Budapest, Mumbai, and Busan have been fraught with problems. The four countries involved have all resorted to martial law with each of the cities now encircled by their own country's military. The military forces enforcing the quarantines have in some instances resorted to lethal force in order to keep individuals from leaving the cordoned areas. There remains concern that some persons who were exposed to the virus exited the quarantined areas before the cordons were fully established. In addition, the encircled populace is panicking, with widespread riots reported in Mumbai. The people there have been demanding vaccine, but availability has been severely limited. President Stockton has said that the United States will supply some vaccine to each of the four locations and called on other developed countries to do so as well. She said, "It is worth some risk to the people of our own countries to keep the breakdown of societal norms from expanding this disaster into a worldwide epidemic…"

LaQua's AI said, "You have a call from Gordito."

"I'll take it... Gordito, our first run with your new gene and methodology's far more efficient at synthesizing the antigen. We haven't confirmed its quality yet, but it's looking good!"

"The quality will be fine as long as the described protocol's followed," Gordito said, giving LaQua the impression that other people were already making the vaccine, but maybe hadn't been following the protocol exactly.

For some reason this gave her the sensation that he was from some other country. *Homeland Security's going to have a cow if it turns out that Gordito's a Russian,* she thought. Then she started wondering about the one change she'd made in the protocol they'd received. *What if that's the reason we're only getting seven times as much protein, not Gordito's claimed ten?* To Gordito, she said, "How can I help you?"

The synthetic voice said, "We'd like to deliver the vaccine I talked about. Could someone come to the entrance and pick it up?"

She was busy and didn't want to take the time to go out there, but would if it gave her a chance to meet Gordito, "Are *you* out there?"

"Um, no. Anonymity and all that, you know? The package's sitting at the end of the reception counter with a bunch of UPS deliveries, but it's unlabeled except for your name. We're a little worried that, in the crisis, someone might just trash it."

"I'll send somebody." Then, suddenly hopeful that it might be a really large amount, she wondered if whoever picked it up might need a rolling table to set it on so they wouldn't have to carry it, "How much does it weigh?"

"Just over 600 grams."

"Oh," she said, disappointed, then worrying that her feelings showed in the tone of her voice.

Obviously it had, because the synthetic voice said, "It's a purified and lyophilized protein powder. Enough for a little over 40 million doses. I know it'll take some work to confirm its purity and sterility, then put it in actual syringes for distribution and vaccination, but we're hoping that, knowing you had this vaccine available for the States, you could immediately free up enough of your own doses to treat the people in Durban, Budapest, Mumbai, and Busan."

LaQua was stunned into silence for a second by the amount of vaccine, then she turned for the door. "I'll be right out to get it," she said, "and once we have initial confirmation that the protein appears to be good, I'll really lean on people above me to free up vaccine for overseas. Um, do you mind if I imply that you made future deliveries of vaccine contingent upon our using our own vaccine to help those poor souls overseas?"

"I don't mind your implying that, but I'm not planning on making any more vaccine right now."

"Why not?! Are you running out of precursors? Something else we can get you to enable you to make more of it?"

"Well, no. I've been working on a way to synthesize some of the antibodies that the vaccine induces. Instead of vaccine, I thought I'd make the antibodies so you'd have something you could use to treat people in the active stages of the disease."

LaQua almost stumbled. Vaccines essentially only prevented the disease by stimulating the patient's own immune system to produce antibodies. They'd often ameliorate and sometimes completely prevent the disease if they were given to the patient after the patient had been exposed—but *before* they were actively sick. However, giving a vaccine to stimulate antibody production to a patient who was already sick and already desperately trying to make his own antibodies to the virus rarely made any difference. Giving actual antibodies would be great but producing antibodies was difficult and expensive.

"You're trying to generate monoclonal antibodies?" she asked, trying to understand what Gordito intended. When a lab grew up a clone of B lymphocytes that'd been sensitized to an antigen, then harvested the antibodies they produced, the product was called a "monoclonal" antibody. Growing sufficient quantities of the lymphocytes to make very much of the antibody was difficult and therefore expensive.

"No, that seemed pretty hard. Instead, I vaccinated myself, then selected some of the antibodies I generated and sequenced them. It took a little while to work out a protocol that would synthesize and assemble actual antibodies in a CFPS but..."

LaQua'd stopped walking so she could try to follow what Gordito was describing. Her mind boggled at the concept of actually constructing an entire antibody in quantity. A complete antibody not only consisted of several proteins, they needed to be assembled to one another in a kind of a "Y" configuration before they functioned correctly. Incomplete fragments of an antibody molecule could attach to the antigenic sites on a virus, but they weren't nearly as good as an entire antibody at "opsonization" of the virus—a process in which the presence of the antibody on the surface of a microbe attracted white blood cells that ingested and destroyed the germ. Scientists had generated synthetic antibodies in the past, but it generally took an extended period of research, then generated small quantities of very expensive molecules that were most commonly used in research. She just couldn't imagine that someone was about to start manufacturing synthetic antibody in quantity this soon after the vaccinia virus had been identified! She suddenly wondered, *Could Gordito be able to do this because* he's *the one who created the virus, and he's been working on the vaccines as well as the antigens and antibodies for years?! It's awfully convenient, the Gordito website suddenly appearing at nearly the same time as this disaster.*

Not noticing her own bias in assigning Gordito a male pronoun when she suspected him of something appalling, LaQua started walking again. Entering the lobby, she looked around for someone who might've delivered the package, but the lobby was empty except for the receptionist. "Where is it?" she asked through her AI.

"Right beside the stack of UPS packages on the end of the counter closest to you," Gordito said, confirming that he had a camera or some other way of watching what she was doing.

When she glanced at the stack of packages she saw a bag like someone might bring their lunch to work in. It had "Dr. Kelso" written on it with a Sharpie. *A brown paper bag?!* she thought in astonishment. She reached in her pocket and pulled out some gloves, realizing it might tip Gordito off to her suspicions, but unwilling to touch the delivery without at least that minimum amount of protection. She picked up the bag, judging the weight to be somewhat more than a pound, which would be in the range of the 600 grams Gordito'd specified. She didn't try to look in the bag, opting to leave its top rolled closed. For just a second, she considered asking the receptionist if he'd seen who delivered the bag, but then she realized she'd do better having someone review the security camera video. She lifted the bag as if toasting Gordito, then turned and headed back into the hallway. "Thanks," she said, "I'll get our people started on confirming the product." She wondered if she should say anything else, then realized she should act as if she believed the therapeutic antibody story. "I'll tell my higher-ups you might give us some antibody if they send some vaccine to the people overseas."

She took the package directly back to the Level IV Biosafety Lab to be opened, at each step dreading the possibility that she was carrying a one-pound bag of modified smallpox virus.

Or perhaps something even worse...

***

Homeland Security, Washington DC—Today, Homeland Security spokesperson Francis Dorchester announced that they've accounted for all but two of the packages sent from the site in Dallas where modified smallpox was being grown. Also, she said that the CDC believes the epidemic has been brought under control in the United States. Early isolation of exposed persons, urgent vaccination of their contacts, and the layered approach policy to containment of disease epicenters appears to have been successful. The isolation of the contained sections of Dallas and Buffalo is expected to be discontinued early next week if no further cases appear…

The news is not as good in the so-called "four cities" around the world where modified smallpox was disseminated by giving children firecrackers. Although intense programs of vaccination are finally underway in those areas, there is little doubt that they were started late enough that many people will develop fulminant forms of the disease. If so, hundreds and likely thousands will die. Perhaps hundreds of thousands or even millions.

Efforts to isolate affected people in the four cities were less successful due to slow implementation of quarantine policies. Finally, with such large populations, especially in Mumbai, the huge numbers of people who have made deliberate efforts to escape quarantine areas have resulted in a moderate number of successes. It is unknown how many of those quarantine escapees harbored latent disease and will serve as new epicenters for further breakouts.

LaQua Kelso and Abe Cohen were meeting with Mary Wu, Homeland Security's representative at CDC. Abe called the meeting when LaQua'd explained her concerns that Gordito might actually be involved in developing and implementing the plague. Perhaps "Gordito" might even be a pseudonym used by the infamous Adin Farsq. LaQua'd just finished outlining the issues that'd raised her concerns:

That the Gordito website'd been set up not long after the vaccination virus appeared on Little Diomede.

That Gordito'd been *unbelievably* quick to recognize the viral genome when LaQua put it up on the Gordito website, and to understand what it might mean in terms of bioterrorism.

That Gordito'd been able to identify antigens on the surface of the virus in a matter of hours.

That he'd been able to provide CDC with a gene sequence for producing a vaccination protein with multiple antigenic sites on it, also within hours.

That Gordito'd been able to recognize that the virus wouldn't grow in bovine serum without even growing the virus himself.

That Gordito'd just delivered a brick of lyophilized protein he claimed contained enough antigen for 40 million vaccination doses.

"Essentially, whoever's behind the Gordito website knew far too much about the virus far too quickly."

Wu frowned, "But it sounds like everything this Gordito's done has been directed at limiting the epidemic?"

LaQua nodded, "Unless it was all just to get us to trust him. Now he's delivered this huge brick of lyophilized antigen that he expects us to vaccinate people with. What if it's only antigen on the surface of the brick and contains active virus in the middle? Or something even worse? We've been keeping it isolated and testing it very carefully."

"Have you found anything bad yet?"

"No, but… I'm still worried. If he's the genius he seems to be, maybe he's slipped some other joker in the deck somehow."

"If he's the astonishing genius he seems to be, then maybe he's capable of doing all these good things. That's really your only source of suspicion, right? That he's done things that don't seem possible for ordinary mortals?"

"Yeah," LaQua laughed, "it's a circular argument. If he's really some kind of super genius, maybe he really is a good guy. If he's not a super genius, he probably isn't smart enough to trick us with something deviously atrocious in that brick of vaccine protein." She shrugged, "I'm bringing it to your attention because Dr. Cohen says that's something we're supposed to do. I really hope he *is* a super genius who's helping us out…" After the little pause, she shook her head and said, "But, I just don't think anybody could actually be that smart."

Wu chewed her lip for a moment, then said, "Okay, I'll look into it. Tracking down that kind of thing's my specialty. You get back to controlling the epidemic. I may need some scientific help to be able to send plausible queries to the Gordito website. Do I need to come to you for advice? Or do you have a minion who could help me do that kind of thing?"

LaQua laughed again, "Send me a query regarding what you're trying to do and I hope I can find a minion to do it for you. Otherwise, I'll have to do it myself."

Chapter Ten

Zage walked into the lab, his eyes immediately going to Carley. He'd found himself thinking about her a lot and didn't quite know what to make of it. He'd done some reading to try to understand what might be happening to him and had learned that children sometimes had infatuations or "crushes" on members of the other sex, though they didn't often happen as early as age five. Also, the crush was usually on someone similar in age to the kid, not someone much older like Carley. Apparently, such feelings were often unrequited, which could lead to a great deal of emotional distress for the person with the crush.

Surprisingly, he'd learned that many children who had these infatuations didn't really know the object of their desires very well. Kids often got crushes on famous musicians or actors whom they didn't know at all. Apparently, there was some thought that the very fact you didn't know the object of your desires allowed you to attribute all kinds of amazing characteristics to that person. Characteristics the person might not actually have.

His analytical approach to understanding his feelings hadn't diminished his attraction to Carley. He obviously knew her much better than a famous person on TV, though not as well as he'd like to. He admitted that probably some of the attraction came from the fact that she was physically very pretty. He realized she might have flaws he didn't know about. Maybe he liked her because she'd given him that big hug and been so appreciative of the fact that he'd rescued her at her party. Whatever it was, attempts to rationally understand his feelings didn't seem to be making them go away.

He stood, enjoying the glistening curl of her auburn hair and admiring the shape of her cheekbone which was all he could see of her face since she was turned mostly away. He even liked the freckles he'd heard her telling Alice she hated.

Suddenly, she seemed to sense him behind her. Turning, her eyes widened as they focused on him, then she stood and strode to him. Like she'd done when she thanked him for rescuing her at the party, she dropped to one knee and threw her arms around him for a hug. "My brother's alive! Thank you so much for suggesting I do a DNA database search."

Zage put his arms around her and hugged her back, hoping she wouldn't let go too soon. "I'm glad. Do you actually know where he is?"

Sadly, she released her hug and leaned back to look at him, her eyes shining. "No, but the database has agreed to forward a message to him. I've sent him my contact info. I might hear from him any day now!"

***

Homeland Security, Washington DC— It was announced today that an investigation has been opened into a website known only as "Gordito." Gordito appears to be a scientific website which was initially set up to help identify antigenic sites on viruses for those wanting to generate vaccines. However, it has become particularly well known amongst researchers who have been using it to predict the folding of proteins. It's apparently able to predict protein folding from gene sequences with great accuracy, a problem which is been plaguing molecular biology for many decades.

Few researchers were using the Gordito site to predict viral antigens until the recent bioterrorism crisis. CDC actually used it to develop the protein-based or "antigenic" vaccine that has been so successful in providing protection against the modified smallpox virus. Apparently, concern has been raised about the fact that the Gordito site came online shortly before the smallpox crisis and that this site was able to recognize the nature of the virus and predict the antigens for a vaccine in a matter of hours—a feat that most investigators believe is impossible—suggesting some foreknowledge of the virus. It must be emphasized that, thus far, the Gordito site has only been helpful, not harmful. Nonetheless, the apparent foreknowledge of the crisis suggests that the Gordito site may be associated with the terrorists and, therefore, Homeland Security is making a concerted effort to identify the site and its operators.

Because the site is walled off with an astonishingly sophisticated firewall and a PGR connection, Homeland Security is asking anyone with knowledge of the Gordito site to come forward with information...

When Zage arrived at the lab, Alice turned to him and spoke in a low tone, "Did you hear about Gordito?"

Zage paused, trying to think about whether anything he'd posted on the Gordito site might've made the news. Not being able to think of anything, he shook his head, "What's up with them?"

"Homeland Security's posted a bulletin suggesting that the website might actually be run by the terrorists!" she said, lifting an eyebrow. "They point out that the site knew far too much about the virus way too early after its dissemination. They're asking for information from anyone who might know who's actually running the site."

"Oh," Zage said, trying not to let his dismay appear on his face. "But… Gordito's been helpful… The vaccine it designed is working to protect people… How can they say…" he shook his head and stopped, unable to comprehend what might be going on.

"I'll bet they're thinking Gordito's trying to worm his way into everyone's confidence," Alice said in a hushed tone, as if describing bloodsucking ghosts that might be nearby trying to listen in. "Then, once everyone's blindly relying on the website, he'll sneak something into a new vaccine that'll *kill* millions of people instead of protecting them!"

"No! He…" Zage stopped before he said too much. "I've got to go read what they're saying…"

~~~

Shan looked away from the screens he and Ell had been studying. Zage had come in the room a few minutes ago, but Shan and Ell'd been so focused on what they were doing they hadn't noticed him. However, Zage's fidgeting had finally gotten to him. "You need something kid?"

Shan glanced at Ell and realized she was grinning at him. "I wondered how much longer you were going to ignore your son," she said.

Shan had his eyes back on Zage and resolutely ignored his wife. Zage said, "Did you see the news about the Gordito site today?"

Shan opened his mouth to say, "No," but noticed Ell nodding out of the corner of his eye. She patted her knee as she said in a sympathetic tone, "It looks like there're some people out there who don't believe you can do what you can do, huh?"

Zage trotted over and hopped up into her lap as he said, "Well, yeah, I can understand that. But, Gordito hasn't done *anything* bad! It told them why they couldn't grow the vaccinia virus, it told them what the antigens were, it gave them 40 million doses of vaccine..." Zage gave his mother a helpless look, "Everything it's done's been good!"

Ell pulled him into a hug, "I know, I know. It's just that people tend to be suspicious of those who can... who can do things they can't do themselves. Well, maybe not so much if they themselves can't do it, but if no one else can either, they're more likely to attribute it to devious tricks than to genius."

"I don't think I'm a genius," Zage said plaintively, "I just seem to have a knack for protein folding. Kind of like some kind of idiot savant who's good at Rubik's cubes."

Ell gave a delighted laugh, "Well, then you're a genius of protein folding. I hear you might be pretty good at optimizing protein synthesis too?"

In a self-conscious tone, Zage protested, "That's all part of the same thing. I'm just good at those kinds of puzzles." He looked at Shan, "Are they going to be able to track me down through the website?"

Speaking carefully, Shan said, "To the best of my knowledge, it'd be physically impossible for them to track you down because of the PGR connection. I don't think they can get past the website firewall to make Osprey give away your location either, but," he shrugged, "history's full of stories about uncrackable codes getting cracked."

Apparently accepting his father's reassurance and ignoring the warning, Zage turned back to his mother, "What can I do? What did you do when President Stockton was accusing you of bad things?"

Ell gave him a sad smile, "My advice would be to just keep being decent and treating others the way you'd like them to treat you. Don't be tempted to deny their words or retaliate against them, just wait for them to figure out for themselves who you are and what you've done." She got a distant look in her eyes, "Once, when someone was saying a lot of wrong and ugly things about me, I took it upon myself to prove how wrong they were. I've regretted it ever since."

Shan looked at his wife and thought she was probably talking about Michael Fentis, the sprinter who'd denied all the evidence Ell could run faster than he did. He'd often thought she'd regretted proving Fentis wrong.

Zage had a very thoughtful look on his face. After a moment longer, he said, as if he'd made a very important decision, "Okay, that's what I'll do." He got down off of his mother's lap and headed down the stairs into the basement.

A moment later Zage came back up and said, "Mom?"

Ell turned back to him, "Uh-huh?"

"I've got some antibody against modified smallpox. They could use it to treat some of the people who're actually sick with the disease."

"Millions of doses again?"

"No. Not even a hundred so far. Treatment with an antibody takes grams of protein, not micrograms like the vaccine. I'm wondering if you have a way to get some to Mumbai? They've got a lot of people who're actually sick, not just exposed." He got a sad look on his face, "Obviously, with their suspicions, I can't send it to the CDC anymore. I'm not sure how to convince the people in Mumbai that it's okay without CDC's stamp of approval on it, but since everyone who actually gets symptoms of modified smallpox dies I thought maybe they'd be willing to try the antibody... even if it didn't have certification."

Ell gave him a thoughtful look, "I'll look into it." Once Zage had gone back down the stairs, she spoke to her AI, "Connect me to Viveka." After a brief pause, she continued, "Viveka, I need a connection in Mumbai. Do you know anybody there?"

***

Adin's room was dark.

He sat staring at several screens, all displaying news about the modified smallpox crisis. His emotions had been on a roller coaster. Sometimes he'd be high over the devastating results of infection with the lethal disease he'd created. Sometimes he'd be horrified as he watched the human suffering his smallpox was causing. Sometimes he felt despair over Islam Akbar's apparent failure to distribute the virus widely enough to significantly decrease the number of non-Muslims in the world. Even worse, the children who'd set off the firecrackers in Durban, South Africa had been from

Muslim families that hadn't been exposed to the vaccination virus in their particular mosque. Durban had rigorously enforced quarantine of exposed persons and limited the outbreak there, but hadn't received vaccines in time to protect those children or their contacts. Although the disease wasn't spreading in Durban, a substantial number of people were dying or dead.

The majority of them were Islamic.

Was he a genius? A failure? A monster? He didn't know.

Even worse, the news was full of reports about a Gordito website that people thought was the source of the virus.

Adin Farsq wasn't even mentioned anymore.

The door opened and once again the man from Islam Akbar walked in without knocking. Adin didn't even have the energy to hide his hate. With undisguised loathing he said, "What do you want?"

"To point out that you've failed us," the man said in a disgusted tone, pulling out a pistol and working the slide.

Heart suddenly beating faster, Adin sat up in the chair. "I created the ultimate weapon. Everyone who catches the disease *dies!* It isn't my fault that Islam Akbar didn't distribute it correctly."

"We distributed it just the way you said. First we wasted tens of thousands of dollars buying and distributing those damned ports that the infidels simply deactivated. Then we spent hundreds of thousands of dollars shipping the virus all over the world, again according to your suggestions, only to have them track down the shipments and sequester them! Islam Akbar's *beggared* itself following your plans, all to little effect!" He began to lift the weapon.

"I can create another bioweapon!" Adin said hurriedly, even while wondering how he'd get access to another pathogen he could modify. Then he thought, *I can just make new modifications to the smallpox virus! I've already got the gene code for it.* "I just need…"

The man cut him off, "Weren't you listening?! Islam Akbar spent *all* its money on this witless plan! Whatever you need, we can't buy it!"

Adin saw a flashing light, heard a series of loud bangs and felt some thumping. It took him several moments to realize that the man had fired the gun over and over and that the thumping resulted from the impacts of the bullets striking his chest. He slumped back in his chair, staring in disbelief as the man from Islam Akbar shook his head in revulsion and stepped back out the door.

The pain in his chest had just begun when Adin's consciousness faded and slipped away…

***

Reggie looked at the ten mice she'd been keeping in the biosafety lab. They looked perfectly healthy, which was astonishing considering the variety of mutagens and radiation they'd been subjected to. Since they were being kept in a single cage, all of them were females in order to keep them from breeding. They'd been several months old when they'd had their DNA modified using the method Donsaii'd brought Reggie from the Virgies.

The Virgies' system was, in fact, much like a very simple virus. The initial viral shell had been created entirely through cell free protein synthesis and self-assembled itself from there. She'd made up a DNA sequence that'd create a viral shell using a modification of the Virgies' recipe and put it in the CFPS system. The outer surface of the created viral particle was coated with a protein that only displayed antigens that were the same as those found on the surface of the red blood cells of the animal to be treated with the virus. The animal wouldn't make antibodies to that protein because that'd result in its rejecting its own blood, so it ignored the virus. Then in an amazing piece of engineering, she only had to expose the Virgies' protein shells to her custom-designed DNA sequences and the shells sucked up the DNA like little syringes.

The DNA sucked into the virus would be injected into the animal's cells as soon as the virus contacted their cell membranes. It had the Virgies' telomere system to keep the virus from replicating endlessly, but would replicate itself enough times to inject its carrier DNA molecules into every cell in the body. Once the DNA was injected into a particular cell, it modified the cell wall receptor where it'd attached so more viral particles couldn't enter that cell. Rejected by cells that'd already been modified, the particles would move on to other cells, thus ensuring not only that every cell would be modified, but that the organism as a whole wouldn't get sick from excessive viral replication. All this, for the end goal of inserting the DNA for the Virgies' DNA error correction system that repaired mutations from radiation and other mutagens.

It'd certainly work for inserting other bits of DNA. Not that DNA couldn't be inserted now, but when you wanted it inserted into every cell in the body, this would be the way to go.

And the error correction system was amazing itself. These ten mice had been exposed to lethal doses of multiple mutagens and were not only alive, but thriving. None of them had even formed a tumor. Subsequently, they'd been exposed to lethal doses of radiation, again without effect.

This was going to protect astronauts.

It would also stop cancer in its tracks...

***

Dr. Tanvi Mishra got home from an agonizing day treating the victims of modified smallpox at the Mumbai children's hospital where she was in training.

None of her patients were surviving. She felt truly grateful that, as a physician caring for such patients, she'd been one of the first to get the vaccine.

However, Tanvi's efforts as a physician had gradually been reduced to lying to the children about their prognosis and giving them medications to make them comfortable. When they got too sick, she often prescribed enough narcotic that it probably sped their inevitable end.

Tanvi was well beyond wondering whether she was violating her oath to "do no harm."

Tomorrow she knew she'd be giving the bad news to Anika's parents. A beautiful little girl until she'd arrived with a fever, malaise, vomiting, and backache. Even as sick as she was, there was something really sweet about the child. Examination had shown Anika had the typical red spots in her mouth. Just before Tanvi left the hospital the skin rash was beginning to appear.

Death was knocking at the beautiful Anika's door.

And no one would be able to deny him entrance.

To her surprise, Tanvi saw she had a package. When

she opened it, she saw it contained a fifteen millimeter port and a printed message. Unfolding the paper, she gazed at it in astonishment.

We'd like to deliver a modified smallpox antibody to you for your use. It should be effective even in patients who already have clinical signs of disease. It hasn't been certified by any agencies. We cannot be certain that it'll work but, since everyone who has developed clinical signs so far has died, it seems that there is little risk in trying it. If you would like a dose of the antibody, just switch on the enclosed port. If you find it effective, just switch it on again and we'll deliver another dose.

Tanvi switched on the port and a syringe immediately dropped into her hand. It had a slip of paper wrapped around it with instructions.

No longer tired, Tanvi got up, opened her door, and started back to the hospital.

***

Raleigh, North Carolina—Duke University announced that several days ago Dr. Regina Barnes' laboratory began producing the vaccine for modified smallpox using a genetic sequence for the vaccine that was published on the Gordito website. Apparently university laboratories at UNC and North Carolina State have also begun producing the vaccine. Dr. Barnes is calling on the CDC to confirm—in view of their recently reported suspicions of Gordito—that the sequence published on the Gordito website is in fact the correct one for the vaccine.

The Infectious Disease departments at both Duke Hospital and the University of North Carolina Hospital

System are planning to initiate vaccination programs for North Carolinians using the locally produced product as soon as CDC confirms that the gene sequence is correct. Some are asking why the CDC hadn't already published the gene sequence for the vaccine so that research laboratories everywhere could've been producing vaccine for use by the public. However, it is thought to be likely that this is due to the fact that research laboratories usually cannot produce large quantities and the CDC prefers to have tight control over manufacturing in order to ensure quality.

When she arrived at the hospital, Tanvi immediately went to Anika's room, anxiety making her heart thump her chest. She'd awoken this morning, suddenly certain that the medication she'd given the girl last night was some kind of toxin. She'd begun imagining the girl dead. Someone would find out what she'd done, and that she'd done it without getting permission. After spending all these years getting her degree and training, she'd be put on trial and denied permission to practice medicine. As she walked quickly down the hall towards Anika's room, one of the girl's nurses, Kiara, saw her. Eyes widening, the nurse rushed toward Tanvi. With her heart in her throat, Tanvi prepared to receive grim news, but instead Kiara said, "Anika's better! Her fever's down and the rash isn't spreading!"

Restraining her own ecstasy, Tanvi accelerated her stride toward Anika's room. When she entered, rather than sprawled prostrate on the bed, Anika was sitting up. The girl offered a smile and said in her little voice, "I feel better! Thank you for giving me that medicine."

Kiara, who'd excitedly followed Tanvi into the room, frowned, "What medicine?"

Bioterror

Tanvi swallowed. Little Anika'd watched Tanvi hook up the filter and inject the antibody into her IV, but she'd been so listless that Tanvi hadn't dreamed she'd remember it. "Um…"

Kiara put a hand on Tanvi's shoulder, "If you've got a medicine that works, don't hide it! You should be telling everyone! There're hundreds of children to save!"

Tanvi pulled Kiara a little bit to one side and whispered, "Someone, I don't even know who, sent me some medicine last night. They *said* it was an antibody to modified smallpox. I… I gave it to Anika even though it's not approved or certified, or whatever they do. I gave it because she was going to die and I just couldn't stand doing nothing."

"Can you get more?"

"I don't know," Tanvi shrugged, her eyes darting about, "maybe?"

"Is it expensive?"

"I don't know, they didn't charge me anything for the medicine I got last night."

"See if you can get some more! I'll help you give it to the children. I'll even help pay for it if it's not too expensive."

"But… it isn't approved!" Tanvi said staring at the floor, "I shouldn't have done it…" she lifted her eyes, "We'll get in trouble!"

"Oh, come on! You had the courage to do it last night for Anika. You *know* it's the right thing to do. I'll help you. We'll do it together and make sure no one sees us!"

"Okay," Tanvi said, reaching into her pocket and feeling for the port she'd left there the night before, "but we can't tell anyone about it until we're sure it's working for more than just Anika, right?"

Kiara pursed her lips, but then nodded, "Okay."

Tanvi pulled out the port and switched it on. As soon as she did it, another syringe dropped into her hand. She looked up and saw Kiara staring at it wide-eyed. "That's what happened last night too," Tanvi whispered.

***

Galveston, Texas—A body found in a low-cost motel here has been confirmed to be that of Adin Farsq, the alleged mastermind of Islam Akbar's bioterror weapon. Farsq was shot six times in the chest and had been dead for one to two days. Although you would think that six gunshots that no one reported to the police is a sign of a sophisticated assassin who used a silencer, apparently this particular hotel has been the scene of other unreported shootings.

Of note, although Farsq has apparently been dead since at least yesterday, overnight the Gordito website responded to numerous requests. These were the same kind of requests from scientists regarding various antigens or protein folding issues that Gordito has answered in the past. Unless Gordito is a simple computer algorithm that's still running, the timing of these responses seems to contradict the opinion held by some that the Gordito website was hosted by Farsq and used for disinformation. Even Dr. LaQua Kelso of CDC— who first brought the possibly unsavory nature of Gordito to the attention of Homeland Security—is now pointing out that Gordito has never engaged in any detrimental activities. In fact, she says Gordito has been nothing but helpful to science in general and to the control of the smallpox epidemic in specific. "The only thing that called Gordito's nature into question was the timing of its establishment, the website's rigidly protected anonymity and its astonishing ability to analyze genomes, understand protein functions, predict protein folding, and describe antigen structure, all much more rapidly than anyone believed could be possible. It may well be that someone has developed a computer algorithm that allows these kinds of things to be done extremely rapidly. If so, hopefully Gordito will make this transformative programming generally available as soon as possible."

In other good news, the Neerja Children's Hospital in the isolation zone of Mumbai, India has suddenly become renowned because a number of children admitted with the signs and symptoms of modified smallpox appear to be recovering! As, so far, everyone with a confirmed diagnosis of modified smallpox has eventually died, this has led to widespread requests for transfer of children and even adults from other hospitals to Neerja. No one seems to be certain what treatment, if any, has led to these amazing outcomes but an intense investigation is underway. Outside experts have been brought in...

"All of the patients who improved are on a single ward," Dr. Vaidya said, "under the care of various nurses, but almost all of them under the care of a single pediatric resident, Tanvi Mishra."

"And do we know if she's doing anything different from the standard supportive regimen used by the other doctors?"

"When I talked to her, she claimed to be following the standard regimen religiously..." Dr. Vaidya broke off, a considering look on his face.

"What?"

"When I talked to her, she seemed quite fearful. You'd think someone with such astonishing results would be ecstatically proud. I just realized that, although she claimed to be following the standard supportive regimen, she could be following the regimen *and* doing something in addition. I didn't specifically ask whether she was engaging in supplementary treatments."

Dr. Jindal stood up, "Let's go ask her, immediately."

Vaidya said, "If I may make a suggestion?"

"Certainly."

"Ask your questions in a very positive fashion. Don't imply that you might be looking for something she's done wrong, rather that you're only trying to find out what she's done that's providing results so much better than anyone else's."

Jindal nodded.

When they arrived on the ward, Vaidya found Dr. Mishra and brought her to meet Jindal. When she entered the room, Jindal stood and enthusiastically greeted her. "I don't know if you're aware, but tests have confirmed that your children who've gotten better were in fact infected with modified smallpox virus! We're very anxious to find out how you've been working this miracle. Dr. Vaidya says you've been following the same protocol that everyone else's using, but is there anything you can think of that you might've been doing in *addition* to the standard protocol? If we have to, we can look through the orders you've submitted for your patients' treatment to try to discern what you might be doing that other doctors aren't, but I'm hoping that you might have some idea and that it'll save us time in getting this miracle out to others."

Mishra looked extremely uncomfortable, so Jindal said, "Don't worry that this's some kind of a witch hunt. We're only trying to find out what you're doing that's working so much better than what everyone else's doing."

Mishra's shoulders sagged, "I... I should've sought permission..."

"Don't worry about that now. What you did *worked!* I only want to tell others how to do the same thing."

"When I got home, there was a package..." she ran down, her eyes downcast. Jindal encouraged her again, and she continued, "The package didn't have any mailing labels or anything to tell me where it came from. When I opened it, it contained a fifteen millimeter port and instructions to switch it on. The instructions said that it'd deliver an antibody for the smallpox virus..."

Dumbfounded, Jindal tried not to let it show. He'd been thinking that the young woman might've treated the patients with some standard medication that killed the virus for reasons that might be difficult to understand, but would eventually be worked out. Not some kind of clandestine delivery of miraculous antibodies! Speaking calmly, he prompted, "And you switched it on?"

She nodded, her eyes still downcast. "A syringe immediately fell out. It contained the antibody in a powder form and had instructions taped around it. The instructions described how to draw fluid into the syringe in order to reconstitute the antibody and said to push the antibody through a two-micron filter into the IV. The IV was to be run at a slow rate and discontinued if anything untoward occurred."

Jindal restrained himself from making a comment on the fact that the powder could've been a virus itself. *I can't afford to frighten her,* he thought. He said, "And so you administered some of this antibody...?"

She nodded, "To Anika. A beautiful little girl who'd just developed the rash." Mishra shrugged, "I liked her so much. And I knew she was going to die. I couldn't bear it. Even the possibility that something *might* work..."

Jindal put his hand on hers and used his most reassuring tone, "It all turned out for the best, didn't it? Where's the port now?"

She reached in the pocket of her white coat and pulled out a port. "Each time I switch it on, another syringe comes out. Would you like to see?"

Jindal nodded, staring at the ordinary fifteen millimeter port like it was a genie's bottle. A few seconds later, she'd given him a syringe as promised. "If you don't mind, I'll take this syringe to the lab and have the powder analyzed. In the meantime," he turned to Dr. Vaidya, "perhaps you and Dr. Vaidya could switch the port on and off, trying to get enough of the syringes for us to treat *all* our patients and perhaps even give some to the other hospitals that've been asking how we're doing it?"

***

Raleigh, North Carolina—People have started showing up at the various research universities here in North Carolina, hoping to get vaccinated against modified smallpox. Duke, UNC, NC State, ECU, and Wake Forest University all report having limited supplies of vaccine that have been manufactured in their laboratories. The four medical schools have established limited programs for the vaccination of people thought to be at high risk due to travel plans or medical conditions, but are otherwise limiting vaccinations in hopes of building up a supply to deal with any impending crises. It's important to note that Homeland Security feels that it does have sufficient quantities of vaccine to deal with any future outbreaks and expects to begin a program to vaccinate every citizen within the next few weeks.

Dr. Jindal switched on the port one more time. Still no further syringes. He reread the message he'd written:

Have you run out of the antibody? If so is there anything we can do to help? Who are you?

Deciding those questions were sufficient, he picked up the pencil, wrapped the piece of paper with the message around it, applied a small piece of tape, and held the pencil in front of the port. He nodded at Dr. Vaidya and as soon as Vaidya'd switched on the port, he pushed the pencil through it in the opposite direction. He nodded at Vaidya again and Vaidya switched off the port, cutting off the pencil. Jindal couldn't help running his finger over the incredibly smooth surface where the pencil'd been transected as the port closed. Turning back to Vaidya, he said, "Let's go get some coffee. We'll open the port and see if we got a reply when we get back."

The two men got up and left the ward in search of the magic brown elixir.

~~~

When they returned and Vaidya powered up the port a small curl of paper fell out, swooping back and forth to neatly avoid Jindal's hand and land on the floor. Picking it up, he read:

Out of antibody at present. Making more. Will post gene sequence so other people can make it as well.

Gordito

***

New York, New York—Reports out of India are that the patients there who've survived actual clinical infections with modified smallpox virus have been treated with an antibody to the virus supplied by the mysterious Gordito. Apparently Gordito has run out of the antibody which must be made by protein synthesis in a similar fashion to the way the vaccine is being manufactured. Of note, Gordito's provided forty million doses of vaccine but only a few hundred doses of the antibody so far. Unfortunately, the antibody must be given in gram doses whereas the vaccine is administered in microgram doses; a million fold difference. The same amount of protein that will provide forty million doses of vaccine will only provide about six hundred doses of antibody and it's thought that patients might require several doses of the antibody to completely eradicate the virus. However, because enough vaccine is needed to vaccinate and protect everyone—billions of people—but the antibody is only needed for those who have actually developed infections, the world will hopefully need much less antibody than vaccine.

Regrettably, at present the only source of the

antibody is Gordito and this has created a bottleneck. However, Gordito has now published the gene sequence and a method for manufacturing the antibody so that anyone with the requisite expertise and equipment— essentially the same people who've been making the protein vaccine—can begin manufacturing antibody as well. It can only be hoped that several vaccine manufacturers will convert over to making antibody in time to treat the several thousand people infected with and dying of the active disease.

It should be noted that Gordito, whoever he or she is, or even whatever group might be represented by the Gordito website, has made the trip from scientific phenomenon, to lowlife evildoer, and back to worldwide hero faster than anyone else in history.

Epilogue

Osprey spoke in Zage's ear, "You have a call from Dr. LaQua Kelso at CDC."

"I'll take it! Use the synthetic voice… Dr. Kelso, how can I help?"

"You can accept my apologies. I feel terrible for doubting you."

"I'm not upset. In retrospect, I can understand why you became concerned. The timing of the website and the quick analysis of the virus must've seemed suspicious."

"Ah yes, that astonishingly fast analysis of the virus still boggles the mind. How did you do it?"

"Um, it does involve an algorithm and a supercomputer, but…"

"But what? Are you going to tell the rest of the world how to do it too?"

"Um, I'd like to but, there're some parts of it that involve… intuition, I guess I'd have to say. A computer can't do it and I don't know how to tell someone else how to do it either."

"So, you're saying that *you're* the only person in the world who can do this?" she said suspiciously.

"Every time I do an analysis, I try to understand how I'm doing it. I'm hoping I can figure out how to have the computer do it, or at least be able to explain it so other people can do the same thing, but so far I haven't had any luck. I just look at the section of the protein sequence that the computer can't predict and, somehow, I just *know* how it'll fold. Once I have the 3D model, a lot of the time I immediately get a feeling for what the protein does. Admittedly, the computer works out most of the folding or each one'd take me days, but the left-over bits that stumped the algorithm seem to be easy for me."

"Uh-huh, and how much money are you making by selling antigens and analyses of protein folding?"

"Well, quite a bit. But the reason we're charging is to decrease the traffic on the site to reasonable levels. When it was free people were just dumping hundreds of amino acid sequences onto the site without trying to discriminate which ones they really needed answers for."

"Oh… I can understand how that might happen," Kelso said, "but still, you're making a tidy profit. That's going to make other people, not just me, think you're just keeping the method to yourself for the money."

"Um, if you look at the website disclosures on the homepage you'll see that the money's all going to Doctors Without Borders. Maybe I should make it more prominent, but if you don't trust that, you could confirm it with the charity."

"Really?" Kelso said in a tone of grudging respect. "How are you supporting yourself?"

"Um… other ways."

"Well, in any case, CDC owes you their thanks for all your help with the smallpox crisis. Is there any way we can repay you?" Zage didn't say anything for a moment, so Kelso said, "Gordito?"

"Yes ma'am, I'm still here. The website has the sequence for an antigen that no one seems to be paying any attention to."

"What antigen's that?"

"It's a single protein molecule with a number of different antigenic sites displayed on it. That one protein should stimulate immunity to all of the known obesity viruses…"

"Really?!" Kelso said, sounding shocked.

"Yes ma'am, I don't have the capability of testing it so I'm hoping you'll fund some testing in animals and hopefully someday in people. I…" after a brief stumble, Zage continued, "I really think it's about time we did something about the obesity epidemic."

"You think *vaccination* will work for obesity?"

"Yes ma'am, I do. Obesity's spreading far too much like a communicable disease to be simple slothfulness."

"NIH usually funds those kinds of studies," she said slowly, "not CDC."

"Oh… could you suggest it to NIH?"

"Let me talk to my bosses. Maybe CDC'd actually like to do the study itself. It is, after all, a national health crisis."

"Okay, thanks."

"Um, would you be interested in a job here at CDC?"

"Oh! No. But I'd be happy to help with any other problems like this one."

Kelso snorted, "Okay, but I seriously hope we don't have any more problems like *this* one."

***

Phil's awakening was a slow and cloudy process. Suddenly, he recognized Carol's face hanging over him.

He felt light.

I'm on Mars again! he thought. "Hi Carol!" he said, his voice sounding unsteady even to him.

"Hi yourself, you big lunk!" she said, her lips trembling up into a smile while a tear ran down her cheek. "It's good to have you back out here." She tilted her head curiously at his vacant look, "You do know where you are, don't you?"

"Sure, this's the moon, right?"

Carol grabbed his nipple and started to twist, "No!" Phil yelped, "Mars! Mars, sorry!"

"That's better," Carol said. "I could've predicted that, even in the midst of the scariest event of our lives, you'd be jackin' around like some kind of idiot."

"Yeah," he gave her a weak smile, "but I'm your idiot, right?"

"I do seem to be stuck with you."

"Can I get up?"

Carol glanced to one side. Mark Wilson, the doctor on the Mars team stepped into view. "No reason we shouldn't give it a try, I guess. You'll probably be dizzy, so we should start by just having you sit up."

***

Reggie looked up at a diffident knock on her door. Zage stood there. "Dr. Barnes?" he said uncertainly.

"Hey Zage," she said, turning her chair toward him and motioning him in. "How're things going?" She wondered if he was about to tell her his Cell and Molecular Biology courses were too much for him, or that he'd decided he really didn't want to do research after all. Having a five-year-old taking those kinds of courses and working in her lab still seemed entirely too bizarre for Reggie to believe. She hoped he wasn't giving up though, he was fun to have around and certainly had odd and perceptive insights into scientific questions. She paused this thought process and chided herself—the kid was really pretty astonishing. *I shouldn't be thinking he might be about to quit, I should be wondering what cool new thing he might've figured out.*

"Pretty well, I think," Zage said. "I've been working on Alzheimer protein misfolding. It does look like a couple of the known Alzheimer's associated genes do code for versions of proteins that have a significant likelihood of folding more than one way."

"And you've determined this how?"

"Well, I selected Alzheimer associated genes that code for proteins and... And I sent them to Gordito with a query about how they'd fold. Gordito said folding at some locations was indeterminate."

"Indeterminate?"

"Yes ma'am. Instead of having a high likelihood of folding one particular way or another, those proteins have a site where the likelihood is, not 50-50, but maybe twenty percent, or even thirty that they'll fold into a nonfunctional state."

"Ah, and for some of them, once one protein misfolds, there might be a crystallization event where neighboring proteins fold the same way and then form clumps?"

"Yes ma'am."

"Okay, how're we going to test that hypothesis?"

"I was thinking that we could use the new system from the Virgies to insert a corrected gene?"

Reggie narrowed her eyes, "And how do you know about that?"

Zage looked startled and didn't say anything for a second, then he said, "My mom said something about it. She might've heard about it from Ell Donsaii. They work together, you know?"

Reggie snorted, "Donsaii's had *me* sign all kinds of secrecy agreements about this, but she's telling an assistant who's spreading the word to her *kid*?!"

Zage shrugged, "Sorry. Um, I might've overheard a conversation I shouldn't have?"

Reggie shook her head, "Okay, let's talk about your idea. You're starting at the hoped for end result, treatment of the disease. I've got to point out that no one's going to approve human testing just because you have a theory it'll work. Therefore, the first thing for us to do is to synthesize some of the proteins you're talking about and see if they actually do misfold sometimes. And if they misfold, do they then crystallize neighboring proteins into clumps?"

"Oh," Zage said, looking disappointed.

"Welcome to science kid. It's a world where you've got to do a lot of dull, rigorous testing before you get to make your moonshot and claim the grand prize."

"Okay," the kid said in a disheartened tone, "I guess I'll get started on synthesizing some of those proteins tomorrow?"

"There you go." As Zage turned and left her office, Reggie looked after him, thinking about how she'd recently learned that most childhood prodigies play instruments or do math astonishingly well as kids, but then don't actually contribute much that's original after they grow up. *But I'll bet* that *kid does something that makes a difference in the world someday. Maybe it won't be something that saves lives or makes the news, but still, something that's somewhat important, at least in its own way...*

***

Carol gave the command through her AI and the third balloon of the triple airlock into the dome deflated. As the atmosphere of the dome rushed into the lock, Phil felt his suit collapsing around him. Stepping forward, he looked out into the dome with awe. "Wow. A dome that's a kilometer in diameter really is huge," he said, staring out across what, after living in the tunnels, felt like a vast distance.

"It's got 194 acres," Carol said, putting it into more familiar terms.

Turning around, he saw Carol had her Mars-suit most of the way off so he started removing his own. He glanced up at the roof of the dome. Mars didn't get a huge amount of sunlight to begin with, and with only about fifty percent of that available light making its way through the graphene layers and a meter of water, it'd have been pretty dim. However, brilliant light from a near-solar parabolic mirror was flooding through a port running on a rail up high against the dome. He understood that if you were standing at a certain spot in the center of the dome, the lighting port would track across the dome directly in front of the sun. Of course, in most locations in the dome it wouldn't hide the sun, but at least it moved across the "sky" like a sun should.

When he got his Mars suit off, the first thing Phil noticed was that the temperature was pleasant. Even though, cognitively, he knew the dome had been set up for months with a meter of water providing insulation and the solar parabolic mirror not only providing light, but significant heat as well, he'd subliminally still expected it to be cold. Mars, after all, was really cold on the surface, and even though he was in the dome, it was so big that it felt like he was outside. Carol took his hand, "Feel like a stroll, big boy?"

"Sure."

She walked him out to show him the "ponds." They'd purposefully set up this second dome on an area of the terrain where there were several depressions. The water they ported in from the oceans of Europa pressed the graphene bottom layer of the dome down into the depressions to make the little lakes where the cyanobacteria did the initial conversion of carbon dioxide ported in from Venus into oxygen and biomass. Once some of the water'd been used up, they brought in machinery to shovel Martian dirt through ports onto the floor of the dome. They mixed organic material from Earth into the Martian dirt according to a recipe that the agricultural scientists recommended. Some early plantings were already starting to grow.

Phil looked out over all of it, overcome by a great feeling of pastoral satisfaction. Turning to Carol, he said, "This could be our home!"

She smacked him on the shoulder. "It could not! First of all, you'll be bored here after a day or so. *Farmers* are the kind of people who'll enjoy living here, not jumped up wrestlers who think they're astronaut adventurers. Besides, inheriting your genes, my kids are going to have one strike against them from the get-go. Lord only knows," she leaped high into the air, then landed softly in the low gravity, "how they'd turn out if they were raised in a low gravity environment too!"

***

White House, Washington DC—Today President Stockton announced victory in the battle against modified smallpox, a disease which medical experts are now telling us could have killed as many as 5-6 billion people worldwide if not for a rapid reaction from Homeland Security and CDC. Not all of the virus created in Dallas has been accounted for, but at this point the vast majority of Americans have been vaccinated and vaccinations are proceeding apace in the rest of the world. Stocks of the Gordito antibody have built up enough that CDC believes they could use them to treat even a significant outbreak of clinically evident disease. The President praised a number of people who were important in preventing this from becoming a disaster. These included Miki Denuit, Mary Aston, and Dr. Nancy Tigner; who first recognized the vaccination virus on Little Diomede island. Dr. LaQua Kelso at CDC was credited with her rapid recognition of the seriousness of the situation and for excellent management of the medical response. D5R got credit for shutting down Islam Akbar's planned method of distribution. And, of course, almost everyone now recognizes the incredible contributions made by the anonymous "Gordito." Stockton begged Gordito to come forward and be recognized. A number of other organizations are offering jobs, lucrative consultation positions and outright prizes as well, but so far the three persons who have claimed to be Gordito have all proven to be impostors. Many have begun to suspect that Gordito may actually be some kind of organization, rather than a single individual.

Bioterror

***

Zage felt a little torn. Carley, Alice, and Rick had invited him to go out for lunch with them to celebrate the end of the semester. It felt good that they were taking him along on a social outing instead of just talking to him in the lab. On the other hand, out here in public, he knew most people just assumed that one of them had brought their child with them. The fact that his legs were so short he practically had to trot to keep up with them made it worse.

He also worried that they'd assume they needed to pay for his lunch. That'd be embarrassing so he'd told Osprey to download the bill and pay his part of it while they ate.

He'd managed to tell Osprey where they were going shortly before they left. When they entered the restaurant, he saw Randy and Linda from his security team sitting at a table near the middle. He'd hoped they'd be able to do that instead of having to follow him to the restaurant from the lab.

After they sat down, the waitress brought three adult menus and a child's menu. He blushed and Carley obviously recognized his discomfort because she asked the waitress to get him an adult menu too. Even worse, he then found he wanted to order off the child's menu because he was worried that some of the adult choices would be too spicy for him. Eventually he settled on a plain hamburger and French fries, then relaxed back to listen to the three grad students talk.

The conversation ranged widely, touching on the basketball team's prospects, whether or not Donsaii'd let them get in on the studies of ET DNA, Rick's new girlfriend, and how the world had gotten off easy with the smallpox thing.

As he'd been taught, Zage had taken the seat with his back to the wall so he could watch the door. Therefore, he noticed when the guy came in the door. The overweight young man looked vaguely familiar, but didn't seem to be sure if he was in the right place. Zage thought the young man was perhaps undergraduate age, which was unusual in this little restaurant that catered more to grads. He didn't really look like a student though.

"What do you think Zage?" Alice asked.

Zage hadn't been paying close attention to the smallpox conversation, but had been following enough to know they'd been talking about who Gordito might be. "I favor the 'weird computer guy sitting in his mother's basement' theory," Zage said.

"Oh come on," Rick said, "that kind of guy wouldn't know enough about protein structure to be able to design an algorithm that predicts folding!"

Zage didn't respond because the young guy who'd come in had focused on their table and started their way. His three friends looked at Zage when he didn't respond, then turned to see what he was looking at.

The young man said, "Carley?"

"Eli!" Carley screamed, leaping to her feet and throwing her arms around her long lost brother.

The End

Hope you liked the book!

Try the next in the series, *Terraform (an Ell Donsaii story #15)*

**To find other books by the author try
Laury.Dahners.com/stories.html**

Author's Afterword

This is a comment on the "science" in this science fiction novel. I've always been partial to science fiction that posed a "what if" question. Not everything in the story has to be scientifically plausible, but you suspend your disbelief regarding one or two things that aren't thought to be possible. Essentially you ask, "what if" something (such as faster than light travel) were possible, how might that change our world? Each of the stories tries to ask such questions.

"Bioterror!" asks what kinds of terrible things a terrorist with some of the new technical skills in gene manipulation might be able to do. Personally I find it difficult to believe that someone with the genius to understand the technology and actually modify a genome would also be evil enough to use that rare ability to harm other human beings, but certainly history is replete with stories of evil geniuses doing just that. The frightening thing is that such a constructed disease could be built to resist treatments and be even more virulent than the disease (smallpox in this case) that it's based on.

"Technology is a two-edged sword" many would say, referring to the fact that, while it can do much good, it can also do terrible things, sometimes even as an unintended consequence. I prefer to think of how technology might solve *even* the problems it creates. For instance, though it's little known, pollution has been reduced by 50% since the 1970s and the price of solar electricity dropped below the average cost of electricity generated by other means in 2016 (meaning that economic forces will now drive the development of solar energy and reduce our dependence on oil and production of CO_2).

I like to hope that if an evil genius fabricates a disease, a benign genius might invent the means by which we contain it.

What if that benign genius was a child prodigy? Not a prodigy who plays piano or does math, but one with a math-like skill for analyzing genes and proteins?

For those of you interested, there actually is evidence that smallpox vaccination protected recipients somewhat against other diseases—HIV, asthma, and others—for reasons that aren't well understood.

Acknowledgements

I would like to acknowledge the editing and advice of Gail Gilman, Nora Dahners, Mike Alsobrook, Allen Dietz, Hamilton Elliott, Jack Hudler, and Stephen Wiley, each of whom significantly improved this story.

CPSIA information can be obtained
at www.ICGtesting.com
Printed in the USA
FSHW020126271221
87191FS